CANDLELIGHT
Supreme

"YOU WHAT?" JASON DREW BACK. "YOU THINK I'M A MURDERER?"

"Well, no, not really." Maris swallowed hard, suddenly feeling suffocated by his nearness. "It's just that you've been treating me so oddly. And I was so frightened, I've never dived in rough seas before. And then, when you went straight to the body . . ."

"You were afraid that you would be my next victim," Jason finished for her, his golden eyes smoldering with anger. Stormy winds shrieked around the boat, but the silence between them stretched tautly. Jason rose, turning his back on her.

"Jason, please, let me explain. . . ." She stared at the corded muscles in his neck.

"You won't ever have to worry about that again."

"Jason!"

But he was already out the door.

CANDLELIGHT SUPREMES

QUANTITY SALES

Most Dell Books are available at special quantity discounts when purchased in bulk by corporations, organizations, and special-interest groups. Custom imprinting or excerpting can also be done to fit special needs. For details write: Dell Publishing Co., Inc., 1 Dag Hammarskjold Plaza, New York, NY 10017, Attn.: Special Sales Dept., or phone: (212) 605-3319.

INDIVIDUAL SALES

Are there any Dell Books you want but cannot find in your local stores? If so, you can order them directly from us. You can get any Dell book in print. Simply include the book's title, author, and ISBN number, if you have it, along with a check or money order (no cash can be accepted) for the full retail price plus 75¢ per copy to cover shipping and handling. Mail to: Dell Readers Service, Dept. FM, 6 Regent Street, Livingston, N.J. 07039.

THE MERMAID'S TOUCH

Lynn Patrick

A CANDLELIGHT SUPREME

Published by
Dell Publishing Co., Inc.
1 Dag Hammarskjold Plaza
New York, New York 10017

ISBN: 0-440-15570-3

Printed in the United States of America

July 1987

10 9 8 7 6 5 4 3 2 1

WFH

*Thanks to Roger Klocek at the Shedd
Aquarium for information.
Thanks to Mel Fisher of Treasure Salvors,
Inc., for inspiration.*

To Our Readers:

We are pleased and excited by your overwhelmingly positive response to our Candlelight Supremes. Unlike all the other series, the Supremes are filled with more passion, adventure, and intrigue, and are obviously the stories you like best.

In months to come we will continue to publish books by many of your favorite authors as well as the very finest work from new authors of romantic fiction. As always, we are striving to present unique, absorbing love stories —the very best love has to offer.

Breathtaking and unforgettable, Supremes follow in the great romantic tradition you've come to expect *only* from Candlelight Romances.

Your suggestions and comments are always welcome. Please let us hear from you.

Sincerely,

The Editors
Candlelight Romances
1 Dag Hammarskjold Plaza
New York, New York 10017

THE
MERMAID'S
TOUCH

PROLOGUE

Gazing down into the dreamlike dark blue depths of the Bahama Banks, Jason Price feared that he was about to die. The rapture of the watery deep beckoned to him, willed him to give in, and it was becoming more and more difficult to fight its lure. His eyelids felt so heavy, he was tempted to let them close, but he knew it would be the last thing he'd ever do.

Breathe! he commanded himself with what was left of his survival instincts. Breathe! To forget would mean certain death, his lungs painfully rupturing inside his chest. He sucked air through his regulator, but his head wouldn't clear. A pounding hammered at his temple and his stomach lurched.

Only one thought penetrated the painful fog behind his eyes—the air in his second tank must have been fouled somehow.

A barracuda appeared suddenly, mere inches from his mask. As Jason tried to focus on the row of sharp teeth projecting from its thrusting lower jaw, the glinting white points seemed to grow larger and more threatening. He shuddered and tried to stifle his fear, an emotion he'd never before experienced during his underwater sojourns. He remained still until, its curiosity satisfied, the menacing fish swam away. Jason sagged

11

with relief and hooked a fin onto a coral shelf so that he could try to get his bearings.

He'd been disoriented for quite a while now, and if he could trust his distorted vision, his depth gauge read only one hundred and twenty feet. From years of diving experience he knew he'd gone down only far enough to undergo mild giddiness and euphoria—symptoms of the first stage of nitrogen narcosis—but not far enough to induce the confusion and hallucinations that made him certain he was doomed.

In any case, he'd head for the surface if only he could figure which way was up. Decreasing the pressure would decrease the effects of the nitrogen in his system. Jason struggled to lift himself from the coral shelf. It was a sloppy attempt, his legs and arms seeming to go in every direction, all without purpose.

Emotions warred within him, equally out of control. *It's no use. Give up,* whispered the voice of exhaustion and despair. *You must make the attempt,* said the voice of reason.

Why? he asked weakly.

So you will live.

No. I'm going to die.

No sooner did he resign himself to his fate than a shimmering vision swam into the circle of his underwater light, one so beautiful, he thought it might not be so bad to die, not if he could do so in her arms. A mermaid —a turquoise water spirit with long curling tendrils of pale hair spreading around her face—beckoned to him, just as sailors' legends told.

She seemed to study him curiously before pointing directly at him, then bringing her fist to her chest. More confused than ever, Jason wondered why she'd signal that she was low on air. The magical creature repeated

12

both gestures, and he finally realized she was asking a question rather than making a statement.

Suspended without any sense of direction, Jason nodded and put his hands to his throat. Help!

She beckoned again, but didn't wait for his approach. Gracefully moving forward, she tapped her mouth to indicate buddy breathing, then wrapped her pale arms around him and started a slow ascent. He allowed her to do what she would, not even fighting when she plucked the regulator from his lips.

It was true, then. She would lure him to the briny depths, enfolding him in her arms. There was no escape for him, after all.

As he accepted the inevitable she put a smooth object in his mouth and, somehow, he reminded himself to breathe. Another intake and she pulled the life-giving force from him, putting it to her own lips. She repeated the action as they floated upward, her hair tangling itself around him, joining them together.

Then she stopped, forcing him to hang suspended for a length of time. Although Jason wanted to continue the ascent immediately, he didn't have the strength to fight her. The mermaid's arms circling his torso and her tail wrapping around his legs were too strong for him, preventing him from moving as he would. Watching the brightly colored fish darting through her hair, he waited until his mermaid was ready to proceed because he could do nothing else.

Floating upward in dreamlike apathy, Jason allowed her to lead him through true blues turning to pale aqua to bright golden light to total darkness. . . .

When his eyes fluttered open sometime later all he could focus on was blue ringed with violet. His mermaid's eyes. And his breath mingled with hers because

13

her mouth covered his own. As he clutched her warm body in his arms, Jason kissed her passionately, not caring what legends willed. For it was said, *Once kissed by a mermaid, a man would be hers forever.* But if he was going to die, what a way to go!

His body racked with sensations that told him he was still very much alive, Jason Price closed his eyes, prepared to meet his fate.

CHAPTER ONE

Finally freeing her silver-blond hair from her diving mask, Maris Collier cursed the hungry fish that had plucked the rubber band holding her single braid together. She'd been working on untangling the waist-length strands since setting foot back on the *Mermaid's Kiss,* the collecting boat owned by the Coral Gardens Aquarium, where she worked.

"You would have been proud of our heroic curator," aquarist Paul Martinez assured the other members of the team as he stripped off his wet suit. "I didn't even see the guy until she had her arms around him and started sharing her air." Her young diving partner's tone was mischievous when he added, "Of course I understood her quick response when we got to the surface and Maris was kissing this guy who looked like a blond Adonis."

"I did not kiss him!" Maris protested indignantly, fixing the newest member of the team with what she hoped was a wicked glare. Paul just laughed, and she was forced to relent. *"He* kissed *me."* And what a kiss it had been!

After setting her mask down next to her tank and fins, she removed her weight belt and buoyancy compensator. The others gathered around her, obviously eager to hear all the details of the rescue. Maris felt odd about everything that had happened—as though the experience had been a movie she'd watched—and she wanted to be alone for a while to think about it. Especially about him. The blond Adonis.

Hoping the other team members would go away if she ignored them, she unzipped her yellow-trimmed turquoise wet suit and began struggling out of it.

"The question is, did you or did you not enjoy his kiss?" Jo Schneider asked, quickly sidestepping the fin Maris picked up and tossed at the senior aquarist. The short, dark-haired woman grinned triumphantly at her reaction. "And how was it he happened to kiss you, anyway?"

"Oh, all right. You obviously won't let me have any peace until I've confessed. The man seemed to be doing okay, but then he passed out while we were still underwater," Maris explained. She sat and pulled one long, tanned leg free of the neoprene wet suit, then the other. "When I got him to the surface I could see his lips were a bright cherry red. I knew he was suffering from carbon monoxide poisoning, but I wasn't sure how serious it might be, so I gave him artificial respiration—"

"And, boy, did that bring him around!" Paul teased, making Maris remember the passionate way the man had embraced her, not to mention the embarrassing way she'd responded.

"The question is, are *you* all right?" asked Brian Nelson, director of the aquarium.

Maris looked up at her boss, who was studying her with serious gray eyes. "Why? Do I look green or something?"

"White is more like it. A rescue like the one you just pulled off is enough to stress anyone out."

"I'm fine. Do I have to swim a few laps around the boat to prove it?"

"Brian is only thinking of your best interests, girl," Matthew Kearns said. The grizzled sea captain placed a calloused hand on her shoulder. "You may not realize what kind of effect the incident had on you now because you're all pumped up with adrenaline. But later you might not be feeling so cocky and chipper."

Seeing this as her chance to escape for some solitude, Maris rose and stretched. "Maybe you're right. I think I'll go to my cabin and rest for a while."

"Don't feel obligated to come to the party tonight if you're not up to it," Brian told her. "I can give Arthur your regrets. He'll understand."

"I'm sure your old friend would never miss me if I didn't attend the affair," Maris stated. "But the only way you'll keep me from going is by locking the door to my cabin. And the porthole! I've never helped christen a boat before. I wouldn't miss this spectacle for the world."

"You overdo it, and you won't be good for nothin' tomorrow," Kearns grumbled.

"You sound like my father," Maris grumbled in return. However, she appreciated the gruff man's concern. Smiling, she patted *him* on the shoulder. "Don't worry, Captain. In case you haven't figured it out yet, I'm a pretty hardy woman. Those black cap basslets aren't safe from me yet. I'll find those little buggers if it's the last thing I do."

"We have more than three weeks before we have to leave the Bahamas for Florida." Jo winked at Maris as she added, "That's more than enough time to chase down our prey, whether fishy or human."

Ignoring Jo's teasing, Maris rose. Heading for the

cabin she shared with the other woman, she skirted the large central stern well, which was currently divided into six compartments, only two of which held the brightly colored tropical fish that Brian and Jo had found. For her, as the curator of this expedition, the day's dive had been a bust. She and Paul had gone deep to find the number one item on her shopping list but had returned empty-handed.

Well, not totally, she thought, remembering how her arms had been filled by a mysterious Adonis.

As she went below she eyed the first mate, a thin man with dark hair that stood out in wild disarray. Leaning on the rail looking out toward the Atlantic, he was the only person on board who hadn't seemed interested in her adventure. An odd duck, Gallagher always stayed to himself. He was a qualified mate and a good worker, Kearns insisted, but there wasn't much more a body could say about him. Neither she nor the other aquarium staff members even knew if Gallagher was the mate's first name or last.

It wasn't Gallagher she wanted to think about, however. Maris entered the tiny cabin and flopped on the lower bunk, not bothering to strip off her damp tank suit. She tucked her hands under her head and stretched out her slender legs, crossing them at the ankles.

Why couldn't she forget the nameless man she'd rescued? The crew members on the boat called the *Argonaut* had said he was their captain. He'd been only half conscious when they'd lifted him from the water. After she'd warned them that he might need a decompression chamber, Paul had suggested they leave so the crew could get their captain to a doctor. She only hoped she'd spent enough time at each decompression stop on the way up to the surface.

18

If she hadn't . . . Maris frowned as she imagined the worst happening—embolisms rupturing the man's lung tissue or blocking arteries or lodging sinisterly in his brain or spinal cord. If any of those things happened, he'd be lucky if he was only paralyzed. It was more than likely that he'd die.

And what a waste of a perfect specimen that would be! the curator in her thought, even as some instinct told her the man was alive and well. Or would be with a little rest.

Closing her eyes, Maris imagined his face as she'd seen it when she'd pulled up his mask to give him mouth-to-mouth respiration. He had a high forehead, a long, straight nose, and full lips that looked every bit as sensual as they'd felt when joined with her own. Only a shade or two darker than his hair and surrounded by long, thick lashes, his golden eyes were without question the most arresting thing about his ruggedly handsome face. And from what she'd been able to tell of his body through the wet suit, it was equally rugged and appealing.

A shiver shot through her as she remembered the feel of him against her. Maris was appalled at her physical reaction to something that had happened almost a half hour before. Instead of rationalizing what had happened, she was allowing her instincts to have the upper hand in this situation—something she'd promised herself she'd never do again. After all, she was thirty-two years old, not some scatterbrained teenager.

First and foremost, she should remember the man had been alone in the water, a foolhardy move that had almost gotten him killed. Hadn't he ever heard of the buddy system? It was dangerous to dive alone.

No, Maris told herself, she wasn't about to get all

moony-eyed over any man, especially not one who was as irresponsible as this one appeared to be. She'd had one such man in her life—the husband who'd stolen her dreams—and as far as Maris was concerned, that had been one too many. Her heart didn't need another disappointment.

Maris frowned at the bunk above. What in the world was she worried about, anyway? All of this intellectualizing was really ridiculous. She decided that she didn't have to worry about her oddly aroused instincts because she was certain that she'd never see her blond Adonis again.

Jason Price awakened, still chasing his mermaid through a coral forest. She disappeared behind a large sea fan. Reluctantly, he allowed the dream to fade. Eyes open, he saw his first mate, Alonzo Ferrara, standing above him and holding an oxygen mask over his nose and mouth.

"Welcome back to the *Argonaut,*" Alonzo said, removing the mask. His dark eyes studied Jason's face for a moment. "At least your color's back to normal."

"What in the hell happened?" Jason tried to focus his blurred vision on the far corners of the small room. They held no seductive sea nymph. "And where is she —my mermaid?"

"Beats me." The mate removed the portable tank and set it against the cabin's wall. When he turned back to his captain his lips were turned down under his thick mustache. "This is unbelievable. The famous Jason Price with carbon monoxide poisoning. I'm going to chew out Eli's ass for being so careless about filling the tanks."

"I can't believe it myself," Jason said distractedly,

20

still wondering how his mermaid had escaped. "The old man knows his business. He's been working with divers half his life."

"Well, there's a first time for everything, even for Eli Hart. The wind must have shifted while he was filling the tanks and he didn't notice. You know how easy it can be to pump exhaust from the compressor into your intake hose."

"Uh-huh."

Jason sat up suddenly, intending to get out of the bed and take off his wet suit, but his head seemed to thud and float simultaneously. With a groan he leaned back against the pile of pillows.

"Hey, it isn't any worse than I thought, is it?" Alonzo stood over him, demanding, "Any pain in the joints? How's your chest feel?"

"I wasn't down there long enough to get the bends." Fighting confusion, Jason remembered that the beautiful sea creature had made him stop at various points on the way to the surface. "At least I don't think so, but she wouldn't let me keep going—"

Before he could consider the idea further his cabin door opened and Carmen Ferrara entered carrying a tray with a pot and three mugs. She wore a pair of deck pants over her bathing suit and a smile on her face.

"Good, you're awake," Alonzo's wife said cheerfully. "I brought us some coffee."

"Maybe it'll help clear my head." Scooting up carefully, Jason gratefully took the first mug she poured. "How long was I out, anyway?"

"Ever since we hauled you up on deck," Alonzo told him. "Fifteen, twenty minutes, maybe."

Carmen handed her husband his coffee and took a sip from her own mug. Her beautiful Spanish-Indian face was still set in a smile, but from experience Jason knew she was worrying about him, as she did about everything.

His assumption proved correct when she said, "We're on our way back to Nassau. I already radioed ahead. A doctor will be waiting for us at the dock."

"That's ridiculous. There's nothing wrong with me that a little fresh sea air won't cure." To prove it Jason tried to sit up once more. The dull ache in his temple intensified, reminding him of how close he'd come to dying. "Help me up so I can get out of this damned wet suit, would you?" he demanded with an impatient growl.

Self-reliant since he'd left his St. Petersburg home at eighteen because his young stepmother had seemed more interested in him than in her new husband, Jason hated asking for help for anything. He'd been a fiercely independent drifter, taking odd jobs for almost a half dozen years before hooking up with Will Gibbons, the Key Largo deep-sea treasure hunter who'd become his mentor. By then he'd been too old to change. And now, at thirty-six, he no longer wanted to.

Setting down his coffee on a nearby shelf, Jason remembered that he *had* asked for help this time, and not only from his crew members. Blue eyes ringed with violet haunted him. With Alonzo's assistance he got to his feet.

"The mermaid!" He saw Alonzo and Carmen exchange startled looks. "Where is she?"

"Who?" Carmen asked.

"The sea sprite who saved me."

Alonzo smothered a laugh. "He's still having fantasies from inhaling all that carbon monoxide."

22

"It's not funny," Carmen told him. "Jason, maybe you should lie down again."

Jason ignored her plea. As the boat gently rocked with the waves below his feet, he went to his desk, shaking his head in an attempt to clear it.

A mermaid? There was no such thing, was there? Then why did he remember the shimmering vision? Her turquoise body? The pale hair and arms that wrapped around a man until he thought he'd be glad to die if only he could feel her against him forever? And her mouth . . . her mouth!

"But she kissed me after she brought me back up to the surface!" he insisted. "Are you telling me the whole thing was an hallucination?"

"The diver," Carmen said. "You must have imagined the diver who rescued you was a mermaid."

"Diver? Then she's human!" The thought left Jason strangely excited. "So she really does exist. She wasn't a figment of my imagination."

Alonzo sat on the edge of the bed. "She was real, all right. Both she and her partner."

"There were two of them? Who are they? Where did they come from?"

"From another boat anchored a couple of hundred yards away. I didn't catch the name," his first mate admitted. "Anyway, the woman diver delivered you. A guy was following close behind her. They swam off while we were busy trying to revive you."

"And while we're on that subject, why in the world were you down below alone?" Carmen demanded. "You knew Davey wasn't feeling well when Alonzo and I went down. You should have come with us."

"I was following a hunch." Suddenly the hazy image of a sunken hull took shape in Jason's memory, but the

23

vision slipped away from him. His illness had erased whatever he'd seen far below the water's surface.

"One of these days a hunch will kill you," Carmen warned.

Jason gritted his teeth so he wouldn't say something sharp in response. He knew the young woman was concerned about him, but it was with difficulty that he held his temper. Though she was almost as seasoned a diver as her husband, Carmen was overcautious, as were many other divers. She liked doing things in an orderly manner, according to a preconceived plan. She didn't understand trusting hunches and taking risks. Certainly not the way he did.

As a matter of fact, he'd built his reputation as a marine insurance investigator and salvor on those very qualities. And Jason was sure that it would be the hunch-trusting, risk-taking part of his nature that would eventually lead him to a sunken treasure ship he'd been seeking off and on for a number of years.

Jason was grateful when a knock at the door gave him an excuse to avoid Carmen's comment. "Come on in."

The door swung open and Eli stepped inside, his wizened black face solemn. "Cap'n, you all right?"

"I'm not dead yet," Jason said, noting Davey hanging back in the passageway. "You can come in too. There's not enough room for a party, but then I wasn't planning on giving one."

"You sure you want me in there?" Davey Watson asked, his expression wary behind his wire-rimmed glasses.

"Why wouldn't I?"

"It's my fault you almost got hurt." His freckles

24

stood out against his pale face more than usual. "If I had gone down with you . . ."

"We *both* would have been in trouble," Jason finished.

Knowing his new, fairly inexperienced partner would have been taking a risk with his own life was the reason Jason had gone down without him. Davey had eaten part of an omelet that morning before realizing that Eli had thrown in bits of shrimp, one of the few things the young man was allergic to. His reaction hadn't been severe, but he'd experienced mild swelling in his throat tissue and Jason had been afraid that Davey would have a problem underwater.

How ironic that it had been Jason who'd ended up having trouble breathing. Now that his head had cleared, he wanted to know why. *Had* Eli been careless or had someone tampered with his tank?

"Listen, Jason, I'm really sorry I wasn't with you," Davey said, his narrow face serious. He ran a nervous hand through his sandy hair. "I feel terrible."

"That makes two of us."

"Three." Eli lowered his grizzled white head and twisted his cap in his bony hands. "Sorry, Cap'n. I'll leave the *Argonaut* when we get to Nassau. Lots of men need hiring—"

"Good lord! You'd think this was a wake!" Jason yelled, startling all four of his crew members. They gaped at their normally calm, good-humored boss. "I don't want to find someone to replace you, Eli. And, Davey, stop acting like a martyr. I'm fine!"

"You will be if you're sensible." Carmen gave him a determined look. "What you need is bed rest."

Shaking his head, Jason leaned back on the edge of his desk and crossed his arms over his chest. "I have

25

nothing against getting some bed rest," he said, the thought reminding him of the sea sprite who'd enchanted him. Of course with a lovely woman in his arms, her pale hair wrapped around their naked bodies, neither of them would get much rest. He'd see to that! Keeping a straight face, Jason added, "I might even take that advice if I can find the lady who rescued me."

Alonzo laughed at his ribald comment, but Carmen's dark eyes flashed as she glared first at her husband, then at Jason. "I should have known you wouldn't take your own health seriously. I don't know why I waste my breath." She headed for the doorway, pushing Eli and Davey back through it before leaving without another word.

"She's probably right, you know." Alonzo rose from the bunk and moved toward the door himself. "Carmen's a little spooked by the rumors of voodoo curses sending those ships down in the Bermuda Triangle—even so, a little rest wouldn't hurt you."

"I don't have time to take a nap," Jason said, shaking his head at the crazy superstitions of an educated woman. "I have to get ready for a party."

That stopped his mate cold. "You kidding?"

"Not in the least." Jason opened the built-in closet and pulled out a lightweight cream-colored suit. "I have a job to do."

"Hey, going to Wilkerson's shindig isn't part of the job. I seriously think you should pass on this one, amigo."

"And I seriously know I shouldn't." After throwing the suit on the bed, Jason began rummaging through a drawer. "I want to meet the possible suspects. What better way than at a social gathering?"

"Wait a minute. We were hired by Intercontinental

Mutual to investigate the missing ships. But Ray Turner is paying us to find the ships and salvage the cargo, if possible. He didn't say anything about suspects."

"Maybe not, but I'd like to get a better idea of whether or not human forces were at work. Three ships owned by Wilkerson Industries all going down in this area of the Bermuda Triangle within a year! Sounds fishy to me, and you know how I like to do a thorough job."

"Yeah, and you're going to get yourself killed if you're not careful," Alonzo muttered.

"You want to explain that one?"

"It's just that neither of us can believe that Eli was so careless, after all. Right, amigo?" Without waiting for his captain's response, Alonzo walked out of the cabin. Jason was left alone to think about the ominous implications of what he'd just said.

If Eli hadn't been careless, that meant someone was out to get him, to stop him from finding the lost ships. It was a discomforting possibility, but one Jason had to consider. Obviously he was going to have to watch his back. And his boat. If someone had tampered with the tanks . . .

He would be forced to leave a twenty-four-hour guard on board. Terrific! That divided the responsibility between Alonzo and himself, since the rest of his crew was made up of an old man, a kid straight out of college who was still wet behind the ears, and a woman!

Woman. His thoughts shifted to the one who'd saved him. Who was she? Where had she come from? And why had she disappeared so quickly? He was determined to find out.

Jason had a hunch his mermaid would turn up again,

and soon. And if not, he was willing to take any risk to find her. . . .

Maris knew her adrenaline high had dissipated by the time the Wilkerson Industries christening party got into full swing. Along with nearly a hundred other people, she'd stood on the docks to watch Caroline Wilkerson, the owner's daughter, smash an expensive bottle of champagne on the prow of the new ship, named the *Caroline* in her honor. Then she'd ridden in one of the horse-drawn surreys that had been hired to transport the throng to one of Nassau's most elegant old hotels, the Sheraton British Colonial.

Once there, Maris was able to drink only one glass of celebratory champagne and share an energetic dance with a particularly frisky Brazilian before making her excuses and heading for the tables and chairs lined up on the edge of the hotel's private beach. She felt dizzy and very tired. The stress of the rescue was finally getting to her.

The low-slung canvas chair she sank into was comfortable enough to sleep in. Forcing her lazy eyelids to stay open, however, she flipped her long cascade of hair over one shoulder, careful to keep it from entangling her elaborate shell necklace. Loosening the slim tulip skirt of her turquoise cocktail dress around her legs, she slipped off one of her high-heeled sandals and gratefully dug her sore foot into the white sand. She wasn't used to executing fast-paced dances in such impractical shoes.

Gazing across the hotel's private beach, where the gala was sure to continue until the early hours of the morning, she noted the number of dancing couples on the beach's wooden dance platform. The Brazilian was there and he'd found another partner, thank goodness.

The steel band's island beat added to the exotic ambience of the setting. Nestled behind the spreading pale pink wings of the Sheraton Colonial, the beach was alive with the glow of pastel hanging lanterns and the colorful dresses of the women. Champagne flowed freely. Dignified white-coated waiters circulated with bottles and trays of tasty hor d'oeuvres.

"No thanks," Maris told the waiter who approached to refill her glass. "I already have enough champagne bubbles pulsing through my veins."

As the waiter moved away the crowd before Maris parted slightly, allowing a couple to pass through. The young woman with fine brown hair and a rather large nose—the most notable Wilkerson family feature—clung tightly to her escort's arm.

"Oh! I'm so-o exhausted," complained Caroline Wilkerson in a soft British accent as she daintily pressed a lacy handkerchief to her forehead. She looked up with an imploring gaze at the flashily dressed man beside her. "I have to rest, Thorpe, dear, if only for a little while. I'm on the verge of collapsing."

"Of course, darling." Thorpe Harris, Caroline's fiancé, placed his arm around her solicitously and helped her to the nearest vacant chair—the one next to Maris. "You've had a very busy and important evening."

As soon as Caroline was settled Thorpe glanced at the blonde, his openly appraising stare making Maris uncomfortable. Caroline seemed to notice her fiancé's shift in interest also and tugged on the sleeve of his bright pink jacket.

"Go to the bar and get me a glass of water, will you,

29

dear?" asked the young Englishwoman urgently. "With ice and lime."

Thorpe frowned slightly. "But we're celebrating tonight, aren't we, Caro? There's champagne . . ."

"I don't feel like drinking champagne at the moment."

With a quick nod Thorpe started for the bar. As he walked away Caroline sighed and turned to Maris with a friendly smile. "Sitting down feels so wonderful." She shrewdly eyed the other woman's outfit. "That's a lovely dress you're wearing. I noticed it earlier this evening. What kind of material is it made of? It positively shimmers."

"Silk," replied Maris, looking down at the dress. "And thank you for the compliment."

"You're with the Florida Aquarium crew, aren't you? Did you buy your dress in Florida too?"

Maris nodded and grinned politely. "In Miami."

"I should take a trip there sometime."

"We certainly should go to Miami, Caro, darling." Thorpe had returned, holding a glass of water in one hand, a stemmed glass and a full bottle of champagne in the other. "We could fix you up with a new wardrobe and buy me some colorful clothes." He handed Caroline the water and filled his wineglass up with the bubbly liquid, his speculative hazel gaze once again fixed on the blond curator.

Maris couldn't help but think that the man's clothing appeared quite Miami-ish enough already. A definite contrast to his fiancée in her unassuming beige print chiffon, Thorpe wore a flamingo-pink Italian suit over a matching silk T-shirt. Sporting the shadow of a beard on his face and a pair of metallic sunglasses atop his slicked-back hair, he was a gaudier version of the fashions made popular by the *Miami Vice* television show. Were the speculations about Thorpe's being a gigolo really true? Was Caroline so shy and insecure that she thought her father had to purchase a man for her?

"Would you care for more champagne?" Thorpe asked Maris, looking down his short, straight nose to sneak an admiring look at the cleavage revealed by her strapless dress.

"No thanks," she told him, subtly rearranging long strands of her shell necklace to block his view.

"Oh, come now, we're celebrating here," insisted Thorpe, filling her glass until she moved it away. Before he could say anymore, a stir in the surrounding crowd caused him to turn away.

"I'd like to make a toast!" boomed Arthur Wilkerson from the nearby table from which he'd just risen.

Caroline's father, president of Nassau-based Wilkerson Industries, was portly, extremely wealthy, and a descendant of four generations who'd lived in the islands. Standing next to him, his son and heir, Harold, made a taller, angular contrast to his rotund sire.

"Toast, toast!" called various people around the area.

"Yes, a toast," repeated Arthur vigorously, drawing himself up importantly and taking a deep breath that expanded his chest. "To success. To Wilkerson Industries—may our setbacks only serve to advance our progress."

"To more profits," seconded Harold, looking tense as he licked his lips. Behind the thick lenses of his eyeglasses, his large eyes sparkled in the lantern light.

"You should make a toast also, Caro," Thorpe whispered to Caroline. Helping his fiancée out of her chair, he hurried her toward the rest of her family.

"To success for everyone, Father," Caroline managed

to say right before glasses clicked and the wine was downed.

To be polite, Maris drank the half glass of wine Thorpe had poured. The potent effect of the champagne probably inspired her to play the what-kind-of-fish game as she watched the Wilkerson clan.

They certainly were a mismatched school. Petite, gray-haired wife in tow, Arthur Wilkerson had left his table to move grandly through the crowd like some kind of puffer fish, able to blow himself up to double size to express his pride and self-importance. Anxiously darting from side to side behind him came Harold, his long nose and physique identifying him as a sharp-snouted needlefish ready to spear any extra attention or cash that had been discarded by his father.

And then, of course, there was Thorpe Harris—a perfect specimen of a clown fish if Maris had ever seen one. Aggressive and brilliantly colored, the clown fish usually hung out in the equally brilliantly hued but deadly tentacles of the sea anemone. Maris frowned as Thorpe hovered over Caroline's slight form. Another mismatch. Instead of an anemone, the young Englishwoman resembled a plain little minnow. . . .

Maris decided it must be time for her to go. Through years of study and work as a curator, she'd frequently played the goofy game of comparing people to fish, but never while attending a colorful, noisy party. If she didn't feel like dancing or meeting new acquaintances tonight, she might as well return to the villa owned by Brian Nelson and go to sleep. Reaching over to place her stemmed glass on the nearest table, she picked up her evening purse. That was when she sighted him.

The tall man seemed to be stalking the school of Wilkersons as they swam through the waters of the

32

crowd. Watching him, Maris thought he had the look of a sleek predator. Trim-figured in his cream-colored suit worn over a gold-shot knit sweater, the man had a deep tan, dark blond hair, and rugged, sharply etched features that resembled the carved profiles on old coins. It took Maris a few seconds to realize that he was familiar, that when she'd last seen him he'd been ill, bedraggled, and not quite so magnificent.

The Adonis from the sea.

Just then, as if he were intuitively aware that he was being watched, Adonis turned toward her. The luminous eyes Maris knew to be deep gold widened. With recognition?

She leaned forward in her chair to rise as the tall man strode purposefully toward her. Her heart beat faster as his hunter's eyes impaled her with a yearning gaze.

"My mermaid," Adonis murmured softly. He knelt by her chair, his intent face only inches away. "You saved my life, lovely creature of the sea, and now have the power to claim it." He leaned closer to her, an inviting smile on his chiseled lips. "I'm all yours. Do with me what you will."

CHAPTER TWO

Jason had had a hunch he'd see his mermaid again, although certainly not this soon. When he'd spotted the beautiful blonde sitting on the fringes of the noisy party —her sleek turquoise dress flaring into a fluted skirt that even resembled a fishy tail—he'd stopped dead in his tracks. Completely forgetting about his self-imposed task of observing the Wilkerson clan, he'd stared in amazement. And strode swiftly to her side.

"You're all mine?" the blonde asked in response to his passionate declaration.

"Totally."

Although her striking blue-violet eyes watched him warily, her low, throaty voice vibrated with laughter. "Thanks, but I think you're a trifle large for the shelves where I keep my collectibles."

He laughed, observing the way she clutched the glittery evening bag in her lap. She looked as if she wanted to escape him, to swim . . . or, rather, run away. For the lady wasn't really a mythical sea creature, only an unusually beautiful human. And one who was obviously startled by his sudden approach.

He leaned back to give her the illusion of space and safety. "Words can't really express how I feel. If you hadn't been out there beneath the water today, I'd be a dead man." Anticipating her touch, he held out his hand. "Jason Price."

Her lips drawing into a genuine smile, she took the proffered handshake, her grip firm. "Maris Collier."

"Maris . . ." he repeated the name, and reluctantly released the smooth hand he wanted to caress. So far he was intrigued by the lady's mixture of cool sophistication and warmth. "Did you know Maris means 'of the sea'? It's very fitting." Rising to his feet, he grabbed a nearby chair and slid it over to sit next to her.

"Fitting?" she asked. "Why? Because I scuba dive? Or have you heard that I work for an aquarium?"

"A caretaker of fish." He nodded knowingly, admiring her long, silvery-blond hair and elaborate shell necklace that made her look like the mermaid he'd imagined her to be. "That makes sense too." Her eyebrows drew together in a puzzled frown, but since he didn't want to tell her about his hallucinatory fantasy at the moment, he explained, "You seemed at home in the sea . . . when I saw you earlier today."

"It's a wonder you remember me in any capacity," she remarked dryly. "As sick as you were."

"Carbon monoxide poisoning isn't much fun," he agreed, preferring instead to remember how exciting their embrace in the water had been.

Her blue-violet eyes traveled over him, and he hoped she was recalling the very same thing. "You appear to have recovered nicely. What happened to your tanks, anyway? Who filled them?"

"One of my staff."

"They made a dangerously careless mistake," she said, seeming genuinely concerned.

"Accidents happen."

"And why were you diving alone in the first place? I

35

wouldn't have had to come to your aid if you'd had a buddy diver."

He didn't like interrogations, but as his rescuer he supposed she had a right to ask questions. That didn't mean he had an obligation to tell her everything. In his kind of business he was used to keeping his own counsel.

"Actually, I had a couple of partners," he explained. "They were diving on the other side of the boat this afternoon."

"That was obviously too far away. You should be more careful." She fingered her necklace. "When you dive below the surface of the water, you're entering a completely different element. It's not at all like land sports."

"I'm not a sport diver. I'm a professional—"

"Jason Price!"

Arthur Wilkerson's booming voice drowned out his words. A champagne glass in his hand, the large Englishman made his way over to the seated couple. He gazed down at Jason with eyes that seemed small and pale in the width of his florid face.

"Thought I spotted you when I was making my speech," said Arthur. "How's the investigation going? Found any of my ships? Located any wreckage?"

Jason shrugged. "I have a few leads."

"Well, I should hope so," admonished Arthur. "Just keep me informed of the details. Heard you're the best in the salvaging business. Intercontinental Mutual was wise to hire you."

Jason merely smiled. Arthur's enthusiasm seemed a trifle too hearty. Could he have scuttled his own ships for the insurance money? Or somehow taken them to another port and sold their cargoes? Of course the radar on the ships had reportedly bleeped out. . . .

"Those bloody freighters have got to be out there somewhere," the Englishman continued. "Don't believe in any of that rubbish about curses or the Bermuda Triangle."

"And what about simple foul play, Father?" asked Harold Wilkerson, who'd suddenly joined the group. "Do you believe in that?" The younger man gazed down his long nose at Jason as if in challenge.

"Something happened to those three freighters," said Arthur, turning toward his son. "But I can't say whether their loss was caused by man or nature. That's for Mr. Price to find out."

"Or for me," said Harold stiffly, giving Jason another cold glance. "At least I seem to remember being appointed head of the in-house investigation. We don't need the help of outsiders."

The company investigation. That was why Harold seemed to regard him as a competitor, Jason realized. When beginning his own inquiries he'd heard rumors about disagreements between father and son. Most people said Arthur distrusted his heir and refused to give him any important responsibilities. Could Harold, undoubtedly resentful, have sunk the family's ships to get even with his father?

"You're in charge of the company's investigation, all right," Arthur told Harold brusquely. "But I don't care who unravels the mystery, the insurance company or us, as long as it's solved. Three ships in less than a year —never lost so many in such a short time span in all the years of Wilkerson Industries."

"You want the insurance company to find the ships?"

said Harold with a derisive snort. "They've practically accused us of sinking those freighters ourselves."

His florid face getting redder, Arthur appeared to be irritated. "Well, of course. Insurance companies have to do a thorough investigation, question everyone. That's what subscribers are paying them to do. And, in this case, there's millions of dollars involved."

"Millions of Wilkerson dollars," muttered the younger man with a pained expression.

"For God's sake, think positive, Harold. We'll get the money back," insisted Arthur. "And double our profits to boot." He swirled the champagne left in his glass and held it up to Jason in a toast. "Here's to success, Mr. Price. You know about success, don't you? I've heard you're a lucky man."

"There's some luck involved in my profession," said Jason, thinking to himself that finding lost ships, whether for salvage or treasure, was damned hard work.

Jason gazed at Maris, who'd been sitting quietly, but her eyes were following Harold as he stalked away. It was impossible to tell what she was thinking, but Jason hoped the talk of sunken freighters hadn't turned her off.

"Harold!" Arthur shouted after his son. "Come back here, I haven't finished talking to you."

But the younger Wilkerson kept going, striding toward the far side of the hotel where there wasn't as much of a crowd. Harold didn't even pause when Thorpe Harris ran up to accost him but only walked faster. Obviously realizing he was being brushed off, Thorpe turned away, scowling.

"Ah, well, I'll talk to Harold later," muttered Arthur. He suddenly seemed to notice Maris. "I see you're lucky in other areas as well, Mr. Price, if this beautiful lady is your companion for the evening."

The blonde smiled up at him. "Actually, I'm Maris Collier, Mr. Wilkerson. Brian Nelson is my boss."

"Oh, so you're with the Coral Gardens Aquarium," remarked Arthur thoughtfully. "Tell Brian I'm sorry I didn't have much time for him. I saw him for only a few minutes when I arrived at the hotel. Maybe we can get together later on in the week."

Jason frowned. Arthur Wilkerson and Maris had a mutual acquaintance? He hoped that fact wouldn't lead to a lengthy discussion between the two of them. He wanted to get his mermaid off someplace alone.

"I'll tell him," Maris promised. "Thanks for the invitation to your party. We're all staying at Brian's house on Paradise Island through the month of April." She yawned. "That's where I should be right now."

As she started to rise from her chair Jason got to his feet and Arthur stepped forward. Both men offered her a helping hand, but it was Jason's strong bronze one that possessively grasped her upper arm. When she wobbled unsteadily he slid his hand upward, placing an arm around her shoulders.

"Too much champagne?" he murmured, inhaling the fresh scent of her hair as she leaned against him.

"No, only one shoe," she replied, her amused smile dazzling him. She stared down at the sand and politely extricated herself from his hold. "I took off my left sandal. I wonder where it is?"

"Well, I guess I'll leave you two alone," Arthur said.

Jason looked up to find the portly man already distracted, waving to some well-dressed influential men at the poolside bar. Almost everyone who was anyone in Nassau had attended the evening's affair.

Arthur turned before walking away. "I'm sure I'll see you both around the city. And I meant what I said about wishing you luck in finding those ships, Mr. Price."

If the Englishman had had anything to do with his own vessels' disappearance, Jason concluded, he was capable of hiding his guilt under the guise of very real-looking sincerity. And it was hard to imagine him or even uptight Harold poisoning a salvage diver's tanks. But someone had done so. . . .

Just thinking about the many possibilities involved in the mystery—family intrigue, rivalry between local companies, piracy—made Jason realize he'd been neglecting the detective work he'd intended to do at the party. Maybe he was a cynic, but he just didn't believe in superstition. The Wilkerson freighters had disappeared in the Bermuda Triangle without a trace—no wreckage, no bodies washing up on some island's shore—but he knew there had to be some very mortal explanation for the incidents. And he might have gotten some leads tonight if he'd wandered around observing everyone. Instead, he'd let himself be distracted by a beautiful siren.

But what a siren, he thought, glancing down at Maris, who'd bent over to shake the sand from the shoe she'd finally found and was slipping it on her foot. Her sweetly curving backside made Jason raise his eyebrows appreciatively.

When she stood up and slung her purse over her shoulder, he accompanied her through the crowd, heading down the concrete walkway that led to the rear entrance of the hotel. Reaching across to take hold of her arm, he quickly slid it through his own before she could resist.

"Where to now?" he asked with a big smile.

She tried to pull away, but he held her captive. "I don't know where *you're* going, but I'm on my way to Paradise Island. I need to get some sleep."

"I know of a nice warm bed that's a lot closer," he said teasingly, thinking of his boat anchored at the dock.

"I said I need to sleep," she repeated meaningfully, trying not to smile.

"Who said you couldn't do that on the *Argonaut?*"

She shook her head, but he could tell she was amused. "I think I'll be safer on Paradise."

The wry glance she gave him from beneath lowered lashes made his heart beat faster. It was about time she reacted to his oft-tested charms.

"You might be safer on Paradise, but you'll be happier on the *Argonaut,*" he said decisively. "In fact, I'd venture to say you might even be ecstatic there if you'd just relax and let yourself go."

"Oh? That's certainly an arrogant statement if I ever heard one."

"I'd prefer to call it self-confident."

"Or conceited."

He decided to change his tactics. "Actually, don't you think it's a little early for sleep? Why don't you let me express my gratitude to you by buying you dinner and drinks somewhere?"

"I'm not in Nassau for the nightlife. I came to the Caribbean to enjoy the water, to dive, and to collect fish," she replied, her sparkling eyes belying her no-nonsense tone of voice. "I already spend most of my life on land." Stopping by the open French doors that led into the hotel's inner bar, she tried once again to escape from his grip. "I have to get back to Paradise Island—I have an early dive tomorrow morning."

"So who says we can't catch a quick bite over there?"

Lord, the man was persistent. Taking a deep breath, Maris was about to explain that she wasn't hungry when she caught sight of someone who evidently was—a thin man busily helping himself to generous servings of the refreshments at the hors d'oeuvres tables nearby. She couldn't help but stare.

"What's he doing here?" she said wonderingly, speaking half to herself. Clad in a dirty T-shirt and old jeans, the seaman from the *Mermaid's Kiss* stood out like a sore thumb among the well-dressed guests.

Finally releasing her arm, Jason turned to look. "That's just crazy Gallagher. He probably wandered into the party, saw the food, and is helping himself."

"You know him? He's the first mate on our boat."

Jason nodded. "He's still a capable seaman, though he used to be a crack diver when we both lived in the Florida keys. Too bad he blew part of his brain cells away by diving too deep."

"Is that what's wrong with him?" For a second Maris wondered how long Jason himself had been a diver.

Gallagher glanced up at the couple as if he didn't recognize either of them, then turned his back to walk away with two heaping platefuls of food. The shabby man ambled right past Caroline Wilkerson, earning a baleful stare.

"At least Gallagher's enjoying himself," Jason said with a chuckle. "Even a goofy guy like him knows how to have fun. Are you sure you don't have time for one drink?" He gazed at her with persuasive amber eyes. "That would only be a drop in the bucket, but I'd like to repay you in some way."

"You don't owe me anything," she assured him once and for all, annoyed that she felt tempted to accept the invitation. "I would have done the same for anyone."

"*Anyone?*"

He obviously didn't like that statement. Probably a man with his looks and practiced charm was used to being fawned over. Although flattered by his attentions, Maris decided she'd better keep him at arm's length. After all, she really didn't know much about him, except for the fact that he'd been careless about diving procedure.

"Mr. Price?" Caroline approached, smiling. "Are you leaving so soon? My father told me to give you our private number at home in case you can't reach him at the office."

Jason raised his brows. "If I need to call him, I won't bother him at home."

"Oh, but you never know," said Caroline, opening the clasp of her velvet evening bag. "I have a card in here . . ." She stiffened, her eyes widening before she dropped the purse like a hot coal. "E-e-e-k!"

Spooked, Maris stepped backward as the contents of the purse spilled across the concrete—a pencil, a compact, a small wallet . . . and a bloody, decapitated chicken head. Without thinking, she grasped Jason's hand.

"Thorpe!" shrilled Caroline.

Thorpe Harris suddenly materialized out of the crowd that was gathering around. "Caro, darling!"

Caroline collapsed into his arms. Shaking, she pointed at the chicken head. "That horrible thing was in my purse! Call the police!"

"Now, Caro," crooned Thorpe. "This is hardly important enough for the police."

"But someone had to have put that thing in there intentionally," Caroline wailed petulantly. "And it isn't as if it were the first time something like this has happened. What will they do next?"

"What will who do next?" a woman guest hissed to another as they stood nearby.

"It's voodoo, mon," muttered one of the hotel's black bartenders, edging away.

"Or maybe not," said Jason, so quietly only Maris heard him.

As Caroline clung to her fiancé and the rest of the gathering stood as if transfixed, Gallagher casually made his way into the center of the crowd. Still munching from a plate, he stooped to pick up the grisly head and held it up to examine it. An elderly lady made a wretching sound and Thorpe raised his eyes to glare at the invader.

"Put that down!" Thorpe demanded.

"Just part of a chicken," Gallagher muttered before throwing it back on the concrete and quietly disappearing.

"Move aside. Let me through, I say," bellowed Arthur Wilkerson, pushing his way to the forefront. He stared at the splotches of red marking Caroline's dress and at the purse and its contents scattered across the walkway. "What's all this rubbish? Has someone hurt my little girl?"

"Daddy!" Moving away from Thorpe, Caroline grabbed her father's arm. "Someone put that thing in my purse!"

"H-r-rmph. Nasty." The elder Wilkerson stared at the chicken head and patted his daughter on the back in an awkward attempt to comfort her. "But nothing too serious. I thought you were being killed."

"Well, it's obvious someone wishes I were dead," stated Caroline.

"Now, now." Her father patted her again and gently pushed her toward her fiancé. "Why don't you let Thorpe take you home, sweetheart?" As the two young people started to leave the portly man motioned to a waiter. "Get over here! Clean this mess up!" Then Arthur gazed around at the gathered guests. "Don't let a small thing like this spoil the evening. Go on!" he commanded. "Mingle! Celebrate!"

Jason laughed low in his throat and looked down at Maris. "A take-charge kind of guy, huh?"

She had to laugh, too, although the whole incident she'd just witnessed had left her feeling uneasy. She didn't even object when, still holding her hand, Jason led her through the quiet, nearly empty darkness of the hotel bar.

"Why don't we take a taxi over to Paradise?" he suggested as they made their way out of the bar toward the lobby.

She had to object to that, however. "I'm really too tired to go out. I want to head straight for my boss's house."

"Then that's exactly where I'll take you."

If she hadn't gotten spooked at the party, Maris knew she would never have accepted a cab ride with Jason Price. Not only was the man a virtual stranger, but he was also dangerously attractive. She'd been fighting the deadly combination of his stunning good looks and pushy charm all evening. She had to keep remembering he wasn't her type, that he was probably an irresponsible thrill-seeker. Why else had she found him venturing alone deep beneath the water, trying to breathe from a fouled tank?

As the taxi sped down Nassau's streets she sneaked a look at Jason's chiseled profile, visible against the passing streetlights and the pale flood of a full tropical moon. Even silent, he radiated raw energy, a vitality that could only be described as . . . primitive or wild.

Wild? Primitive? She frowned. Wasn't she letting her imagination get away with her? Couldn't she be overreacting to the first man who'd really appealed to her since the husband she'd divorced a little more than a year before?

"Did the voodoo stunt scare you?"

"Hmm?" she mumbled, startled by Jason's deep voice.

"You've been so quiet, I was wondering if you were shook up by the sight of that chicken head." He turned toward her, sliding his arm across the back of the seat within inches of her bare shoulders. "You have to realize there are still a lot of native Bahamians who resent the English because they continue to control most of the money on the islands, even though the Bahamas are now independent."

"You think that's why someone used voodoo tonight?"

"Maybe. And then someone might have a personal vendetta against Caroline Wilkerson. Maybe she fired a household servant and he or she decided to put a curse on her. Of course it's all a bunch of superstition."

Almost imagining that she could feel the heat emanating from the bronzed arm behind her, Maris told him, "You don't have to reassure me. I'm all right. My nerves were a little jangled, that's all. I startle easily when I'm exhausted."

He nodded. "Diving can take a lot out of you, especially when you're not used to doing it as an everyday activity."

"Do you dive every day?" she asked, feeling envious.

"Pretty much, unless there's a storm."

The taxi rounded a sharp corner near the high, curving bridge that connected Nassau to the smaller Paradise Island—site of numerous resorts, a casino, and many homes of the wealthy—and Jason slid a little closer, his muscular thigh brushing against her own turquoise silk-covered one. She tried to ignore the electric sensations that the glancing touch produced in her.

When the taxi stopped at the top of the bridge, Jason leaned forward to hand the driver money for the crossing fee. Maris glanced away from the sight of his broad back and gazed out the rear window at the moon-kissed water of Nassau's deep-water harbor and the huge cruise ships anchored there. Built on a gentle hill, the city nestled around the harbor, twinkling with lights that were only a little brighter than the canopy of stars above. It was a perfect setting for romance. Too bad she wasn't having any.

But she'd thank herself for her resolve tomorrow, she thought. She had to keep remembering she'd been telling the truth when she'd said she had no time for social life, what with all the work she had to do. Trying to remember just what her duties were for the following day, she quietly slid farther across the seat, placing more space between her and Jason. He didn't seem to notice, making small talk as the taxi barreled down darkened, palm-lined streets until they reached the address she'd given.

"Is this it?" asked the driver.

The house was unfamiliar in the darkness, and Maris

peered through the wrought-iron gates at the tree- and shrub-filled garden that fronted the place. Many yards away, down by the private beach, a lonely light glowed above the doorway of Brian's multileveled structure. Obviously most of the crew were asleep and the rest hadn't yet returned from the christening party.

"This is it." She gathered up her purse. "Thanks for escorting me here," she told Jason, relieved she was finally home free. "I'll be happy to help out with the taxi fare."

He grinned. "No way. A gentleman doesn't take a lady's money . . . and he doesn't let her walk through a dark garden by herself either." He handed the driver a couple of bills. "Pull the car over and wait for me," he told the man. "I'll make it worth your while."

"But I'll be fine," insisted Maris.

Her objection was to no avail. Jason had already gotten out of the taxi and was striding around to her side. She managed to open her own door, but he was standing right outside it, ready to give her a helping hand.

"Seriously, it's not dangerous here."

He raised his thick eyebrows above glittering eyes. "No monsters lurking behind the bushes?" he asked in a hushed tone. "No ghosts—chickcharneys the natives call them—floating around in the trees? Not even a couple of snakes or huge island cockroaches—"

"Stop it," she demanded. "Quit trying to scare me or I'll tell you what sharks do to arrogant divers."

He laughed, and in spite of herself she couldn't help but appreciate his sense of humor. Closing the taxi door, he walked beside her to open the gate. "I'm only offering my protective services. You were kind enough to look out for my safety today. I'd like to do the same for you."

48

"Well, I suppose if you put it that way," she said, entering the garden first and gazing around at the shadows. Without him, she privately conceded, the overgrown place could look a little eerie.

Besides, he sounded sincere. She had no real reason to distrust him. And, after all, she'd already refused to go out to dinner with the man. So she supposed a short walk couldn't hurt. Of course that walk would wind down a narrow path through a dark, flower-laden garden under a full romantic moon, all to the tune of not-so-distant waves and the balmy sigh of the tradewind. But the taxi was waiting. What's the worst he would do? Kiss her?

Unfortunately, it was herself she distrusted most. It was too easy for her to imagine those sensuous lips roaming over her own, his breath mingling with hers, his arms molding her against the length of his body. . . . Distracted by her fantasies, she almost stumbled.

"Watch out," he warned, catching hold of her waist.

She was embarrassed and all too aware of the strong fingers holding on to her. "I'm usually not this clumsy. It's just the fatigue and these shoes."

"Uh-huh. A fish out of water—I've seen you move like a dream in the sea."

"You think I'm a fish?" She decided that conversation would help reduce the tension that was rife between them. "Actually, I guess I was always better at swimming than walking. That's why I love coming to the islands." She paused meaningfully. "And why I have no time for nightlife while I'm here." She was relieved when he let go of her to walk by her side. Focusing on the light above the house's door, she lengthened her stride. "I have to get up very early tomorrow morning. We're going out to the Bahama Banks again to dive."

"Yes, I know how it is. I'll be getting up early too," he told her, easily keeping pace. "I've been working about six days out of seven the past few weeks. I was feeling tired when I first got to the party, but then I saw you—"

"Working six or seven days in your search for those lost ships?" she interrupted swiftly, seeking a topic that would divert him from any thought of taking her in his arms. If she could only get him talking, she could slip her keys out and be ready to enter the waiting door. "Wreck diving can be dangerous, can't it?"

"Almost as dangerous as love."

She ignored that remark as she fumbled in her purse. "Have you really got any idea of where those ships went?"

"I have lots of ideas."

Unfortunately, at the moment she was sure they didn't concern lost ships at all. Struggling to remember the conversation about the freighters at the party, she stubbornly persisted with her questions. "Do you think there's foul play involved?"

"Maybe." He brushed against her as they skirted some low-leafed palms. "But they say all's fair in love and war."

"We're not talking about love or war," she pointed out, becoming irritated with the way he kept turning her questions around. "We're talking about missing ships. And if there's crime involved, crime involving lots of money, you'd better watch out. You could be in danger."

"At the moment I'm certainly in danger of losing my heart."

They'd almost reached the house when he stopped to gaze at her, barring the path. "Do you believe in magical things?"

She stepped back, pulse racing, aware that she probably wasn't going to escape him tonight. "What are you talking about now? The Bermuda Triangle? Chickcharneys?"

"No, I'm talking about kisses . . . and mermaids. I saw a mermaid this very day. She had beautiful long blond hair with fish swimming through it and violet eyes. She saved my life and kissed me. You know what that means, don't you, Maris of the Sea?"

She caught her breath as he towered solidly over her. "You thought I was a mermaid?"

"I imagined it for a few moments. And the kiss was so good, I could believe the old legend was true . . . if a mermaid kisses a man, he'll belong to her forever. After tasting your lips I was ready to let you take me to the bottom of the sea. It was positively magical."

He placed his hands around her waist while she stood frozen, unable to move away. Sighing helplessly, she offered one last excuse. "But you weren't in your right mind."

"You mean I only imagined the kiss was that good?" he asked huskily. "Well, let's try another one right now."

He pulled her tightly against him, covering her half-open mouth seductively with his own. The embrace seemed so inevitable and natural, she wondered why she'd bothered to fight against it for so long. She sighed as she let her arms slide up around his neck. Full breasts pressed against the hard wall of his chest, she could feel the outline of something round beneath his lightweight sweater—a medal? A coin?

Then the sensations he was causing with his lips and tongue made her lose track of any logical thought. Exploring the deepest surfaces of her mouth, he seemed to be searching for treasure there. At the same time his large hands caressed her spine beneath the thin silk dress. Their bodies touched sweetly from breast to thigh.

Dreamily, Maris recalled what he'd said about his vision of her as a mermaid. No wonder he'd had visions. As they kissed she found it easy to imagine a fabulous watery otherworld, complete with jewel-toned fish, thrones and castles made of shells, and an immortal prince of a merman who could lure her to the depths and keep her there. But for now she preferred real flesh and blood. Kneading the muscles of Jason's back, she moved her hips sensuously against him, gratified when she felt his response.

He groaned. Then he lifted his head to look at her. "It's just as magical," he said softly, breathing heavily.

"Yes," she agreed simply, wanting more.

But he just stood there, staring down at her, his expression unreadable in the darkness. The pause brought her back to her senses. Over his shoulder she glimpsed the moon . . . and the house with its lighted door. The light was the beacon she'd been heading for and should be heading for still. What had she been thinking of?

Or, rather, the problem was that she hadn't been thinking at all. Erotic arousal was just a physical response. And the merman and his underwater kingdom had been mere fantasy. Jason Price wasn't her type, if it could be said she had a type. She hadn't even decided what she wanted from another man. Gathering all her willpower, she pushed against his chest.

"I have to go inside now."

She was surprised and a little disappointed when he loosened his grip so easily. She wriggled free and stepped past him to head toward the door.

"Can we do this again? Tomorrow night?"

Having just inserted the key in the lock, she whipped around to see him standing in the same place on the path. "I told you I have to work."

"But you've also got to have some time off. When are you free? I want to see you." His eyes looked imploring in the dusky light.

"I'll see you only when and if we're in the same area of the water," she said with an air of finality as she hurried inside to close the door.

On the other side, she felt like a fish that had escaped one of her own traps. She leaned back against the wood and sighed as his footsteps faded away. Then she headed for her room, telling herself over and over again that she was tired, busy, and reluctant to get involved with the man. She only wished his embrace hadn't felt so good.

CHAPTER THREE

White foam churning up around her prow, the sixty-five-foot *Mermaid's Kiss* cut smoothly through the turquoise waters of Nassau's harbor. Standing at the rail, letting the sun and wind dry her loosened hair, Maris drank in the brilliant sunset glowing directly ahead.

It had been a very productive day. Diving near the area they'd tried yesterday, she and Paul had captured a pair of the elusive and shimmering black cap basslets. Some of the crew had trawled shallow waters near an uninhabited island—using a net held open by lead weights at the bottom and buoys at the top—coming up with a couple of small lobsters and a scorpion fish, all important items on the aquarium's shopping list.

"Good day, huh?" asked Jo Schneider, echoing Maris's thoughts as she joined her at the rail. "I told you we'd do well on this trip. I take it you didn't sight any more Adonises while you were down there, though."

"No, thank heavens," said Maris with a broad smile. One rescue had been enough.

"Well, if you find another one and want to throw him back, aim him at one of your single friends, okay?"

"I'll be sure to do that."

Maris only wished she could throw aside her memories of Jason Price. She'd been having second, third, and even fourth thoughts after sending him away the night before. Any other woman certainly would have jumped at the chance to go out with such a gorgeous man, would have made time for him in the busiest schedule. If she hadn't been so exhausted, perhaps she would have agreed to see him again. She'd be in the islands for only a short while. It wasn't as if the relationship had to be serious.

Considering the possibilities, Maris scanned the Nassau docks as they went by, searching for a white boat called the *Argonaut*. But she needn't have bothered—there were far too many crafts tied up in the teeming harbor to pick out any particular one.

As the research vessel left the harbor, making a wide, curving turn toward the Paradise Island docks, Maris told herself again that she was better off without any romance to mess up her Bahamas plans. Tomorrow, on Sunday, her only day off, she wanted to spend most of her time snorkeling and scuba diving in the clear, shallow blue waters off nearby Rose Island, known for its lovely coral reefs.

"Hey, watch out!" yelled Paul from behind the women, near the stern of the aquarium boat. "What are you doing, buddy? Trying to kill someone?"

Jo and Maris turned to look back. A speedboat was roaring directly toward them. And the smaller craft didn't seem to be allowing sufficient room to maneuver around them. It was going to ram into their boat! At the last possible second the speedboat's driver took it bouncing across the *Mermaid's* choppy wake, then zoomed up to within a hair's breadth of the side of the research vessel.

Maris's eyes widened behind her sunglasses and her

heart beat faster as she recognized the man behind the wheel of the speedboat—Jason Price. Was he showing off? For her? He smiled up at the women standing near the rail as he cut his speedboat's motor. She supposed she shouldn't be surprised that he was acting like a daredevil. His solo dive had proven he liked to take unnecessary risks.

Bare-chested, wearing only a pair of cutoffs and a chain and pendant around his neck, Jason kept the speedboat parallel with the *Mermaid's Kiss* as it headed for the dock. "Is this close enough, Maris of the Sea?" he called.

"Close enough for what?" Maris shouted down at him.

He pointed at the narrow ribbon of water separating the two boats. "Isn't this what you meant by 'the same area of the water'? Or do you want me to jump in?"

"Jump, by all means," she suggested, unable to keep herself from smiling.

"Ah, come on," said Jo, gazing down at Jason admiringly. "Don't be cruel to such a gorgeous man."

"It won't hurt him," Maris assured her co-worker. "He looks the same, wet or dry."

"I'll take that remark as a backhanded compliment." Jason aimed a sexy grin at the blonde, his straight teeth appearing startlingly white against his tan. "And since I've heard your boat is staying in port tomorrow, how about coming out with me—*on* and *in* the water?"

"What do you have in mind?" Maris asked, wondering who he'd spoken to about the *Mermaid's* schedule.

"I've got a lot of things in mind, but I'll settle for some diving." Jason laughed and turned the speedboat to the side as the research vessel slowed, getting ready to edge into its dock space. As the distance between the boats increased he shouted, "How would you like to go looking for sunken treasure?"

"Treasure?" called Maris, intrigued.

"Spanish gold!" he yelled back over his shoulder before turning around to concentrate on docking his own boat.

"Diving for gold? Sounds like fun," remarked Jo. "But then, I'd go visit a tar pit with the likes of him. Is this someone you met around Nassau?"

"That's the Adonis I pulled from the sea yesterday." A little irritated with the senior aquarist's wholehearted approval of Jason, a man she didn't even know, Maris added, "He's attractive, but appearances aren't everything."

"No, but he also sounds charming. And how do you know he doesn't have a big gorgeous heart to match that face and body?"

Agreed. She didn't know about Jason's heart yet. But she wouldn't be in the islands long enough to probe the deeper side of his personality. Meanwhile, it wouldn't hurt to spend a diverting day with the man. She'd made up her mind to do so long before the *Mermaid's Kiss* was securely tied up and Jason came striding toward her.

"Well? What do you say?" He looked at her expectantly after she jumped down from the high deck of the boat to the dock below.

"Sure, I'd like to go. I've never been treasure diving before."

"Wonderful. I'll pick you up here at eight in the morning." He stepped closer, his eyes gleaming with pleasure. "I promise you'll spend plenty of time in the water."

And plenty of time with him, Maris thought, noting

the gold coin hanging from a long chain around his neck, obviously the object she'd felt through his sweater the night before. It was on display now, shining as it lay upon his broad muscular chest with its light mat of golden hair.

"Like it?" he asked.

At first she thought he was referring to his muscular physique. Then, realizing he meant the coin, she nodded appreciatively. "Is that a piece of eight?"

"A doubloon." He fingered the ancient-looking coin, lifting it from his chest. "Pieces of eight are made of silver."

"Oh." She knew little of antiquities.

"I wear it for good luck. Maybe we'll find some more of these tomorrow."

"That would be interesting. But aren't you afraid to wear that everywhere? It must be worth a small fortune."

He gazed down at the coin again. "Hmm. Doubloons are solid gold. And this one was in particularly good condition, so I'd say it was worth ten to twelve thousand. Of course I destroyed its true value when I had a hole drilled through it."

He was wearing a solid gold coin, worth at least ten thousand dollars . . . in broad daylight? Wasn't he afraid of being mugged? Not knowing quite whether to believe him, she asked another question. "Did you pick that up on a treasure dive?"

"A long time ago."

Before she could inquire as to exactly when and where, Brian Nelson called to her from the top deck of the research vessel. "We'll have that planning meeting in a couple of hours, all right, Maris?"

"I'll be there," she agreed.

"A couple of hours?" remarked Jason. "That gives us time for a drink. How about taking a ride across the harbor for a quick one?"

"Sure, go ahead, Maris," Jo urged her, sidling by with a wink. "The rest of us are probably going to indulge in some liquid refreshment when we get back to the house."

Maris looked inquiringly at Jason. "You'll get me back in two hours?"

"No problem. Just let me know when you have to leave."

"And we aren't going anywhere fancy, are we?" she asked, indicating the casual printed shorts and matching blouse she'd changed into after the afternoon's dive.

"It's not a dressy place, but you'd look great anywhere," he assured her as he admired her face and figure, caressing her curves with his eyes.

Whatever else he was, Jason Price was definitely sexy, Maris thought, wondering what it was going to be like to spend an entire day with him.

The speedboat ride back across the harbor took only a few minutes. On the way Jason gave Maris the wheel while he slipped on a shirt. Enjoying the power of the craft's motor, she sent it hurtling along whenever there was enough open space, throwing spray up on both sides. Then, jokingly calling her reckless, Jason placed both arms around her to help steer the boat into the dock. She shivered as his warm breath feathered the back of her neck.

"Cold?" he asked.

"In a refreshing way," she lied, actually feeling overheated. "The spray from the boat hit me."

"Well, let's go warm you up."

Leaping from the speedboat, he held out a hand to

help her onto the dock. Then he pointed out a bar only a short distance away. It had a peeling painted sign hanging above its doorway.

"The Rum Keg," Maris read aloud.

She needn't have worried about her clothing because the place looked pretty seedy. Why had Jason wanted to bring her here? Maris asked herself. As they approached the Rum Keg two grimy-looking seamen came out. Jason drew her arm through his protectively.

"This is the kind of bar where local sailors and fishermen hang out," he explained. "And where you go if you want to hear harbor gossip. Someone in the Rum Keg told me the captain of the *Mermaid's Kiss* doesn't take her out on Sundays. That's why I figured you'd be off tomorrow."

"I wondered how you knew."

"I'll take you to a nicer bar or restaurant next time."

Just how often did he think he'd get to see her? she wondered. Then she concentrated on trying to see as they entered the dark, smoky establishment. When her vision had adjusted she observed several men hunched over the long bar that paralleled the main wall. A row of low-backed booths lined another wall, candles flickering on some of the tables. As soon as they'd taken a few steps inside, a dark-haired woman leaned out from one of the booths to motion to them.

"Carmen! I didn't know if you'd still be here." Jason guided Maris toward the woman and seated her on the opposite side of the table. "This is Carmen Ferrara, one of my crew. Her husband is my first mate. Carmen, this is—"

"Jason's very own personal mermaid," a mustached man came up from behind Jason to finish the statement. His dark eyes snapping with humor, he was carrying a pitcher of beer and a basket of potato chips from the bar. "Actually, I'm just teasing." He put the food down and held out his hand. "Alonzo Ferrara."

"Maris Collier," said Maris, introducing herself.

Having seen him the day of the rescue, she now recognized Jason's first mate. Shaking his hand, then Carmen's, she guessed that it wasn't surprising that Jason's crew knew about his hallucinatory fantasies. He'd probably been raving after she'd left him on the boat.

Getting two beer mugs from the bar, Jason slid into the booth beside her. Alonzo sat next to his wife, Carmen, on the other side. Maris leaned into the warmth of Jason's arm as he slipped it across the back of the booth. It felt good, though not as titillating as the close proximity of their bare thighs beneath the table.

"Monte wants to talk to you, amigo," Alonzo told Jason quietly, nodding toward the bartender, a small red-haired man with a huge handlebar mustache. "Whenever you have time."

"I know. I told him I'll see him after I take Maris back to Paradise Island," said Jason, a sober look on his face.

Was Monte a friend of Jason's? Maris wondered. She supposed a bartender would be a great source of gossip.

"So, I hear you're a curator of fish . . . when you're not saving drowning divers," Carmen said, smiling warmly at Maris. Then her expression grew more serious. "Let me assure you, Jason's usually not down there alone."

That was interesting. Jason's own crew had been concerned about him. Giving the man a sidelong glance, Maris made no comment, joining in only when Alonzo launched into a discussion of rare tropical fish and diving in the Bahamas. Maris liked the Ferraras, especially

61

Carmen, who was friendly, intelligent, and down to earth. She was amused when the woman told her she'd first met Alonzo while swimming during a vacation, then found out they both had taught at the same university in Puerto Rico.

"What were you teaching?" asked Maris, slowly sipping her beer.

"Latin American history and literature," explained Carmen. "And Alonzo was teaching marine science. Neither of us knew we'd eventually get into professional diving, although amateur diving was an avid interest of my husband's at the time."

"Then they ran into me and I stole them both away from serious academic careers," explained Jason, lightly touching the shoulder exposed by Maris's sleeveless blouse.

She turned toward him to find his lips only inches away and took a deep breath. They might have been able to share a kiss if the other couple hadn't been present. But Maris also liked the fact that the Ferraras were there. The warmth and trust obvious among the three—Alonzo mentioned they'd all worked together for several years—cast a positive light on Jason's character.

Alonzo definitely loved diving—he told Maris he'd dived on nearly every coral reef in the world, including the Great Barrier Reef of Australia and the one in the Red Sea. Fascinated, she asked him about his experiences in these more exotic locales, places she'd like to visit herself someday. Everyone got so involved in the ensuing conversation that no one noticed Monte Adams standing near their table until the bartender spoke.

"Jason?"

The entire group looked up.

"You know, on second thought, I think you should

taste that special rum over at the bar," said Monte, twirling his mustache.

"That special, huh?" asked Jason. "It can't wait?" He turned to Maris after the bartender nodded and turned to walk away. "I'll be back in a minute. I'm a rum connoisseur."

When Jason rose Alonzo followed suit. "I'd like to taste that rum too," the first mate told his wife.

Carmen looked at Maris and rolled her eyes. "Rum! What a secret code. As if we couldn't guess they're talking about those missing ships."

"The Wilkerson freighters?"

"Yes. I'm not supposed to mention the case—and I wouldn't if I weren't certain you're a disinterested party."

"I'd never even heard about the ships until last night," Maris assured the woman, glancing over at the door as someone entered. "I guess their disappearance —three in one year—is very odd."

"Uncanny is more like it."

Maris shifted uncomfortably as she recognized the man who'd just come inside. Standing at the bar, Gallagher stared at her for a few unsmiling seconds, just as he'd stared at her from time to time on shipboard all day, giving her the creeps.

"Is something the matter?" Carmen asked, glancing in the direction of Maris's stare.

Maris shook her head. "I don't particularly like that man—Gallagher—he's the mate on our research boat."

"Oh, that guy," said Carmen. "Don't worry, Jason knows him and says he's harmless enough."

"I'm sure Jason's right. It's just that I work on the boat with Gallagher and then I seem to find him everywhere else as well. He was even at the party last night.

He picked up the severed chicken head Caroline Wilkerson found in her purse."

"Chicken head?" Carmen's eyes widened.

"Yes, I guess the repulsive thing was some kind of voodoo stunt."

Carmen shuddered. "Jason didn't tell me about that incident, but then he already thinks I'm too superstitious. I know he believes someone intentionally sunk or stole those freighters . . . rather than cursed them into the oblivion of the Bermuda Triangle. But why are they so difficult to find and what happened to the wreckage?"

"Do you believe in curses?"

"Maybe. Maybe not." A strange expression passed across the other woman's face. "I've seen and experienced things in my life that make even an educated woman wonder."

"Like what?" Maris asked curiously.

Carmen leaned closer and spoke in a hushed tone. "Voodoo . . . obeah . . . satanism. Different words for the same kind of witchcraft. It's all over the islands. My family once had a Cuban woman as a neighbor— she used to do secret rituals in a special room in her second-floor apartment."

"Did you see her doing that?"

"Not exactly, but one evening my little brother and I made the mistake of visiting her at the wrong time. When we crept up the front stairs and opened her door —it wasn't locked—we saw the sacred room all ablaze with light and filled with horrible-looking statues and . . ."

"And?" Maris urged her on breathlessly.

"And then the worst part happened. That Cuban woman rose up, glared at us, and we were . . . blown . . . literally blown down the stairs by some force. I

64

was never so scared in my life." Carmen shuddered again as she relived the experience. "That woman could put her hands on your head and tell you everything about yourself. Voodoo is nothing to mess around with."

"That's something I have no intention of doing!" said Maris, aware of the goose bumps that had broken out on her skin.

She didn't believe in the supernatural, but Carmen's story had been very convincing. Undoubtedly there'd been some logical explanation—one the kids had never figured out—for the incident, though.

"I didn't mean to scare you," the Hispanic woman said in a contrite voice.

Maris reached across to pat Carmen's hand. "I'm not scared. I know there's a lot in this world that's still unexplainable."

"It was thinking about those missing ships that got me onto the topic. I should try to be more scientific about the whole affair, like my husband or Jason."

Jason? What was keeping him? Looking toward the end of the bar, Maris saw him with Alonzo and Monte, deep in conversation. When was he coming back to the booth? As a matter of fact, shouldn't she be leaving? She glanced at her watch and was appalled to see the time had passed so fast. She had less than half an hour to get to Brian's house on Paradise Island.

"You'll have to excuse me," she told Carmen. "I need to be going. I have to be at a planning meeting with the rest of the aquarium crew."

"I'm sure we'll see each other again." Carmen's gaze flicked from Maris to Jason and back again meaningfully.

Would they? Maris rose and headed directly for the

bar. "I'm taking a taxi back to Paradise Island," she told Jason, who turned at her approach.

He glanced at his watch. "Why didn't you tell me it was so late?"

"I got involved in our talking and forgot." Pushing away from the bar, he followed her as she made her way toward the door. "I can get back by myself," she assured him. "You don't have to interrupt your own conversation."

"A boat ride will be faster than a taxi," he said persuasively. "Besides, you may not find a taxi around here too quickly."

She didn't object when he opened the door for her. From the evening before, she knew he was a difficult man to argue with.

They had just stepped outside when he stopped short. Following the direction of his stare, Maris saw two men talking quietly in the shadows of the building. She recognized Gallagher, then quickly realized that his well-dressed companion was none other than Harold Wilkerson. A surprising duo if there ever was one.

"What the hell is *he* doing here?" muttered Jason under his breath.

"Who? Gallagher or Harold?" she whispered. When he didn't answer she thought that he might now want to stay. "Are you sure you wouldn't prefer that I take a taxi?"

"I'll take you over on my boat," he insisted stubbornly, taking her arm and leading her away.

Hurrying down the dock, Maris was so intent on reaching Jason's speedboat that it took her a few moments to realize that someone was calling to her.

"Maris! Maris Collier, over here!"

"Wait," she told Jason, peering into the evening darkness of the harbor. The lights on a small boat were quickly growing closer.

"Maris!" yelled Paul Martinez as he brought the motored launch nearer the dock. "You're going to be late if we don't hurry. Jo suggested that I come get you."

"Good idea," said Maris. "Bring the boat just a little closer and I'll jump in." She felt Jason's hand tighten on her arm and gazed up into his shadowed eyes.

"Guess I'll see you tomorrow." He sounded disappointed. Then he leaned forward to kiss her quickly, his lips and breath warm.

"Hey, Maris, you can give the guy some more of your special artificial respiration tomorrow, can't you?" called Paul mischievously. "Come on."

"Artificial respiration?" mumbled Jason.

"See you tomorrow," Maris told her Adonis, smiling as she left him, his brows quirked in puzzlement.

Sticking his hands in the pockets of his cutoffs, Jason strode quickly back to the Rum Keg. He was disappointed that he hadn't been able to enjoy much of Maris's company during the last half hour, but he'd found out some very interesting gossip from Monte Adams.

What did Gallagher know about the missing Wilkerson freighters? Important information he'd claimed to have found out from some native seamen? Did the strange man really know something or was he having deluded fantasies? Monte had believed him, saying Gallagher was able to understand the native patter, a mixture of English and other languages.

Reaching the spot where he'd glimpsed Gallagher in conversation with Harold Wilkerson, Jason looked up and down the street and saw that the two men had gone. Why had Harold been talking to the seaman? Had the Wilkerson heir heard rumors too? Gallagher had better be careful.

Entering the Rum Keg again, Jason saw that Carmen and Alonzo were still seated in the booth. Going to join them, he paused as he sighted Gallagher alone on a stool at the very end of the bar. The skilled diver he'd once known in Key West was now laughing and staring down into his glass of beer.

"Gallagher," said Jason, approaching the man.

The seaman didn't look up. "The man's a stuffed shirt," Gallagher muttered before laughing again. "And cheap too."

Jason leaned casually against the bar. "Who's cheap? Harold Wilkerson? I didn't know you and Harold were friends, Gallagher."

"I don't like him at all." The seaman frowned.

"Then what were you doing talking to him?" Jason looked around, catching Alonzo's eye and nodding to his mate. "Where did Harold go anyhow?"

"Harold lives in a mansion but he's too cheap to pay me for anything I know," said Gallagher, either unable or unwilling to answer questions directly, as usual.

"But he *is* gone . . ."

"He took off for his mansion."

Jason moved a little closer, making sure no one could overhear. "I've heard you may know some useful information, Gallagher. Are you saying you'll tell your secrets for the right amount of money?"

The crazy ex-diver grinned and lifted his beer glass to swirl the liquid around. "I need lots of money."

"Before I give you money, I have to know if your information's worth it."

Placing his beer back on the bar, Gallagher gazed up at him with an expression that looked almost as intelligent as Jason had once known him to be. "You want to know where those ships went, don't you?" Then he chuckled slyly and glanced away. "You didn't know someone was killed, did you? But I do. I always listen to the fishermen and the other islanders on the wharf. The Wilkersons are going to pay someday, whether Harold wants to part with his money or not."

"A murder. Someone was killed?" Jason asked smoothly.

Gallagher shrugged. "I need money."

Deciding to go along with the strange man—what could it hurt?—Jason pulled his wallet from his pocket. He placed a couple of bills on the bar. "Is that enough?"

Gallagher picked up the money and inspected it carefully. "It's enough for today."

"So, what's this about a murder?"

The seaman tucked Jason's money inside his shirt. "A man's dead, but someone knows more about it than me."

"I'm paying you to know about it."

"I'll have to take you to this certain person . . . as soon as I find out where the person lives." Gallagher grinned. "Not everyone owns a big mansion with the address written out nice and bold in front."

"This person knows about the murder?"

"The murder and other things about everyone."

What kind of double-talk was this? Was the seaman putting him on? Or had he gone completely over the edge? Despite his logical reservations, Jason could feel his intuition urging him to give Gallagher a try. The strange man was always hanging around the wharf and

69

downtown Nassau. And since he was considered harmless, people would talk freely around him.

"Okay, you find out where this person lives. If his information pans out for me, I'll pay you more."

"I need money," Gallagher insisted.

"Okay, okay," Jason agreed. "I'll pay you up front as soon as you tell me where he lives." He paused, suddenly concerned that the information he was seeking could become widespread. "Does Harold Wilkerson know about this person?"

"Harold's too cheap to pay."

"I guess that means he doesn't know."

Jason scowled, realizing that Harold might be protecting his own interests by feeling Gallagher out. What if the Wilkerson heir were guilty of sinking his own father's ships? And what if he'd gone so far as to commit murder?

Jason told Gallagher, "I think you'd better keep your mouth shut about this if you want to remain healthy." He paused, deciding to use a more specific threat. "And if you give anybody else the information I'm paying you to tell me . . . I'll wring your scrawny neck myself."

"Wring my neck?" Instead of appearing afraid, Gallagher smiled. "Just like a chicken."

"Look me up as soon as you find out where this mysterious person lives," Jason ordered the seaman as he eased himself away from the bar.

"I need money. It'll be soon."

Wondering if his intuition was correct or if he'd just wasted his money, Jason went to join the Ferraras. When he glanced around at the bar again Gallagher was gone.

CHAPTER FOUR

"Do you ever get discouraged, constantly searching for lost ships that are almost impossible to find?" Maris asked Jason, thinking about the Wilkerson freighters. They were leaning against the rail of the *Argonaut*, on its way to the treasure-diving site. "I've searched for rare species of fish and failed to find them. It can be frustrating and I don't even go out looking every day. You must have a lot of patience."

"It takes more faith than patience," Jason told her with a smile. "I believe—implicitly—that I'll find what I go looking for. If a particular method doesn't work, I just try another one. No matter what happens, I have faith that I'll reach my goal in the end."

What confidence. Or was it merely self-delusion? Maris wondered which as she stared at the man next to her, his bronze profile crisp against the blue of the late morning sky. At the moment she couldn't help thinking that he sounded and looked like the perfect hero from a men's adventure magazine.

"Lost ships are like unrealized dreams. And sometimes just as hazy and far away," Jason went on thoughtfully, gazing down at the crystalline turquoise water as if he expected a submerged vessel to appear at any moment. "But I never give up on either. I know I'll find those ships . . . and make my dreams come true, if not today, then tomorrow."

"You have faith all right," said Maris dryly, remembering the dreams she'd surrendered through the years.

"You should have faith, too, Maris of the Sea." His golden gaze swung toward her. Then his voice softened. "I have a hunch you're going to find something wonderful."

What did he have in mind? She looked at him archly. "You mean you think I'll run onto a treasure chest of doubloons today?"

He laughed. "If it were that easy to find, everyone would be wealthy. Chances are the worms have already eaten those wooden treasure chests, along with the ships that carried them."

Maris nodded. "I figured as much. What are we really going to be looking for, anyway?"

"Roundish-shaped ballast stones that were placed in the hold of a Spanish galleon to balance it, unusual outcroppings of coral that may have grown around debris, cannonballs, shards of pottery. . . ."

He pushed away from the rail. The doubloon he always wore—with only a trim-fitting blue swimsuit today—swung gently against his tanned muscular chest, capturing her rapt attention. "Want to help me fill up the tanks?"

They walked toward the stern of the boat. As Maris followed him she couldn't help appreciating the sight of his broad back tapering into shapely, narrow hips. His swimmer's legs were long and muscular.

"Why do you even suspect there might be treasure where we're going today?" she asked, attempting to get her mind on a more intellectual topic. "How do you decide where to look?"

"I've magged—used a magnetometer or boat-drawn metal detector—at least several square miles of this area and kept a chart of high metal readings. We'll dive down to see what we can find." He stopped to glance over at the water. "And we've got a great day for seeking the treasure of the *Isabella.* Look at that ocean bottom. With the sea this calm and the sun so bright, underwater visibility will be perfect."

Maris smiled, already imagining the pleasure she'd feel upon plunging into the sun-kissed water. And that should be soon. Jason had told her the diving site was only an hour out from Nassau. They must have been traveling almost that long. She helped him remove tanks from the rack he kept at the rear of the boat so he could fill them with the compressor.

"What happened to the *Isabella?*" she asked. "Was the ship wrecked by a storm?"

"A storm finished the galleon off on September 21, 1675, but not until she'd been damaged in a battle and got stuck on the submerged reef that's not far from here."

"You know the exact date?"

He nodded, concentrating on his task. "The Spanish were very exacting about records, especially when they wanted to keep track of ships that carried a king's ransom in doubloons, silver bars, emeralds, and, in the *Isabella*'s case, a wealthy bride's dowry as well." He paused to make a wide, sweeping gesture at the surrounding open water. "You can bet that particular ship's still out here or the Spanish officials would have made note of her salvage."

As he continued to fill tanks Maris gathered their equipment together on the deck and checked it carefully. Since the sea was warm and they wouldn't be diving deep—Jason had said no more than thirty feet—they wouldn't be needing wet suits. She glanced up when Davey Watson suddenly came on deck.

"Jason?" Davey said, eyeing Maris covertly. "Eli says he's almost on top of the spot you marked for him. Want us to put down anchor?" When he realized that Maris was aware of his glances, the kid pushed his glasses up the short bridge of his nose and focused his hazel gaze entirely on Jason.

"Anywhere along here will be fine," Jason told him. "Then I want you to watch the deck while we take a dive."

Nodding, Davey went back inside. Only one of the two crew members Jason had on board that day, Davey hadn't said two words to Maris, although she'd caught him staring at her off and on all morning. It was almost as if he knew her, Maris thought, even though she was sure she'd never met the clean-cut young man before.

As Eli cut the *Argonaut*'s motors, swinging it around in a half circle, Maris forgot about Davey and strapped her dive knife on the calf of her leg, then picked up her weight belt to fasten it around her waist.

"Let me help you," murmured Jason from behind, covering her hands with his own.

He fastened the belt, then helped her strap on her buoyancy compensator and tanks, adjusting the buckles until they were tight enough. She liked the sure touch of his hands. Trying to get her mind off the fantasies they inspired, she focused on the history Jason had been relating. "You mentioned the *Isabella* was damaged in battle. Who was she fighting with? The English?"

"No, it wasn't political. The ship was first captured by an amorous Frenchman who wanted the bride, then the *Isabella* was engaged in battle by the prospective bridegroom—a Spanish planter who was enraged at the loss of the dowry he was supposed to receive."

"He was upset about the dowry? What about the bride?" Maris asked, now helping Jason with his tanks.

"Doña Maria's wealthy father had been open about the fact that he was buying his daughter a husband."

"What happened to Doña Maria and the Frenchman?" she asked as they moved out onto the small dive platform that had been custom-built into the side of the boat.

"They went down with the sinking ship." He glanced at his watch. "But their story is long and complicated— and romantic. Why don't I fill you in on the rest of the details when we come back up for lunch?" He gazed at her. "The tale might inspire you."

Inspire her to do what? she thought as they synchronized their watches to make sure they would both know the exact amount of time they'd been under.

"I'm taking this along," he said, indicating the small underwater metal detector he held in his hand. "Ladies first."

Slipping on her fins and adjusting her mask so it didn't entangle her braided hair, she drew on the gloves that would protect her hands from the stings of coral. Then she stepped directly out from the platform, taking a giant stride into the water. With a solid splash and the gurgle of escaping oxygen bubbles, she sank deep. A blue-green veil seemed to close around her. Hovering in the water for a moment, she stabilized herself, breathing evenly and gazing around to get her bearings. A huge bubbly splash a few feet away told her that Jason had joined her.

He soon moved toward her, his eyes glowing amber in the aqua-tinted light. Beckoning for her to come along, he took off, swimming above the sandy ocean floor and holding the metal detector in front of him. Maris followed for a few seconds, then quickly caught up. Swimming side by side, fins moving gently, they propelled themselves forward, heading for the patches of coral up ahead.

As usual when entering the tropical undersea world, Maris felt like sighing with pleasure. The warm buoyant water seemed to caress her skin. Colors were peaceful to her eye, yet magical. She anticipated the brilliantly hued fish that could appear at any moment to flit about against the muted purples, golds, and greens of sand and coral. And the only sound that she could hear was the soft flutter of passing bubbles.

Even in the relative silence, however, Maris was fully aware of her companion diver. Turning to find Jason staring at her, she gazed in the direction of his pointing hand. Beyond some waving amethyst-hued sea fans was a sunken boat.

They could see in an instant that it wasn't the *Isabella*. The peeling wooden hull of the small, decrepit-looking vessel bore no encrusting coral as yet, proof it was a relatively new wreck. Perhaps it had been a derelict fishing boat that had taken on too much water and sunk.

Swimming on, gliding between more sea fans, Maris spotted several blue-head wrasses hovering around the tall plants' flat blades. As the divers continued forward the coral grew thicker and the water more heavily populated. A large school of bright yellow sea bass darted away before them, followed by at least a half dozen pouty-lipped blue tangs. A black-and-white banded butterfly fish stuck its head out of some nearby

76

branches of elkhorn coral to stare, then shyly retreated when Maris came too close.

But she wasn't down here to study tropical fish today. Following Jason's example, she paused and dived downward. Hovering over the surface of a clear spot of sand, she saw him check the metal detector, then extract his knife and begin to dig around some rocks. Could they be ballast stones? They looked like plain old rocks to her. Trusting his greater knowledge, she removed her own knife from its sheath and helped him dig. Maybe they'd uncover a nest of precious coins!

After several minutes, however, they'd found only a couple of buried shells and more rocks. When they started digging at the site from another side, Jason suddenly stopped and made a peculiar gurgling sound. She looked up to see his eyes crinkling behind his mask. He was laughing! What was so funny?

She found out when he dragged several rusty beer cans out of the sand—the "treasure" indicated by the metal detector.

Maris smiled. At least she did the best she could with the bulky regulator in her mouth. Shaking her head in mock disgust, she spread out her arms as if to say "What now?"

Jason pointed up. Although they still had plenty of air left in their tanks, he obviously wanted to return to the boat. Acquiescing good-naturedly, Maris replaced her knife and headed back in the direction from which they'd come.

Their return journey went faster. It seemed only seconds until Maris sighted the shadowy bulk of the *Argonaut* overhead. Taking a last glance at the seabed below, her eyes widened when she saw a large, flat-shaped form wriggling through the sand. A stingray! She grabbed

Jason's arm and pointed. Exhilarated by the sight, Maris swam down for a better look.

Startled, the stingray broke out of its cover to take off, flying away through the sea on its great, undulating, winglike pectoral fins. Maris turned to see Jason treading water where they'd been. Didn't he think the creature magically beautiful, she wondered. She rose toward him and together they floated up to the boat.

They broke the surface at the same time. Removing his regulator and lifting his mask as they hung on to the boat's dive ladder, he asked, "What were you doing? Trying to get yourself stung by that thing's tail? It must have been seven feet across."

"Wasn't it beautiful?" She spit out some salty water. "Though stingrays can be a little paranoid, they don't harm humans unless they're stepped on."

"Well, I was worried because I knew someone who did just that."

"I wouldn't be that careless! Don't forget, I'm an expert in the area of tropical fish."

"True. Of course any mermaid would be."

Was he still identifying her with his wild fantasy? Not knowing how else to react, Maris joked, "I only wish I had a set of gills. I could stay underwater for days instead of hours."

Deciding to try another spot closer to the submerged reef and the Tongue of the Ocean—a strange area of the Atlantic where the seabed suddenly plunges to depths of hundreds of feet—Jason directed Eli to take the boat a mile farther on. A year before, following a reading from the magnetometer, Jason had dived down and found an ornately engraved cannon that could have belonged to the *Isabella*. Unfortunately, a storm had come up the very same day and blown away the buoy he'd set out as well as covered his find. In the months since he'd searched the same spot several times but had managed to uncover only a few worthless cannonballs. The cannon itself had remained lost.

But perhaps his luck would change today. Anchoring at midday, Jason brought out the special picnic lunch he'd packed for them to eat on deck.

"Lobster!" She gazed appreciatively at the tray he carried. "Hmm . . . and French bread, melon, grapes, mangoes."

"Glad you like it. I chilled the lobster—kept it in the cooler with the rest of the food on the way out," he said. "I have some wine for later—we'd better stick to mineral water while we're diving."

She helped herself to several grapes when he placed the tray down on the deck and sat beside her. He'd sliced everything else into bite-sized pieces and arranged them on communal plates so they could eat lunch with their fingers. Opening a bottle of imported mineral water, he poured out two glasses and handed one to her.

"Delicious," she murmured as she chewed a piece of lobster and reached for more fruit and a hunk of bread. "Diving always makes me hungry."

"Eat hearty. There's plenty," he told her, noting her healthy appetite with pleasure.

But then, so far, he'd approved of everything about her, starting with her appearance. Admiring the silvery hair that haloed an almost perfectly oval face, he let his eyes sweep past her graceful neck and shoulders down to the curvy but athletic figure revealed by her strapless swimsuit. The garment was made of an iridescent silvery-greenish-bronze fabric . . . and when he realized it resembled mermaid's scales, he almost laughed.

Luckily, however, Maris had legs rather than a tail! And what legs, he thought, glancing at the tanned shapely limbs stretched out beside him.

"Aren't you going to have some melon?" she asked, interrupting his appreciative inspection of her by holding the plate almost directly under his nose. "If you don't help yourself quickly, I'm going to eat all of it."

"Thanks," he said, taking a piece of the fruit.

He had a momentary fear that she might think his attraction to her was merely physical. But she needn't worry. He also liked Maris's underlying warmth, not that he didn't intend to heat it up to full-blown passion!

Furthermore, he admired her courage and cool self-assurance. Having known too many women who freaked out at the sight of spiny lobsters or small eels, he was delightfully surprised by one that chased after full-grown stingrays. And saved hallucinating divers.

"Are you going to tell me the rest of that story now?" she asked him. "About the *Isabella* and her treasure?"

Jason couldn't help but think that his mermaid also resembled a treasure—with her silver hair and golden tanned skin—one he wanted for his very own. He murmured, "What would you like to know?"

She gazed at him curiously and took a sip of water. "You said there was a lot more to the story."

He nodded. "True, I gave you only the barest details."

"So, tell me the rest. It's fascinating."

At the moment he felt like doing anything she wanted. Would she like him to fall in love? That wouldn't be the least bit difficult, he realized with surprise.

"It all started in Havana, in the days when the Spanish owned Cuba. Doña Maria was the daughter of an

80

important government official who was disgraced when she was caught walking in a garden with a man, without a chaperone."

"And nice girls didn't do such things in 1675."

"Not a wealthy unmarried Spanish lady. To make things worse, Doña Maria's admirer was French, not Spanish. The lady's wealthy father sold his 'damaged goods' to a planter from one of the nearby islands, a Don José Cardona, by offering the man a rich dowry. Doña Maria was on her way to her wedding when her Frenchman, an adventurer named Louis Duhamel, daringly captured the *Isabella* with a smaller ship and a handful of men."

"But weren't galleons heavily armed?"

"This one had over thirty cannons and was guarded by soldiers. The *Isabella* was to sail for Spain with a hold full of silver bars, gold, and emeralds after dropping the lady and her dowry off. Louis managed to take the ship only because he attacked by night and caught the soldiers by surprise."

"He must have been crazy about Doña Maria."

"So besotted, he wanted to take her off the *Isabella* and leave those tons of treasure behind," said Jason, for the first time in his life able to empathize with Louis's feelings. Sitting across from Maris, his foot only inches away from her, he let his bare toe touch the calf of her leg and was pleased when she didn't move away. "The weight of gold and silver on the galleon would slow Louis down, you see."

"What happened next?" she asked intently.

He liked her rapt attention, only wishing it was himself that interested her rather than the story he told. "Louis never had the chance to get back to his own ship. Don José couldn't wait to get his hands on his bride's dowry and had sailed out to meet her. When Don José realized the galleon was in 'pirate' hands, he immediately attacked. The smaller French ship was sunk and the *Isabella* lost her mainmast in the cannon fire."

"Then the galleon blew onto a reef?" Helping herself to more lobster, Maris passed the plate to him.

Their fingers grazed as he took the dish from her, making Jason want to pull her closer as he continued the romantic tale. "Louis tried to get away and took the crippled galleon north—to a spot right around here." Jason pointed. "There's a submerged reef over there, one that's taken many ships through the years, even in modern times. And that's where the *Isabella* ran aground . . . or was blown by the rising winds of the oncoming storm."

"Right around here, huh?" She looked out at the sea with a bemused expression, as if she were envisioning the shipwreck. He was entranced by the subtle lights dancing in her unusual violet-blue eyes.

Recapturing her immediate attention, Jason said, "Of course Don José was furious because he wouldn't be getting his gold. Louis Duhamel was wounded by the time the ship struck the reef and some of his men had been killed. Everyone left on the *Isabella,* including the soldiers locked in the hold, was facing certain death."

"Even Doña Maria."

"Yes, though she called to Don José across the waves, begging him to send rowboats out to rescue them. But José refused. Now, if there'd been some way to save the treasure . . ." He paused. "Did I mention Don José Cardona had a reputation for greed and cruelty?"

"And he wanted to live up to it, obviously," Maris remarked with a wry smile. She scooted over to lean against the cabin's outer wall and flipped her blond braid over one shoulder.

Sliding back, Jason leaned against the wall as well, moving close enough to feel her body heat. "Louis ordered his remaining men to set the soldiers free and told them all to swim for it. Some even made it to Don José's ships—the Spaniards were taken aboard, the Frenchmen left to drown. Don José called to Doña Maria and advised her to swim too. But he'd throw a rope down for her only if she brought him her own weight in gold."

"He didn't!"

"I told you he was a winner."

"So Doña Maria went down with the ship!"

"Along with her Frenchman and several tons of treasure. Hopefully they made the most of their last night together." Their shoulders only inches apart, Jason gazed at Maris meaningfully, imagining how he'd spend his last living hours with her.

"I'm sure they had plenty of Spanish wine."

"And cabin space. They were alone on a sinking ship."

He could almost see the rising waves, the shredded sails, the desperate and passionate woman in his arms. But instead of Doña Maria's raven hair, he pictured blond strands whipping around the lady's face, tossed by the wind. . . .

"So, that's the whole story?"

"Hmm?" Yanked abruptly back to the present, he stared at his glass of mineral water, then looked at Maris. "Not quite. According to legend, Doña Maria called upon all the names of the saints and the angels to curse Don José, praying he'd suffer for his greed and come to a terrible end—which he did a few weeks later when a slave he'd been torturing killed him. And the night of September 21, after Doña Maria's curse, the storm worsened, pulling the *Isabella* down, probably spilling her contents onto the reef and off in who knows how many other directions—perhaps into the Tongue of the Ocean."

"Do you think the part about the curse is true or is it a romanticized version of what really happened?"

"The storm and the wreck are historical fact. Who knows about curses. Some natives believe Doña Maria's saints and angels are the same gods they worship in obeah or voodoo. Maybe that's why, over on Andros Island—which isn't that far from here—they claim the drowned lovers walk out of the sea on moonlit nights, hand in hand."

"Well, I'm glad they can be together in some way," Maris said softly.

"So am I." Her wistful expression made him yearn to take her in his arms. "I can see the romance of the tale has gotten to you," he said hopefully, leaning closer.

"It's definitely romantic, if sad. Like Romeo and Juliet. It's too bad families—like Doña Maria's father—can mess up their children's lives sometimes."

"It wasn't the family's fault," he insisted, irritated that she seemed determined to focus on the tragedy of the story instead of the romance. "If you don't like a situation, you get out of it. Doña Maria had a chance to go with Louis while they were still in Havana but she wouldn't leave because he wasn't rich and couldn't guarantee her a secure life. In a way the tragedy was her own fault."

"That's rather judgmental," she said, lifting her eyebrows in challenge. "Wealthy women were raised in a sheltered environment in Doña Maria's culture. It's a wonder she ever met Louis in her garden in the first place."

"Agreed. But everyone makes their own destiny, whatever the culture or age. There comes a time when you have to believe in your gut feelings and act on them, even if that means taking a big risk."

Maris shook her head wryly. "Taking risks doesn't always work out."

"Are you speaking from experience?"

Leaning forward, she wrapped her arms around her knees and met his interested gaze with an openly honest expression. "I took a chance on a man . . . and lost. I'm divorced."

"Then you married the wrong man," Jason stated firmly. "And now you're free to find someone better."

Was he the right man for Maris? he wondered, becoming more and more aware that he'd been without the love of a woman for far too long.

"If one person doesn't work out, just go find another, is that it?" asked Maris. Though she smiled, he could tell she was quite serious.

"You'll never find anything if you don't look," he said, equally serious. "What you're seeking might be right under your nose."

She gave an uneasy laugh. "But I'm on a break from seeking anything but fish . . . or treasure right now."

"Really? Maybe you'll change your mind."

When he gazed at her intently she looked away, then took one of the grapes left on the plate of fruit. She popped it in her mouth and chewed thoughtfully.

"All this information about the *Isabella* has been very interesting," she said finally, obviously trying to change the subject to something less personal. "I'm impressed with your knowledge. You could write a master's thesis on it."

"A thesis? I didn't go to college. Everything I know I learned from experience and from reading on my own."

"You certainly know a lot about the *Isabella*."

"Sure." He was a professional treasure hunter, why shouldn't he? But at the moment he'd prefer to learn a lot more about Maris, possibly memorizing every inch of her delectable body. He plucked another grape from the plate and slid forward to get closer to her. "Has my story inspired you?"

"To do what, find treasure?"

"Or love." He held the grape before her beautifully shaped lips. "Want a taste?"

She didn't answer as he moved even nearer to cover her mouth with his own. He was gratified when she responded, making a low sound in her throat and slipping her arms up around his neck. Allowing one hand to glide along the sleek satin of her thigh, he used the other to press her against him. Her mouth tasted of mango and melon. He took a deep breath and let his tongue delve deeper.

"Cap'n?"

The voice was a rude interruption. Feeling Maris stiffen, Jason reluctantly raised his head and turned to find Eli standing a few feet away. The old man stepped backward, obviously embarrassed.

"Sorry to bother you, Cap'n. But there was a boat that seemed to be following us for quite a while. . . ."

Jason became more alert. "What boat?" Lately he'd gotten the eerie feeling someone was constantly watching them. He couldn't help but frown as Maris slipped her arms from his neck and moved quietly away. "Did you get a good look at it?"

Eli stepped back another pace. "Ah, no, sir. It didn't get that close. You've always said to tell you if I see anybody else around, but it's probably only fishermen."

"Probably," Jason agreed, though he still felt uneasy.

"Yes, Cap'n. I wouldn't have disturbed you. I just thought you were preparing the tanks. . . ."

No, Jason had been preparing Maris, utilizing one of his infrequent days off to pursue romance. But when he glanced at her now he saw the spell he'd been weaving was broken.

During the day's second dive Jason had little time to think about the aborted love scene with Maris. Almost as soon as they'd hit the water she'd spotted a pile of cannonballs and had swum directly toward them, all the while motioning wildly to him. He'd signaled back to forget it and to follow him, but he didn't know if she'd understood.

The metal detector had gone crazy and he'd surged forward to find the source. After skirting a jagged outcrop of the submerged coral reef, he'd turned in the water to find she'd disappeared.

Damn. She'd stopped to look at those useless cannonballs, the same ones Jason had dug up several months before when he'd blown the sand around them down to bedrock with his boat's prop wash. There'd been no sight of gold or the lost cannon.

Jason peered around the other side of the coral outcrop, his eyes widening at what he saw there. He hesitated, torn between duty and impatience. Should he go back and find Maris? Surely she'd seen the direction he'd taken and would soon follow. Meanwhile, he was anxious to inspect his find, though the object couldn't exactly be called treasure.

He swam forward, stopping to hover a few feet from the huge, bulky metal cylinder resting on the sand. Large enough to contain several men, it was definitely a freighter's boiler. And it hadn't been down long. Rubbing the curving edge of the smooth, nonencrusted cylinder, Jason examined the fresh grease stain spreading across his glove's palm. Then he moved lower to look at the ragged hole piercing the side of the boiler.

Explosives? Had explosives been used on the ship to which the boiler had belonged? Could that ship have been one of Wilkerson's freighters? If so, where was the rest of the vessel? At the bottom of the Tongue of the Ocean?

Mulling over the possibilities, the most exciting he'd turned up in his investigation so far, Jason glided around to the other side of the boiler to look for a brand name and serial numbers. He planned to surface as soon as he checked out the immediate area surrounding the boiler, figuring that Maris would find him eventually.

Where was Jason? Maris wondered irritably, looking up from the pile of cannonballs she'd stopped to examine. Why had he ignored her and swum away to swiftly disappear? It was dangerous for divers to work separately. And she'd found the cannonballs, hadn't she? He'd told her they were something to look for on a treasure dive.

She gazed around for a few more seconds but was unable to see her companion diver anywhere in the surrounding water. Surely he'd return. In the meantime, instead of searching in what might easily turn out to be the wrong direction, she'd dig around. Withdrawing her knife, she thought about the *Isabella,* awed that these very cannonballs could have sunk with the galleon more than three hundred years before, along with Doña Maria and Louis Duhamel.

Feeling sad, Maris once again hoped the doomed lovers were together somewhere and scratched at the sand with her knife. After almost twenty minutes, however, she'd turned up only the usual shells and several small stones. She examined the objects beside her, one of them roundish and blackened.

Blackened? Bringing the round stone up closer to her mask, Maris peered intently at it. Hitting it with the hilt of her knife, she was intrigued when black flakes fell away to reveal a hole piercing the object's center.

Could she possibly have found a silver ring, tarnished and blackened by salt water? How exciting! Securing her find by threading it with one of the strings of her net bag and tying a knot, she dug enthusiastically for several minutes more, uncovering more shells. Then she checked her watch and looked around. Still no Jason. Where on earth was he? Floating a few feet above the ocean bed, she gazed upward hopefully when a large shadow passed overhead.

But the shadowy form that glided so easily under the surface of the water high above was fish-shaped, not human. And Maris's heart beat faster as she realized that fish was probably a shark. A big one. When another large shadow followed the first, then a third, she panicked. Where was Jason? Especially now, when she needed him?

Sharks usually didn't attack humans, but she knew they were highly unpredictable. The safest way to face the predators was to rise slowly to the surface back-to-back with another diver. Except that she didn't have another diver! Jason had been irresponsible to go off and leave her alone.

She had to do something and it would be best to get out of the water. She wasn't about to wait for Jason to find her. Willing herself to remain cool, Maris began to swim up toward the larger and darker shadow of the *Argonaut*. Pausing so she wouldn't rise too fast, she scanned the water above, below, and on either side.

That's when she spotted Jason swimming toward her from below. Finally! Sighing with relief, she signaled "danger" and "come." As soon as he reached her, he enclosed her in his arms.

"No! The other way!" she signaled, trying to turn around so they'd be back-to-back. She pointed at the shadows circling above them. As she did so one of the fish took a deep dive.

In spite of the diver's precautions against doing so, Maris held her breath. She let it out again as the fish— or, rather, mammal—swam swiftly past her and Jason, emitting a series of high-pitched chirps and clicks. A spotted dolphin! Its two companions followed, full-sized adults weighing at least two hundred pounds. As they passed they turned on their sides to stare curiously with round mischievous-looking eyes. What she had feared were sharks were actually wild dolphins!

Feeling foolish, Maris chided herself for not more quickly recognizing the animals. Still wrapped in Jason's arms, she saw his eyes crinkle behind his mask. Was he laughing at her signal of danger? He'd made the situation seem twice as deadly by going off and leaving her to fend for herself! She pushed away from him angrily, her hands firm against his chest.

Obviously still amused, he held out his arms imploringly, dangling the metal detector in one hand and his red net collecting bag in the other. Then he wiggled his eyebrows teasingly and motioned for her to come back.

She had a sudden crazy thought that maybe he wanted to cuddle underwater, losing all track of time . . . until the air in their tanks ran out.

Ignoring him, she swam upward. Jason followed until they both broke the surface near the hull of the boat. He took the regulator from his mouth to shout, "What's the matter? Why did you signal danger?"

"Those dolphins could have been sharks!" she shouted back as soon as she'd paddled over to the dive ladder.

He followed, shoving his mask to the top of his golden head with a grin. "But they weren't sharks. I would think a curator could tell the difference."

Why was he smiling? His refusal to take the situation seriously was making her even more angry. "Even curators can make mistakes! And my judgment wasn't helped by the fact that I thought I was alone down there."

His grin faded. He finally seemed to understand that she didn't want to joke. "Why didn't you follow me when I swam away? I thought you were right behind me."

Maris had to admit that she'd seen him motion for her to come with him. Used to taking the lead on a dive, she also had to admit she'd conveniently ignored his signal. And underwater, where communication was limited, it was essential that someone be in charge. Suddenly she realized that she'd contributed to the situation too.

A little embarrassed, she let her anger dissipate and tried another tack. "But didn't you think those cannonballs were important?"

"They're worthless. I dug them up several months ago."

"Oh." She should have known he'd had a reason, and he was the one who knew about treasure hunting. Turning away from him to remove her fins, she climbed the ladder.

"I didn't intend to leave you alone," Jason said, climbing up right behind her.

It seemed that he was making an apology of sorts and she hastened to add her own. "I should have followed when you signaled."

"We're just not used to diving together yet, that's all."

Were they going to dive together again? She wondered with a rush of excitement. Maris glanced up at the sound of a splash near the prow of the boat. She caught sight of a tail fluke before it disappeared beneath the water.

"The dolphins are playful today." Jason laughed. "It might interest you to know that I also thought I was being trailed by sharks the first time I ran into Freckles and her kids."

"Freckles? You know these dolphins?"

"They've been hanging around this area for years. When I first saw them Spot was a youngster and Puff a baby. There're other dolphins around sometimes, but these three are the tamest. I think Freckles may have been a research animal at one time."

As Jason spoke another member of the sleek trio—the one with the biggest spots on his hide—leaped out of the water a few yards away, arching back in with a tremendous splash.

"I think they want to play with us," said Jason. "They're especially crazy about keep-away. Want to pit your wits against some dolphins?"

Quickly regaining her good humor, Maris agreed,

"Of course, I'll try a game." She'd always loved the intelligent mammals. "They'll probably win, but what fun!"

Jason looked up at the boat. "Hey, Davey!"

At his boss's call the young diver came to the platform to get the metal detector Jason handed up. Following Jason's example, Maris removed her tank and buoyancy compensator, regulator, and weight belt, retaining only enough equipment for snorkeling.

In the water Jason tossed the empty net collecting bag away from him. Lightweight, it floated until Freckles zoomed around to pick it up with her pectoral fin. She hurtled away, followed closely by Spot and Puff. Circling back toward the boat, she dropped the bag in the same place, where it was taken up by Spot.

Maris and Jason spent the next ten minutes trying to take the bag from the dolphins, who, as if realizing that humans were vastly handicapped when it came to swimming skills, brought it within inches of their fingertips.

Maris laughed delightedly when she finally caught hold of the red bag. But she hadn't so much as grazed Puff, who'd personally delivered it with her tail fluke. One of the rules of dolphin keep-away seemed to be that a player was not allowed to touch any of the others.

After an hour of the strenuous game, the humans had to call it quits. Jason helped Maris up the ladder, throwing her fins to one side.

"Tired?" he asked.

"Delightfully so," she answered. "But I think you've lost your collecting bag." She gazed out at the water where the dolphins were still playing with their new toy.

"I can get another one."

Before she and Jason had retreated from the edge of the deck, Maris was surprised to see one dolphin break away and swim back to the boat. It made a quick pass by the ladder to drop the bag off on a step.

"How polite!" said Maris, laughing delightedly.

As she leaned over to pick up the bag, Jason yelled, "Davey, where are you?"

"Here." The young diver popped up from where he'd been sitting on the deck and crossed to the rail. "You need help with the equipment?"

"No, we can handle it. I want you to toss a buoy over the side here before the *Argonaut* heads back to Nassau."

Davey pushed his glasses up the short bridge of his nose as he scanned the water. "A buoy? What did you find? Something from the *Isabella?*"

"Not exactly," Jason said, picking up diving gear off the platform and heaving it into the boat. "But something else that could be important. We'll have to come back as soon as we can get a crane to hoist it out of the water."

"That heavy, huh?" Davey studied his employer's face with interest, but Jason didn't elaborate. The young diver shrugged and went to get the buoy. Maris was curious, too, but she decided to let her own questions rest for the moment and help Jason with the equipment.

A few minutes later the *Argonaut* left the site and she and Jason changed from swimsuits to street clothes. Then Maris showed him the blackened ring she'd found.

"What do you think? Is it silver?" she asked.

He turned it around, studying it carefully. "Probably, though we'll have to wait until it's cleaned to examine it fully. In the meantime, I'll keep the ring immersed in salt water. Old silver starts to deteriorate when exposed to the air," he explained.

"Do you really think it's old?"

"It certainly looks like it is."

"And do you think it might have been part of the *Isabella*'s treasure?" she asked eagerly, realizing that treasure hunting was beginning to get under her skin.

"Maybe." He carefully placed the ring in a container of salt water he must have been keeping in his cabin for such a purpose. "If it's worth anything, I'll make sure you get the full price of it."

"I don't care about the money," she assured him. "I'll be happy to find out I've recovered something old and historically important. Treasure from a sunken ship of 1675 has got to be of interest to underwater archaeologists."

"It definitely is, but I think you should have the money for the ring anyway."

She didn't want to bother arguing. Instead, she changed the subject. "Speaking of finds, what kept you busy for so long while I was digging? Why did you tell Davey to leave that buoy out there? You said it wasn't exactly from the *Isabella.*"

"I located something more modern," he said casually, looking away as he opened the bottle of white wine he'd taken from the cooler in one corner of the cabin.

"Something from a modern sunken ship?"

"Possibly."

"What kind of ship?"

"I'm not sure."

He seemed to be avoiding her eyes. Was he intentionally withholding the truth? Irritated and now suspicious that his discovery had something to do with the Wilkerson case, she asked right out, "Do you think what you found could have come from a freighter?"

He shrugged. "Maybe. I have no actual proof."

"And I suppose you wouldn't tell me if you did have proof," she said, needling him. Was he always going to play this avoidance game when it came to his investigation? Surely he didn't think she'd spread the information.

"My find isn't as interesting as yours as far as history or treasure is concerned." He poured out two glasses of white wine. "It definitely had nothing to do with the *Isabella.* It was just a piece of soon-to-be rusty metal."

"From a Wilkerson freighter," she declared. "Wasn't it? Even though you won't admit it."

He made no comment. Instead, he handed her a glass, their eyes meeting and their fingers touching for a second before she pulled away. He reached over to click his glass against hers.

"To the *Isabella,* her treasure, and the romance of Doña Maria," he said softly.

Letting her irritation ebb away with the warmth of his tone and the gleam of his golden eyes, she told herself he probably had professional reasons for keeping quiet. It really wasn't any of her business. Still, she couldn't help but chide him with her own toast:

"To a maddening man who obviously knows how to keep secrets."

They sipped at the wine, Jason gazing quietly at her over the rim of his glass. "I'm merely mad about you."

Was he? What could she say?

"Would you like to spend this evening with me on land, lovely mermaid?" he asked with a smile.

She hesitated. "Well, I don't have any plans. . . ."

"You might as well make some then," he urged. "There's going to be a full moon tonight and I know of an outdoor restaurant where we can dine and dance under the stars. What do you say?"

Why not accept his invitation? Strong, determined, virile, and attractive, with a love of the sea and a penchant for romantic stories, Jason was fascinating. Maris couldn't resist.

"All right, it sounds nice," she told him, imagining the pleasure of moving to soft island music in his arms.

His smile grew wider. "Great. But I'll make sure any time you spend with me is much more than nice."

Anticipating an especially romantic evening, she let him lead her outside the cabin to watch the boat swiftly approaching the city's harbor. When he slid an arm around her shoulders, his callused palm caressing the flesh of her upper arm, she turned toward him, raising her willing mouth for the kiss to come.

It was intense and sweet, his lips moving over hers possessively as he drew her tightly against him. She could feel the strong, even beat of his heart through the thin shirt he wore. And taste the salt water from their day's diving on his skin. A strong wave of desire coursed through her, making her want even more.

"Maris," he breathed.

They parted slowly as the boat neared the dock. Jason moved down the rail to call to Davey. As the *Argonaut* swung around Maris swayed with the boat's choppy motion and the strength of the passions Jason had aroused. What would she do later, when he would undoubtedly ask for more than just a good-night kiss from her? Would she be able to say no?

Intoxicated with her first experience treasure hunting, buoyant from the thrill of spending a day in the ocean, warmed by Jason's kisses, Maris definitely wasn't in her usual state of mind. That's what she kept telling herself anyway, after they'd tied the boat up and Gallagher, of all people, approached to steal her escort away.

The two men conversed on the dock for only a few seconds before Jason came back to her to make his apologies. "I have to go," he said simply. "It's important."

"You're going off with Gallagher?" she asked in disbelief. What about their romantic evening?

"I'm really sorry about this," he assured her hastily, at least having the grace to look regretful. "I'll get you a taxi to take you to Brian's and be back to see you later."

"Don't . . ." she began before Jason placed a swift kiss on her surprised lips. ". . . bother," she finished.

But he'd already signaled one. The taxi pulled up as Jason strode away.

CHAPTER FIVE

Maris just couldn't believe it. Deep in conversation with Gallagher, Jason walked off toward a beat-up old car and got in without even looking back at her. So much for the romantic evening she'd expected to spend. She couldn't help but feel disgruntled when the car moved away with a squeal of tires.

Maybe it was for the best, she thought, watching the vehicle careen around the corner and out of sight. She'd let herself get carried away, allowed herself to like the man too much, could get involved with him too easily, despite the time limits imposed by her stay in the Bahamas. She wasn't ready for such a heady involvement yet. She should be relieved she'd never see Jason again once she returned to Coral Gardens. Too bad her logic couldn't assuage the empty feeling that crept through her after he'd left her to do what she assumed was his investigative work.

"You getting in?" the taxi driver asked good-humoredly. "Or should I take a nap?"

"Yes, of course."

She slid into the backseat and closed the door, then looked out through the window at the *Argonaut*. In spite of her disappointment, she couldn't help but remember the pleasure of the day.

"Where to, lady?"

The question interrupting her reverie was a good one. Maris had no desire to take the short ride to Brian's home. She was too keyed up. Everyone else had made plans away from the place for the day, and she didn't feel like returning there only to be alone.

"Take me to the straw market on Bay Street," she impulsively commanded the driver.

The activity there should keep her mind off of Jason, she reasoned as they pulled away from the docks. Rather than wondering where he was and what he was doing, she could enjoy herself, poking through the stalls and bargaining with the wily native women for their goods. She'd been meaning to find a few souvenirs to take home, anyway. Shopping in the straw market would be a lot more entertaining than the regular stores. Besides, it was practically the only place open on Sunday.

The driver quickly got her onto Bay Street and took her to Rawson Square, beautiful with its colonial structure housing the Bahamian's Parliament and off of which stood the straw market. No sooner had she alighted from the taxi than women who had the stalls facing the sidewalk began hawking their wares.

"Here, darling. Look," one black woman said, holding out a sample. "The best-made straw bags in Nassau. Only ten dollars American."

"No, I don't think so."

"Nine dollars, then," came the reduced offer. Maris smiled but shook her head as she went inside the market. "How much do you want to pay, darling?" the woman called after her.

Maris took her time looking around, trying to decide what she wanted to buy. It was getting late, however, and some of the merchants were already packing up their wares. Looking through a rack of necklaces, she finally spotted one she really liked. She tried it on and inspected herself in the small, cracked mirror above the rack. A white shell carved into the shape of a dolphin hung from a short string of purple beads. Not only did it match the silk-screened purple and white Androsian shirt she was wearing, it would be a wonderful reminder of the special day she'd shared with Jason.

"It's beautiful like the lady," the young woman running the stall told her. "It was made for you."

"It's nice," Maris said nonchalantly, as though she didn't care whether or not she got it. That was part of the bargaining process—pretending only mild interest. She took off the necklace, adding, "But probably too expensive."

The woman stayed Maris's hand from putting the item back on its hook. "Twelve dollars."

Maris firmly disengaged her hand and replaced the necklace. "I think I'll look around some more. I'm trying to find one I like for eight."

"I'll save you the walk, honey. Ten. That's a good price."

"Nine would be better."

The woman flashed her a broad grin, her teeth a slash of brightness against her ebony face. "All right, but only because I'm going home now."

Maris smiled in return and took out a ten-dollar bill. While the woman got her change Maris put on the necklace, admiring her purchase in the small mirror. Turning sideways to see it from a different angle, she noticed the image of a man behind her. He was turning away quickly, as though he'd been watching her but didn't want to be seen. She whirled around as he disappeared between a couple of stalls. Funny, but the guy's lime-green sport jacket made her think of Thorpe Harris, Caroline Wilkerson's fiancé. . . .

"Here's your change, honey."

Reluctantly turning back to the satisfied saleswoman, Maris took her money. Then she continued looking through the stalls, trying to ignore her growing unease. Every once in a while she had the weird sensation of being followed. But by whom? she wondered, feeling a little ridiculous when she turned and saw nothing unusual. Thorpe Harris? Why in the world would he want to follow her?

Even though she could think of no good reason for her anxiety, Maris couldn't relax so she decided to leave. Her stomach growled, reminding her she'd had more physical activity than usual and that lunch had been too long ago. The Sheraton British Colonial was only a few short blocks away so she headed for the old hotel. The Bayside Restaurant, which overlooked the entrance to Nassau's deep-water harbor, would be a picturesque place to have a quiet dinner.

Since it was early, the place was virtually empty and Maris had no trouble getting a window table. She could eat while watching the color of the water change hues with the setting sun. She ordered Bahamian specialties. The Goombay Smash was a wicked mixture of rums cloaked in tropical juices, and the cracked conch was one of her favorite shellfish dishes, second only to broiled crayfish.

She was relaxing over her drink and watching a small boat maneuver its way through the harbor when she instinctively felt someone standing behind her. Lifting her gaze, she saw the gaudy reflection of none other than Thorpe Harris.

"Hello, lovely lady. You're alone, so I assume you won't mind if I join you," he said, swiftly suiting words to action by sliding into the seat next to her before she could protest. "I told the waitress to bring my drink to this table."

His leg rubbed against hers—purposely, no doubt—making Maris shift away quickly. She remembered the way the man had tried to stare down the front of her dress the first time she'd met him. And there was no question that it was Thorpe she'd seen in the straw market. He had been following her. But why?

"What are you doing here?" she asked, trying to keep any hint of suspicion out of her voice.

"Meeting Caro for dinner." Thorpe made a show of checking his watch. "I was having a few drinks with a business associate of Arthur's earlier, at the man's place up from Parliament Square. I walked here, but I guess I'm still a trifle early. My good fortune," he added, leaning forward and gazing at her intently, "since I can enjoy your charming company alone for a while."

"How do you know I'm alone? My dinner companion could be in the men's room."

Thorpe looked around quickly, then glanced at the table with its single drink, evidence of her lie. His laugh was one that Maris could only describe as leering.

"Oh, I get it. You were teasing me." He slid his hand across the table and boldly covered hers, confirming her suspicions as to why he'd followed her. "I like an amusing woman."

Maris had the distinct feeling he'd like any woman he could get. She pulled her hand free with a deliberate movement and lifted her Goombay Smash just as the waitress set down his drink. He turned and began to flirt shamelessly with the woman, as boldly as he had with Maris.

Maris sipped her drink slowly, eyeing Thorpe over the rim of her glass. He still sported a five o'clock shadow and had mirrored sunglasses stuck in his styled sandy-blond hair. She almost laughed when she realized the streaks in it looked as if they'd been bleached by peroxide rather than by nature. He was rather like the colorful male of certain species of fish—except that he used artificial means to achieve his looks. Did he really think his splendor would draw positive female attention?

"A sense of humor is a valuable asset," she said in amusement when she finally lowered her drink.

Probably thinking she was flirting with him, he eyed her boldly. "Almost as much as beauty. You're a gorgeous woman, Maris Collier. I've had my eye on you."

In the market? she wanted to ask. "How flattering," she said instead, keeping the sarcasm out of her voice in an effort to make him confide in her freely. How she'd love to tell him a thing or two! Poor Caroline!

"If I weren't an engaged man . . ." He let the words trail off his tongue as his fingers trailed up her arm. He leaned closer, more fully cupping her shoulder with his hand. Maris steeled herself from shivering in disgust and got ready to tell the man off. "But then some women don't mind sharing a *good* man," he added in what she guessed was supposed to be a seductive tone. "What about you, Maris? How do you feel?"

"How does she feel about what?" Caroline Wilkerson's strained voice came from behind them.

"Caro, darling!" Thorpe stood and embraced his stiff-backed fiancée in one fluid, practiced motion. He even kissed her cheek affectionately. "We were just talking about the Bahamas. I was wondering if Maris was as enchanted by the islands as tourists are."

"How quaint," Caroline said, not yet allowing herself to be pacified by her lover's lie. She stared down at Maris. "And are you enchanted . . . by the islands?"

"I think they're almost as wonderful as the waters surrounding them," Maris said tactfully. "It's nice to see you again, Caroline."

"Sit over here, Caro," Thorpe insisted, steering his bride-to-be toward the chair in front of the window. "I think we should take pity on Maris and join her for dinner or she'll have to eat all by herself."

Maris didn't know why she couldn't politely say she'd rather have dinner alone. She was already missing the sunset. But poor Caroline didn't need to be embarrassed further, so she couldn't very well object. "It would be nice to chat with someone who's lived here all her life," Maris heard herself saying.

"Yes, we could have a nice talk," Caroline agreed, though there wasn't much friendliness in her tone. She wasn't able to hide the fact that she was jealous. Maris couldn't keep feeling sorry for such an insecure woman —perhaps a shiftless gold digger like Thorpe was all Caroline thought she could get.

Allowing Thorpe to seat her, Caroline gave him another dirty look before turning to Maris. "So, what did you do with your Sunday?"

"I spent it diving."

The Englishwoman frowned, her expression of disbelief making her plain face look pinched. "You were working?"

"It wasn't work. I went treasure diving," Maris admitted, still wondering if Caroline really thought she was interested in her fiancé. "Jason Price took me to the site of a sunken ship called the *Isabella* that he'd done some research on."

"Some research?" Caroline raised her eyebrows. "You make it sound so casual. I'd hardly call researching the archives in Seville for galleon wrecks *some* research. Jason sent that Puerto Rican woman to Spain for several weeks."

Maris frowned. "He paid for a trip to Spain? That's a little costly for a hobby."

"Hobby?" Caroline's brows rose yet again. She stared intently at Maris for a moment before suddenly lowering her lids as though she were hiding her thoughts. She turned to Thorpe. "Darling, I'm very thirsty. Go get me a rum punch. That's a dear."

"Our waitress is right over there, Caro, taking an order—"

"I would like a drink to refresh me when I need it, not when it's convenient for the hired help."

Caroline dismissed her fiancé by turning abruptly away from him. Maris couldn't believe the other woman's petulant tone. It made her sound like a rather spoiled child, one used to getting everything she wanted. But perhaps that wasn't unusual for someone with wealth. To Maris's further surprise, Thorpe rose and headed toward the bar, a scowl pasted on his narrow, handsome face.

"Now, where were we?" Caroline asked pleasantly.

Distracted by her thoughts, Maris shrugged. "Um . . . talking about Jason's hobby."

"It's hardly a hobby." Shaking her head and clucking, Caroline reached across the table and patted Maris's hand. "My dear, sunken ships are never a hobby with professional treasure divers."

"But Jason doesn't go after treasure professionally."

"You really don't know?" Caroline's tone immediately became sympathetic. "Jason Price *is* a professional at it. He was one of the crew members when Will Gibbons made his big find a decade ago in Florida off of Key Largo."

Maris was thoughtful. "The Key Largo find? I remember reading about it in all the papers. Gibbons became world-famous, the treasure he located was one of the most extensive and intact in history."

"Well, it's not intact anymore. At the least it's too bad all the jewelry couldn't have been kept together as a legacy for people to see. All that history gone, sold piece by piece to pay off investors and crew members." Her expression sad, Caroline shook her head. "Jason used his cut to get himself started in the business on his own. Everyone in Nassau probably knows he's been looking for the *Isabella* for six or seven years."

"But Jason's an insurance investigator and salvor," Maris insisted, certain the statement was true. "One with a fine reputation."

"Of course, and he's a lot better at salvaging than he is at locating treasure. When he can't find backers to sink their money into his questionable personal quest, he has to earn some kind of living merely to eat—as well as to finance his obsession as best he can."

"Obsession?" Maris echoed uneasily, noticing that the other woman seemed to perk up at her discomfort. "You make it sound like some kind of disease."

"Treasure fever is, once it gets in your blood . . . or so they say. That's why I've found it impossible to listen to Thorpe on the topic. He wants to find the *Isabella* himself, but I cut him off when he even mentions it. I'm not about to ask Daddy to throw his money away on a ridiculous pipe dream that'll never pan out."

107

Maris tried to keep her voice even in spite of her stomach's warning twinge. "I guess it would cost a lot to finance."

"That's an understatement," Caroline assured her. "You have to buy expensive equipment, have aerial views taken of the area, do a great deal of research, perhaps send someone to Spain to get to the original documents. How much do you think all that cost some unknowing investor?"

"I haven't the faintest idea."

"I really don't either, but altogether Jason has undoubtedly gone through hundreds of thousands of dollars of other people's money," Caroline told her, making Maris feel sick inside. "And who knows how much more of his own. If you ask me, he wouldn't stop at anything to get at a treasure worth millions. Maybe billions."

Wishing she could shout at Caroline that none of this was true, Maris gripped her drink and shook her head. "It just doesn't sound like the Jason I know."

Or did it? Hadn't she already seen that he could be something of a daredevil? Hadn't she suspected that he was optimistic to the point of delusion?

"And how well can a woman really know a man she's just met a few days before?" True. The soft-spoken and sensible question made Maris doubt even more. "Jason is certainly a good storyteller," Caroline continued. "That's how he gets his investors. Perhaps he didn't tell you how deeply he's committed to finding the *Isabella* because he guessed you were a sensible sort and was afraid it would scare you off."

Caroline was right again. If Maris had had the slightest idea . . .

"But, my goodness. What have I done? You look positively pale," Caroline said, appearing contrite. "I've upset you, haven't I? I just know it." She peered over her shoulder to see Thorpe heading their way, then turned back to Maris with a conspiratorial air. "I can sympathize with you, my dear. No matter how outrageous they are, these virile, handsome men are dangerously attractive for a few of us unlucky women. We just have to be careful. If you ever want someone to confide in . . ."

Maris was sure she wouldn't. In fact, she was relieved when Thorpe reached their table, effectively ending Caroline's disturbing revelations. She had no desire to hear more.

"Here you are, Caro, darling," Thorpe said as he placed a tall drink in front of her. He slid back into his seat, boldly nudging Maris's leg with his knee in spite of Caroline's presence. "The waitress is coming to take our food orders."

"Excuse me, please," Maris said, suddenly needing to get away from them both. "I'm not feeling well. Too much fun in the sun for one day, I think." She fumbled in her purse for her wallet. Withdrawing a couple of bills, she set them on the table. "This will cover what I ordered. I couldn't possibly eat anything right now, but you go ahead and have my cracked conch if you want."

"I'm so sorry you have to rush off," Caroline murmured, not even looking at her, while Thorpe's eyes slid to surreptitiously inspect her figure.

But Maris was already on her way out of the restaurant and heading through the shopping arcade toward the hotel in search of a taxi, too distracted to be annoyed with Thorpe. Thinking about what might have happened between her and Jason if Gallagher hadn't come to get him, she shivered.

There was no way in the deep blue sea she'd ever get involved with another irresponsible fast talker who saw a pot of gold at the end of every rainbow, who was more interested in his own gratification for adventure than he was in her feelings on the matter. Her ex-husband had cured her of being attracted to that sort of man. Bob Collier had stolen her dreams.

Entering the hotel through the back door, Maris remembered her youth. While growing up she'd dreamed of owning her own boat, imagining that her life would be one dedicated to searching for unexplored islands and lost ships, living in and on the sea. But somewhere along the line she'd lost that youthful exuberance and had become practical about life. She'd grown up and realized that trying to live out her fantasies could be terribly risky and that her impulsive emotions could easily get her in trouble.

So Maris had decided to compromise, to approach her dream in a mature and practical manner—like working toward a career that would be close to, if not exactly, what she wanted. The job at the aquarium would also let her save money to buy a boat sometime in the future. She'd saved a good portion of every paycheck toward that end for eight years.

Crossing the lobby, Maris remembered that when she had met Bob she had let her heart freely and impulsively choose the easygoing, impulsive fast talker. He appealed to the secret part of her that she'd put on hold while she made a sensible living. She didn't even care that he was often without a means of support.

During their four-year marriage Bob was always going to "hit it big" with some scheme. He'd quit several jobs to pursue the end of the rainbow. Maris had herself convinced that Bob's schemes were harmless, actually part of his charm. And yet, later, she realized that she'd been in the process of falling out of love for nearly half of their marriage. To Maris, love and trust went hand in hand.

Then she lost her life's savings—almost enough money to buy her boat—when he withdrew all their money without consulting her. She realized with sudden clarity that she couldn't go on fooling herself any longer. She had to see her husband for what he was. Bob had invested her money in worthless Florida swampland in hopes that it would be turned into the next Disney World. Instead, he couldn't find backers and he couldn't resell the land. Bob was cheerfully philosophical about the loss.

But Maris couldn't view her husband's actions so casually. She realized that her love for her husband had finally gone the way of her boat—both dreams sucked into that swampland, buried forever. Since she couldn't continue to love a man she couldn't depend upon and couldn't trust, she filed for divorce. And now, a year later, she was still smarting from his betrayal.

As the hotel's doorman flagged down a taxi for her, the sensible part of her realized she was fortunate that she'd found out about Jason. But the other part of her— the free spirit she'd thought was buried forever—wished Caroline had kept her mouth shut, allowing Maris to dream a little while longer.

Gallagher gunned the old beater and, with a squeal of tires, sped away from a stop sign on the road out of town. Sorely tempted to jump out even as the car moved, Jason kept his grip on the window frame and steadied himself.

The quirky diver had been a menace on wheels from

the moment he'd pulled out of the dock area. Instead of joining the traffic pattern around a hub that lined cars up directly with the Nassau bridge, he'd cut in from the side, earning the ire of other drivers. Then, once back in Nassau, he'd sped up and down side streets, backtracking, finally heading out to the west end of the island. He'd excused himself by saying he was trying to lose anyone who might be following them. Jason thought it was the man's marbles that were lost altogether. He had second thoughts about continuing on what would undoubtedly turn out to be a fool's quest.

As they sped along the beach west of town, they passed other cars at a dizzying speed. "Gallagher," Jason growled, "slow down before I rip that wheel out of your hands!"

Though he didn't answer, Gallagher obviously believed him, because the man let up on the accelerator slightly.

To keep himself from getting too steamed up over the wild driving, Jason thought about the change of luck that had brought him more than one clue that day. But he'd have to go back out with a crane to bring up the boiler since he hadn't found a serial number.

Gazing out of the car window at the passing gold sand and turquoise water reminded Jason of another bit of luck—finding Maris. He'd enjoyed the time he'd spent on and in the ocean with her. His leaving her had been regrettable but necessary, and he chided himself for letting her take his mind off of his work. Suddenly realizing they were approaching the Cable Beach properties—and Arthur Wilkerson's seaside mansion— Jason grew uneasy.

"Do you think you might tell me where we're going

now, Gallagher? You can talk freely since there's no one around."

"We're going to see Annie," the man answered just before cutting a sharp left turn across the path of an oncoming car.

"Lord help me if I ever get in a car with this maniac driving again," he muttered as they headed toward the interior of the island, away from the wealthy Cable Beach area. He took a calming breath, willed his pounding heart to return to normal, then asked, "Annie's the person who knows about the murder?"

But, as usual, Gallagher couldn't answer a question directly. "I hope you have plenty of money on you. Annie's very expensive, but the most powerful obeah woman in New Providence is worth it."

"Dammit, Gallagher!" Jason exploded. "I'm paying you to get information, not to take me to some woman who does voodoo magic. Do you think she can look into her bowl of chicken blood and see what happened to those ships and to some unknown man?"

He was irritated further when Gallagher refused to answer the question, rather muttered under his breath about disbelievers and kept driving, once more speeding up as if the devil himself were behind him. Or in front of them, Jason thought wryly. An obeah woman. One who made potions with curative powers, who rid believers of unwanted acquaintances, who supposedly had the power to create zombies—the living dead. He should have known better than to have trusted a man with half a brain!

A few minutes later Gallagher slowed as they passed houses that belonged to the island workers. Old men and women sat on porches watching small barefoot children playing in the streets, shrieking in the universal voice of children across the world. The structures themselves, many of them no bigger than a single large room, were painted in pastel pink or yellow or bright turquoise, their colors now muted by the setting sun. Even so, and in spite of the boxes and hanging baskets of flowers decorating them, few could compete with the buildings in town. The elements were hard at work here, peeling paint from the walls, rotting wooden doors and window trims.

Jason knew that the owners of these small homes lacked the time and the money to keep them in good repair. They were hard workers for the most part, spending long days scrambling for the money it took to feed and clothe their families on an island where the cost of living was incredibly high, where a person had to pay more than two dollars for a simple loaf of bread. It was no wonder there were so many entrepreneurs roaming the streets of Nassau trying to make a buck off the tourists.

When Gallagher stopped the car suddenly it was in front of one of the shabbier buildings, its deep red paint peeling off in large strips, its closed wooden shutters hanging crookedly over the single window. Surrounded by dusk and a charged atmosphere that Jason told himself he was merely imagining, the place seemed almost ominous. He got out of the car reluctantly. Although unafraid, he doubted that this visit would be fruitful. Yet something kept him from ordering Gallagher to take him back to town.

"What now?" he asked, crossing his arms over his chest. "Do you think she'll draw on some magic sight to lead us to those sunken ships? Or will she tell us the Bermuda Triangle swallowed them?"

"The obeah woman has many powers," Gallagher

said, once more avoiding a direct answer. "Her knowledge of voodoo is well known and respected by the islanders. Ask her about that."

Shaking his head, Jason took the few remaining steps to the decrepit little house. Why was he going through with this? He didn't believe in superstition. Before he could knock, the screen door opened.

"I'm looking for Annie," he choked out, momentarily overcome by the heavy smell of incense.

The large young man stared at him with vacant eyes through the screen. He didn't answer, merely stepped back out of the way. Jason entered, aware that Gallagher remained outside. It took a moment to adjust to the interior, dark except for the flickering candlelight coming from a curtained-off area at the other end of the single room. A slight human form stood facing him, silhouetted by the light.

"You're Annie?" Jason asked.

"No other." The lilting island voice was forceful yet ancient. "Why do you seek me out?"

"You're the obeah woman. You tell me."

She let her head drop back and the candles behind her washed her dark face with a muted light. Although it was wrinkled, it was strong, determined. Frail lids closed over sharp brown eyes and she muttered something unintelligible. Then she lifted her head and, with a sharp intake of breath, dramatically whispered, "Death and destruction. You are here . . . because you need information, are you not?"

Gallagher could have primed her, of course. This could be part of a scam to make more money. Jason stepped closer to one side so he could see the old woman better.

She was clothed in a long, shapeless garment billowing with gauzy folds. Jason noticed the wealth of jewelry around her neck, many of the chains hung with amulets. The altar behind her was decorated with statues of demonic-looking saints—chained, as though their spirits were bound by the woman—as well as a few wax figures, chicken bones, and a shallow bowl of thick red liquid. He looked down at the signs drawn with the chicken blood and at the sprinkling of a white powder on the dirt floor.

Then he met her eyes steadily and repeated what Gallagher suggested. "I was told to ask you about the islanders' belief in your knowledge of voodoo."

She raised a hand, palm flattened toward him. "Ah, but you think you are too intelligent to believe in things you cannot see. You think the people who come to me are children, easily fooled." The lilting voice held anger and she made a sharp gesture of dismissal with the raised hand. "So my telling you about spells and curses is a waste of both our time."

On a hunch he said, "I may not believe in your power, but I respect the fact that many others do. I'm not sure what you know that would be important to me, but I'd be willing to pay for the knowledge."

"You want to know why I used voodoo against the Wilkersons."

Jason was startled by such a bald admission of fact, but he tried not to show it. He remembered the bloody chicken head falling out of Caroline Wilkerson's purse. So Annie had been responsible for that in addition to incidents against other members of the family that he hadn't heard about.

"That's a good start," Jason said, taking a bill of large denomination out of his pocket and placing it on a nearby table.

"I was paid to make sure the guilty one was punished."

"Who paid you? Guilty of what?" Jason reached into his pocket to withdraw another bill, but the shake of Annie's head stayed his hand.

"I cannot reveal the name of my client. I may only tell you it was one with a great personal loss, a life taken away by the greed and evil of the Wilkersons. You must find the connection yourself. The incident happened the night before the last ship disappeared."

The mysterious murder? Knowing that not every death was reported to the island police, Jason was tempted to offer her more money than she could refuse, but there was such pride in the woman's demeanor that he couldn't bring himself to try to compromise her. He would do as she suggested. Nodding, he backed away. "Thank you."

Annie reached to either side of her, and taking hold of the curtains, drew them shut. As Jason headed for the door he saw that the young man who'd let him in was sitting stiffly in a far corner of the dark room, his vacant eyes wide open. A chill passed through him as he opened the screen door and escaped into the night. Gallagher was already waiting for him in the car with the engine running.

On the way back to town Jason was thoughtful. In spite of his disbelief in her powers, he believed what the obeah woman had told him. He'd had a hunch all along that one of the Wilkersons was somehow responsible for the disappearance of the freighters. And now they were implicated in a murder, *if* he could prove it happened. But which Wilkerson, how and why?

He planned to plant those very questions around the Rum Keg and a few other spots as soon as they got back to the dock area, but he knew he wouldn't get any answers before morning. That's when he could begin more extensive inquiries, perhaps starting with the police.

In the meantime, Jason was too pumped up to sleep —unless it was with a mermaid who was beginning to haunt him. A clear image of Maris came to his mind: her luscious body was wrapped in her waist-length silver-blond hair . . . and nothing else.

Jason hoped he didn't get detoured for too long before he could go to her and apologize again for running off.

CHAPTER SIX

Damn, why hadn't he realized how late it was getting to be? Glancing at his watch, Jason stopped the car and leaned across the seat to peer at Brian Nelson's house, barely visible beyond the garden's wrought-iron gates. It looked completely dark. Had everyone gone to sleep, including Maris?

Deciding he'd check things out anyway, Jason pulled Alonzo's car to the side of the road and parked it. The jaunt with Gallagher had taken much longer than he'd expected and then he'd gotten into an involved discussion with the Ferraras when he'd stopped by their rented house. All in all, he was arriving on Maris's doorstep several hours later than he'd planned. Would he be able to talk her into having a late dinner with him anyway? She'd looked as disappointed as he'd felt when he'd had to leave her at the dock.

Slamming the car door when he got out, Jason strode toward the gates and let himself into the garden. Only one dim streetlight and the glow of the moon illuminated the surrounding foliage. The multileveled house was quiet, its windows blank and dark.

Cursing softly to himself, Jason walked swiftly down the path. When he reached the house he skirted around the building, then stopped beneath some tall palm trees growing on the other side. His scowl disappeared as he gazed at the lighted screened door on the rear second floor. Opening to that level's balcony, the door revealed little but the white walls inside and the edge of some furniture. That was all Jason thought he'd be able to see from that angle until a woman glided past—someone with long blond hair and, it appeared, wearing little else. Maris! What luck! Should he call out to her?

He hastily decided against that, as he didn't want to wake up everyone else in the house. He gazed around him. There was no stairway to the second-floor balcony, but surely he could find something to climb.

Stopping by the table in her bedroom, Maris riffled through the professional journals she'd brought to the Bahamas but could find nothing she wanted to read. She wasn't in the mood for fish. Or a lot of other things. The novel she'd borrowed earlier from Jo had turned out to be a romance, and Maris had only needed to encounter the hero and heroine's first sensual kiss to become irritated enough to throw the book across the room. She didn't want to read about a loving couple. Any current expectations she'd had concerning romance had been squelched when she'd watched Jason walk away at the docks earlier that evening.

She was still upset over the truths he'd neglected to tell her, so upset she'd been unable to sleep. Anything was likely to get on her nerves. Even the sound of the gentle wind rustling the leaves of the palms outside grated on her. She paced restlessly from one end of the room to the other, her mind in a whirl.

The day had started out pleasantly enough. She'd enjoyed Jason's company immensely, as well as the adventure of the dive and the story of the *Isabella*. Treasure hunting had gotten into her blood with her discovery of the old silver ring. She'd been looking forward to treasure diving again and would have tried to fit another day of diving with Jason into her busy Bahamas schedule . . . until she'd learned that he pursued the activity for more than mere fun.

A professional treasure hunter. The name connoted a modern-day looter who dug up antiquities—legally or illegally—and split up his finds, selling treasure to the highest bidders. Such irresponsible practices deprived the rest of humanity of their historical heritage. Furthermore, many treasure hunters were next to being professional con men, people who used all kinds of tricks to get money from investors.

At least that's what Maris had always heard. Pausing in mid-stride, she glanced at the mirror hanging above the room's low chest of drawers and glimpsed her disheveled reflection staring back at her. She quirked her brows doubtfully. She wasn't exactly an expert on the subject of treasure hunters. She'd gotten all her information second- and thirdhand. Wasn't there some possibility that her sources were wrong?

Maris thought about what Caroline Wilkerson had said. She was obviously insecure when it came to men, if taking up with a gigolo like Thorpe were any proof. Couldn't Caroline be jealous of Maris and Jason? Unlike his daughter, Arthur Wilkerson seemed to trust the salvor, his sincere friendliness at the christening party a clear indication of his respect. And Jason was working for a reputable insurance company. Would such a firm hire a semi-con man to investigate a case worth millions of dollars?

Turning to pace back to the bedside table, Maris riffled through the magazines again. Besides the newspaper articles, she was fairly certain she'd once read a magazine feature about Will Gibbons. She frowned, trying to remember the details of the Key Largo find. Hadn't there been a lot of publicity concerning Gibbons's honesty, about how he'd documented his find and paid every single one of his investors? Paying everyone back didn't sound like something a con man would do. Perhaps only some treasure hunters were irresponsible looters.

Unbidden, images of Bob Collier came to Maris's mind. Was she letting her distrust for her ex-husband color her view of Jason? As a divorced woman, she knew she was doubly wary. Still, why hadn't Jason told her about his profession? Wasn't withholding the truth a form of indirect lying? How could she help being suspicious of him?

Maris shook her head as if to clear it, then glanced toward the screened door. Were the palms rustling louder? She could swear she'd just heard a scraping sound. But her senses were probably doing strange things, following the example of her unruly emotions. She was simply going to have to get a handle on herself. Perhaps some warm milk might make her feel sleepier. She could sneak down to the kitchen and . . .

"Maris!"

The hoarse whisper coming from outside almost made her jump out of her skin. Her heart pounded erratically as she whirled toward the door.

"Maris!" the voice rasped again.

It sounded uncannily familiar. Certain that only one man she knew had the nerve to come calling in the middle of the night, she forgot to grab her robe in her haste to dispatch him. She ran out onto the balcony to behold Jason perched in the palm tree a few feet away.

"Are you crazy?" she cried.

"Sh-h-h." Grinning from ear to ear, he placed his fingers against his lips. "Quiet, or you'll wake everyone."

"What . . ." She carefully lowered her voice to an outraged whisper. "What are you doing here?"

"I'm here to see you." He gazed at her with hooded eyes, let them wander down her body to her legs. "And I appreciate seeing so much of you."

Glancing down at the sheer nightgown that only grazed the tops of her thighs, Maris suddenly felt naked. Clinging softly to her curves, the garment's pale pink satin hid little of her body. Even her nipples were fully outlined.

Crossing her arms over her chest but refusing to retreat from the confrontation, she insisted, "Well, I don't want to see you. It's late and I'm going to bed."

"Alone?" Hanging on to the palm's smooth trunk, he tried to swing a foot over to the balcony.

"Stay over there!" she cried, backing away. "Yes, I'm going to bed alone."

He shook his head mournfully. "How sad. Such a waste of a good nightgown, not to mention the woman inside it."

"You're the one who's going to be wasted if you don't get out of here," she threatened. She had no intention of having anything more to do with the man until she knew a lot more about him.

"I'll leave if you'll come with me. How about a late dinner?"

"No!"

"Or a nice, cool drink . . . with a warm, admiring man?"

"Absolutely not."

123

He glanced below him, then back at her. "How about a walk in the garden then? You sound tense, like you could use some exercise. I can think of some special movements we can do."

"I'll just bet you can. And I can think of a few movements to speed you on your way if you don't get out of here right now!"

His brows drew together in a puzzled frown. "Are you angry about something?"

"You noticed!" she exclaimed, sure she'd had enough of Jason Price for one day.

He swung a foot toward the balcony again. "I guess you're disappointed about our time together being interrupted. Now that I'm here, let's talk about it."

Disappointed? Is that all he thought it was? "I don't want to talk." She came to the edge of the balcony, holding on to the railing to kick at the toe that was reaching for a foothold on her turf. "Stay away."

"I can't stay away from you. What will make you feel better? Would you like me to recite some poetry? We *are* in a Romeo and Juliet type of setting here."

"How about shimmying down that palm real fast and picking up some splinters?"

"You'd like to see me in pain? You *must be* angry! Is it because you had the same kind of fantasies I did about how this evening would end?" His voice grew huskier. "It's not too late to make them come true."

Gripping the tree trunk tightly with his legs and one arm, he quickly leaned across the space between the tree and the house to grab her.

"Let go!" she said, jerking her arm away and swiftly moving back. "Whoops!" She sprang forward the next instant to keep him from falling, her heart pounding. Gripping the tree with one arm, her shoulder with the other, a foot on the edge of the balcony, he teetered over open space. "Now look what you've done!" she complained. "You're going to break your neck."

"I knew . . . you didn't really want me to be hurt," he gasped, "since you went out of your way to save my life in the first place." Drawing himself together, he released her and managed to leap precariously to the outside of the railing.

"Oh, no!" She stepped back.

"Oh, yes." He grinned wolfishly, swinging one leg, then the other over the railing. Securely on the balcony now, he paced toward her as she continued to edge closer to the open door. "I know you're a gutsy woman. So why are you running away?"

Indeed, why was she? She stopped, her resolve hardening, her hands balling into fists at her side. "This has gone far enough. How many times do I have to tell you to leave?"

"Until you decide you'd like to go with me. Or else invite me to stay." He paused to stare down at her, his expression more serious. "Surely we can talk for a little while."

"About what? All the information you withheld from me today?"

He looked surprised. "You insist on hearing about the Wilkerson ships?"

Now it was her turn to be surprised. Did he really think she was stupid? "I'm not referring to the Wilkerson ships. Why didn't you tell me you were a professional treasure hunter?"

"I don't know." He leaned back against the railing. "I figured you'd probably heard about me around town. What does it matter? You're not a competitor going after the same shipwreck, are you?"

"Hardly." She didn't want to tell him the real reason she was concerned, that she was afraid she'd almost gotten herself mixed up with another irresponsible man. She said meaningfully, "I'm not a potential investor either."

He shrugged. "Fine. But you probably helped me uncover a piece of treasure. And you can rest assured you'll get the money for that ring."

"I don't care about the money. I told you that."

"It's a point of honor with me—I always make sure all the people involved with my search are paid."

His open sincerity almost made her feel guilty. She was reminded of the article she'd read that touted Will Gibbons's honesty. Had Jason guessed she suspected treasure hunters of being con men? Had he understood her hidden meaning about not being a potential investor?

"What's the real problem, Maris?" he asked softly, pushing away from the railing. "What else would you like to know about me?"

She felt flustered, at a loss for words. When he placed a warm hand on her bare arm, she looked up at him. "I don't like to be lied to."

"I haven't lied to you." Placing his other hand on her waist, he drew her nearer. "And I'll whisper whatever truth you want to know about me right into your beautiful ear."

What could she do? His chin grazed her temple as he lowered his mouth. But instead of whispering in her ear, he kissed it, then nibbled her tender earlobe, making her shiver.

He embraced her even more tightly, drawing his warm mouth across her cheek to settle it over her waiting lips. At the same time his strong hands caressed her back, molding her body against his harder one.

Sensations spiraled wildly from her core, and Maris felt as if she'd been set on fire, her careful logic burned to a crisp. Running her palms up Jason's hair-roughened muscular arms, she threw her head back and opened her mouth to receive more of him. His tongue tangled with hers sweetly.

Moving sensuously against him, she felt his hands slide down to caress her brief-clad hips, then move upward beneath her nightgown, gliding over her warm bare flesh. She caught her breath when he cupped a swelling breast, teasing the nipple with one finger. Currents surged and waves crashed. The merman had taken hold of her body and soul and was drawing her down to the bottom of the sea again.

She felt intensely bereft when he suddenly released her to draw the nightgown up. He was ready to slip it over her head when she heard the sound of a window being cranked open. Window?

"Jason!" she whispered loudly, grabbing the nightgown to pull it back down, suddenly remembering where they were.

The entire crew had bedrooms at the rear of the house and obviously not everyone was asleep. But Jason reached for her again, his gold eyes looking fiery even in the dim light.

"Stop that!" She slapped at his hands. "This is no place for . . ." She paused, realizing that whoever had cranked the window open was certain to be listening. She whispered, "You have to leave."

"What?" He frowned.

"I said you have to go."

He took a deep breath. "Are you coming with me?"

She shook her head. Before she could make a comment, however, a voice scratchy with sleep called out from below, "For Pete's sake, either go with him or send him away, Maris. Some of us are trying to sleep!"

Was that Brian? Maris wondered with embarrassment. The director's bedroom was on the first floor.

"Ah, gee." Paul's voice came from a window nearby. "Don't make them leave. I want to catch the second act."

"Me too," agreed Jo from another window.

Her face burning, Maris backed away from Jason.

At last realizing that the night's tryst was over, he asked pointedly, "Can I see you another time, since you don't seem to want to continue this discussion at the moment?"

"I'll think about it . . . seriously," she assured him, hoping that her response was positive enough to get rid of him for the moment.

"Only your heart can tell you what you really want to know, Maris," he murmured before hoisting himself over the railing again. "Hope you dream of me." With a parting smile he leaned down to grasp the edge of the balcony and, with agile grace, swung out and leaped to the ground.

Maris listened to the sound of his muffled footsteps retreating through the garden before she turned to go back inside. How on earth was she going to face the crew tomorrow? What had people heard? What must they think? She only hoped the light had been too dim for them to see anything.

CHAPTER SEVEN

"Hey, boss, glad you suggested coming out tonight," Paul said as he led the aquarium crew toward the Cable Beach Casino, stopping at the top of the steps.

Next to him, Brian nodded. "I thought we could all use a break even if it is the middle of the week. I know I need to unwind before heading out to sea for three days."

But Paul didn't seem to be listening. Maris followed the direction of his rapt gaze and smiled when she caught sight of the sultry dark-haired beauty playing poker against a machine. Even from where they stood several yards away, she could see the image of cards laid out on the giant video screen.

"She lost," Paul murmured, straightening the collar of his dress shirt. "I think I'll see what I can do to console her. I've got a feeling this is gonna be my lucky night."

"Don't get yourself too tired out to get up early tomorrow morning!" Jo called after him as he sauntered down the steps and over to the woman, who seemed to be cursing the poker machine. She chuckled loudly and turned to Maris. "Think he'll get to show off his *G.Q.* nightwear?"

"His what?" Brian asked distractedly. But before either of the women could explain, he pointed to the right side of the room. "There's Arthur at that craps table."

Maris's eyes grew wide when she recognized not only Arthur Wilkerson and Thorpe Harris but Jason Price as well. She'd done a lot of thinking since the episode on her balcony two nights before, but she hadn't come to any sure conclusions about the man.

She knew one thing, however: She didn't need aerobics to get her pulse rate up. All she had to do was look at Jason. Tonight he was as gorgeous as ever in pleated beige trousers and a white cotton sport jacket. He'd left the top two buttons of his yellow and white island print shirt open, revealing the gold chain and coin nestled in the pale curls on his chest. Jason Price was a *G.Q.* man if ever she'd seen one.

"I think I'll say hello to Arthur and join the craps game." Brian rubbed his hands as though they were itching to hold the dice. "Either of you ladies care to join me?"

"Nah, I like blackjack myself," Jo stated, checking out the table, which lay in the opposite direction. "Oooh, not to mention blackjack dealers."

"Maris, you seem to be very interested in the craps table. Are you thinking of playing?"

Maris was thinking about playing, all right, but not with a pair of dice. She tore her eyes from the table and managed to give her boss a nonchalant answer.

"Actually, Brian, I just want to walk around and look at everything." Although the only thing she wanted to look at was Jason, she'd control herself this evening. "Maybe I'll try the slot machines."

"All right. See you two later."

"Slots?" Jo took Maris's arm. "Come on with me. A slot machine is a sucker's bet. You can't win. That's why they call them one-armed bandits. I can teach you the basics of blackjack in a couple of minutes."

"You go ahead. Maybe I'll join you later."

"Are you sure?"

"Positive. Now go." When Jo still hesitated Maris firmly pushed at the shorter woman's shoulder until she moved down the few steps. "Go have fun."

Shrugging good-naturedly, Jo headed off in one direction while Maris slowly wandered in the other. She wove in and out of the banks of slot machines, always aware of her proximity to Jason. She caught glimpses of him every now and then as he placed bets and exchanged words with Arthur and Thorpe. Jason didn't seem to notice her. Maybe he was merely ignoring her, which she guessed he'd be justified in doing after the way she'd treated him the other night.

Turning her concentration to the one-armed bandits, she noted the many variations in the machines—numbers, bars, fruits, single-line through five-line bets, the possible winnings multiplied by the number of coins plugged in for a single pull. The slot machines were new, shiny, high tech, though not so different from those she'd played the last time she'd been in a casino when she and Bob had honeymooned in Freeport several years before.

Maris frowned. Why did she have to think of Bob when memories would only mar the pleasure of the evening's outing? Her ex-husband had seen the casino as another "opportunity." But even when he'd gambled away their week's spending money in a single night, she hadn't guessed the true depth of his obsession to get rich quick. Or maybe she hadn't wanted to recognize such a profound weakness in the man she'd just married.

Glancing over at Jason as he picked up the dice, she knew why her thoughts had wandered to her ex-husband. She was still subconsciously comparing them, and it wasn't fair to Jason. As Jo had said during one of their frequent talks, Jason might very well be the exception to the rule when it came to treasure hunters. Maris was beginning to realize how very much she wished that were true.

After trading a ten-dollar bill for a roll of coins, she pulled up a stool in front of a slot machine with a five-way betting pattern. Her seat just happened to give her a direct view of Jason as he rolled the dice. Maris dropped five quarters into the slot, pulled the handle, and turned back to the craps table even before the mechanism in her machine stopped. She vaguely heard the plink of coins as they dropped into the tray. Her attention continued to be diverted by the action at the craps table and she barely noticed that her cache of coins steadily grew in bulk.

Jason was gambling much more conservatively than she might have expected, remaining good-natured even in the face of loss. That was more than could be said for Arthur Wilkerson, who was becoming increasingly loud and obnoxious as his chips ran out and he had to replenish them time and again. Arthur was the one who was reminding her of Bob.

Maris grimaced at the realization. First she'd thought Jason was like her ex-husband, and now she was picking on Arthur. That said something about the validity of the way she'd judged the man who filled her thoughts.

She now knew that she'd been wrong to take the discussion with Caroline so seriously. She'd been too eager to assume the worst about Jason because of her own past experiences. If he were such a con man, blithely swindling investors, why would he have offered to pay her for the ring she'd found? He'd insisted that he always paid his debts. How could she have forgotten that, believing so readily a generalization that Caroline had made about irresponsible professional treasure divers?

Maris looked over at Jason. He was staring at her, his gaze unwavering. Anticipation made her stomach flutter, forcing Maris to be honest with herself. She had wanted to see Jason the other night, to feel his arms around her, no matter what she had supposed about him. It was too bad that the need to protect herself had been so overwhelming.

Thorpe jostled Jason, breaking their invisible contact. He turned his attention back to the dice. Maris felt bereft somehow. If Jason were to approach her about seeing him tonight, she would agree wholeheartedly. It was time to trust her instincts, time to find out for herself whether or not this man was an exception to the rules.

With that settled she tugged at the slot machine's handle, deriving only cursory satisfaction when she hit a minor jackpot, two hundred coins in return for the five she'd played. She remembered the saying—lucky at cards, unlucky in love. Did that apply to slot machines?

Arthur Wilkerson was making an ass of himself, Jason thought, watching the large man shoulder another player aside as he reached across the table to throw down ten one-thousand-dollar bills in front of the boxman.

"Give me five hundreds!" The boxman stuffed the bills through the slot in the table and gave Arthur a stack of twenty chips worth five hundred dollars each. As the stickman pushed five dice in front of him, Arthur boomed, "I want new dice. I don't need someone

133

else's bad luck to rub off on me. I've had enough of that tonight."

"Yes, sir," the stickman said, signaling a runner to bring him new dice while several other players grumbled about the delay.

Jason studied Arthur's florid face, which was slicked with sweat, not from the heat but from gambling fever. After all, that was what he was here for—to verify the rumors that Wilkerson was often strapped for funds because of his consistently large gambling losses.

Although Jason himself was a great believer in luck, he considered it wrong to sink large amounts of his or his investors' money into a casino. Gambling could be an entertaining diversion in moderation, but tonight he'd come only because he knew Arthur, Harold, and Thorpe would be here. He'd had a hunch that seeing them off their usual turf would lend him some valuable insights.

The hunch had paid off, because the last two hours had been a real eye-opener. Arthur was into the house for nearly twenty thousand dollars, and he was willing to throw away another ten. Harold hadn't bet a cent for the half hour he'd stuck around. He'd seemed ill at ease and had constantly looked over his shoulder before he'd finally left, with a weak excuse about catching up with some paperwork. Thorpe had played cagily, feeding his future father-in-law's ego while betting against him.

Jason wouldn't put it past any one of them to be involved with the disappearing freighters. And since not one of the men liked either of the others, collusion was unlikely. Arthur Wilkerson's gambling losses put him at the top of Jason's list of suspects. It was quite possible that the old man had figured out the angles so that sabotaging his own freighters for the insurance money would work to his benefit.

"It's about time!"

Arthur's loud pronouncement meant that the dice had arrived and the game was about to resume. Jason slipped his chips into his pocket and stepped away from the table, indicating he was withdrawing from the game. He moved to stand opposite the older Wilkerson. Bets were placed, Arthur setting five chips on the pass line. Then he picked up his pair of dice, blew on them, rubbed them on his tie, and mumbled something over them before throwing them across the center of the table.

"Eight," one of the dealers called before placing bets for several of the gamblers.

Since Jason was no longer betting and had learned what he'd come for, his attention wandered over to Maris. She still sat in front of the same slot machine. He'd known exactly when she'd arrived, and he'd been conscious of her presence ever since. He could only be thankful that the aquarium team hadn't shown up before he'd been satisfied with the night's work. Not only was Maris herself distracting, but Brian Nelson had seemed to have a calming influence on Arthur for a while, until it had been Arthur's turn to be shooter, that is.

One glance at the table assured him that the old man was losing control again. He was ordering the dealer to place his chips on several numbers as well as "hard-way" combinations. Staying here any longer wouldn't accomplish a thing as far as Jason was concerned. He was tired, but he didn't want to go back to the *Argonaut* to sleep. At least not alone.

Jason wondered if he should approach Maris immediately. Maybe he should let her worry a little while longer about whether or not he would come on to her at all. He hadn't forgotten the way she'd thrown him off her balcony—not that he couldn't have stolen her away if he hadn't been interrupted by several eavesdroppers!

From the way she'd been covertly eyeing him while pretending to play the slot machines, he was fairly certain she'd gotten over the snit she'd been in. But before he could decide what he wanted to do, pandemonium broke loose at the table.

"Craps!" the dealer called.

"No, not again!" Arthur roared as his chips were cleared. Jason saw that there wasn't one left in front of the man. He'd bet the entire ten thousand. "It's those dice. I want to check them!" he shouted at the stickman. "You've switched the ones I picked from the new batch with loaded dice!"

Activity around the table stopped and the boxman quietly spoke to one of the dealers. "Get the manager." Then he told everyone around the table, "Don't touch anything."

"They run a clean house here, Arthur," Brian assured him. "You just had a run of bad luck."

"No one's luck is this bad!"

"Maybe it's the voodoo," Thorpe said with a snicker. "The curse must be working on you, Art."

"How many times have I told you not to call me Art, you poor excuse for a man!"

Arthur lunged awkwardly for his daughter's fiancé. Brian stepped between them before the older man could do any harm and Jason stopped next to Thorpe. "Arthur, calm down," Brian pleaded. "Let's go for a drink and talk about this."

"But the dice—"

"Aren't loaded and you know it." He took Arthur's arm and tugged. "Come on."

Swearing under his breath, Arthur allowed Brian to lead him away. Jason decided to take advantage of a white-faced Thorpe. "Voodoo, huh?" he murmured. "So, someone has reason to curse the head of Wilkerson Industries?"

Thorpe's face pulled into a grimace resembling a laugh. "It was a joke, that's all."

"Then no one's sent Arthur little presents—like that chicken head someone put in Caroline's purse? Or was that a joke too?"

The grotesque laugh faded. "Poor Caroline," Thorpe said, backing away from Jason. "She probably made some superstitious island black angry at her. Well, it was a slice playing with you, Price. We'll have to do it again sometime."

With that Thorpe turned and fled from him, leaving his chips behind. Jason went to the cashier's window to exchange his own for money. He was pleased that he'd come out a few bucks ahead, enough to treat Maris to any restaurant her heart desired. If she preferred eating to coming back to the boat with him, that is.

The thought made him grin with anticipation. Jason headed for the bank of slot machines, sure that Maris would still be there. What he hadn't counted on was Thorpe's presence. Apparently the man irritated her as much as he did everyone else. Jason saw her expression go from annoyed to furious. When Thorpe put his hand on her shoulder she rose so fast that she nearly knocked over her stool.

As Jason reached them he heard Maris hiss, "So help me, you touch me one more time and I'll feed you to a nasty, hungry shark!"

Rather than flattening the other man, as he was tempted to do, Jason smoothly insinuated himself between them. "But, darling," he said, wrapping an arm around her waist, "I'm not all that hungry. Besides, I leave the garbage for the barracudas." Staring steadily at Thorpe, he bared his teeth in a predatory smile, his stance telling the other man in no uncertain terms to stay away from his woman. "Let's discuss this further in private."

For the second time that night Thorpe backed off. Although he left without comment, he shot them a venomous parting glance. Jason stared after him thoughtfully.

"You can let go now."

Jason turned at the softly issued words. "You don't like *my* touch, either?"

The corners of her lips twitched. "I thought you wanted to discuss it in private."

"Well, what are we waiting for?" Jason started to move off, but Maris firmly refused to budge. "Something wrong?"

"Yes. No. I mean, I have to do something with these." She indicated a cup of coins and what looked like hundreds more in the tray under the slot machine. "Some sucker bet, huh?"

Jason found another cup and helped her scoop the quarters into it. They took both cups to a cashier who dumped their contents into a coin counter.

"One hundred and three dollars," the woman said, reading the total.

"Good lord, this is my lucky night," Maris murmured.

"And mine," Jason added, already imagining the details. Before he could get very far he heard a hiss from

138

behind him. Turning, he spotted a disembodied hand signaling him from one of the banks of slot machines. "Who the hell . . ."

"Psst!" The hand waved more frantically.

"I'll be right back," Jason assured Maris as she waited for the cashier to count out her money. He was reluctant to let her out of his sight for even a second. "Don't forget where we were."

"Jason!" she protested. "Wait a minute!"

But he'd already followed the hand and was face-to-face with Gallagher. "What's going on?" Jason demanded.

"I hope you've had a good night gambling."

"I assume that means you want more money. You don't get another cent until you come up with something I can use."

Gallagher looked around furtively, as though he were making sure they were alone. "Can you use a widow?"

"Widow? The wife of the seaman who was supposedly murdered?" Jason had tried to investigate the story on his own, but the islanders couldn't or wouldn't tell him anything. The police had merely laughed at his allegation. "Where?"

"She'll be at the back door of the Rum Keg in half an hour."

"Who will?" came a curious voice from behind him.

"Maris," Jason groaned, realizing that his plans for the evening were blown. She stared at Gallagher suspiciously. "I hate to do this to you again, but I'm afraid I have some business to take care of."

"Business? It's after eleven."

"Investigations don't necessarily fall into the usual nine-to-five work schedule. I'm meeting a woman who may have some information I need."

139

"Fine. I'll go with you."

"You can't."

"Of course I can." Now she was looking at *him* with that same suspicious gleam in her eyes. "Unless you're trying to hide something from me."

Or trying to protect you, Jason thought grimly. He didn't want to involve her in a situation that might already have led to one murder. "It could be dangerous."

She raised an eyebrow as well as her voice. "I'm not afraid."

"Shh!" Gallagher's eyes rolled as he looked around them. "There are interested ears everywhere."

"Do you want me to call a taxi for you?" Jason whispered. "Or do you want to stay here with your friends and leave with them?"

Maris crossed her arms over her chest defiantly. "The taxi, please. That way I can follow you."

Jason swore softly. "You're the most stubborn woman. . . . I'm only trying to protect you."

"And I'm trying to protect my interests. And that's what you should want too. Unless our interests are too different to ever coincide, that is." They stared at each other in silence, the seconds seeming to stretch into minutes before she demanded, "Well?"

"All right. You can come, but it's against my better judgment."

Though she didn't smile, there was a gleam of victory in her eyes that irritated him. Jason took her arm before he realized that Gallagher had disappeared. He wasn't worried. The seaman was greedy, so he wouldn't be far away. In the meantime, he'd score a little victory of his own.

"Look at me lovingly," he instructed Maris, crushing her closer to his side. From what he could tell about their encounter on her balcony, she hated audiences even more than he, and they were surrounded by people. "When we get to the foot of the stairs I'm going to kiss you to throw off suspicion in case anyone is watching me. Make it look good."

"But—"

That was all she had time to say before he zeroed in on his target, plundering her mouth in the same way he'd dreamed of doing to her body. Maris hesitated at first, then kissed him in return with all the passion a man would want from a woman.

Sliding her luscious curves up against him, she wrapped her arms around his neck and ran her fingers through his hair. She pulled her head away only to nip at his lips. Then her mouth sought his once more. There was no way in the world Jason could have held back his very real physical response. He was so hot for her, he could set the casino on fire!

If he didn't stop this now, they'd never get to the Rum Keg. He'd throw the investigation and take Maris to the registration desk of the hotel instead!

Grasping her shoulders, he pushed her away and studied her expression. He scowled, not at all sure he liked what he saw—passion mixed with smugness. She'd known what he was about and meant to get to him, using his own technique.

"Is it safe to go now?" she whispered.

"It's safer than staying," he muttered, rushing her up the stairs and toward the entrance, where the doorman got them a taxi. Just in case there were "interested ears" around, he said, "Take us to Parliament Square."

He would tell the driver he'd changed his mind once they were on Bay Street. Maris was staring at him questioningly, but she didn't challenge him. Wrapping his

141

arm around her shoulders, Jason settled back in his seat, prepared to spend one of the most uncomfortable nights in his life.

As they alighted from the taxi in front of the Rum Keg, Maris reflected on the amount of persistence it had taken her to be included as part of this expedition. She was probably crazy for insisting on coming along, but how could she ever learn more about Jason if he kept running off on her? Besides, she was curious about the information this unnamed woman could give him concerning the missing ships.

It wasn't the investigation she was thinking of, however, when Jason placed his warm palm in the middle of her back and guided her through the front door of the Rum Keg. Maris looked around the dimly lit interior, nervous now that she'd had time to think about the possible danger he'd mentioned earlier. But the wharfside tavern was half empty, and only a few of the customers bothered to look up as she and Jason crossed to the bar.

"Monte," Jason said, nodding. "Two pints of stout."

Monte Adams filled two pints while staring at Maris from under his bushy red eyebrows. He was obviously curious about her presence, but he merely shoved her drink at her, then turned his attention to Jason. Maris grimaced when she tasted the bitter dark beer.

"Have you received any new goods lately?" Jason asked.

"Took delivery just a few minutes ago." Monte's eyes flashed to the right of the bar where a doorway led to the back room. "Gallagher's going over the inventory right now."

"Anyone else interested?" Jason murmured softly, casually sipping at his stout.

"Don't seem to be, but to be safe I'll create a diversion." A bushy brow bobbed as Monte winked at Maris. He went to an old jukebox on the far wall. "Anyone have any requests, you cheap sons-of-the-sea?" he shouted, and all eyes in the room turned to him. He plugged the jukebox with coins. "I'm tired of listening to your bilge."

"Stuff it, Monte," one of the seamen shouted back, "or I'll trim your ears so you won't be able to listen to nothin'!"

While the other customers laughed uproariously and made ribald comments, Jason grabbed their pints and indicated that Maris should precede him into the back room. Once on the other side of the threshold, he handed her the drinks and closed the door to the tavern.

"Hang on to those and let me do all the talking."

About to protest that she didn't have to take orders from him, Maris chose to remain silent when she saw Gallagher talking to someone in the shadows at the other end of the room. As she drew closer she could see the woman was young, perhaps in her early twenties. Her dark face was a mask of anxiety. Maris sat on a crate a few yards away and set the pints down next to her.

"Elizabeth Rawlings is willing to talk to you," Gallagher told Jason. "But first you pay."

"I don't want any cursed money. I want justice!" the woman cried. She seemed to be personally involved in the mystery.

"I'll take enough for both of us."

Gallagher held his hand out till Jason filled it. Then

143

the seaman wandered deeper into the shadows where he counted the wad of bills.

"I understand you've suffered a great loss recently," Jason began gently. "I'm very sorry."

"Why?" Elizabeth's voice was filled with suspicion. "You're white like them. You didn't know my man."

Maris thought he'd ask who "them" was. Instead, Jason said, "I regret any waste of human life, white or black," making her assume the woman's husband had disappeared along with one of the ships.

The island woman seemed satisfied by the answer. "My John, he wasn't a bad man. He only wanted good things for his family."

"Is that why he got a job with Wilkerson Industries?"

She nodded. "And that's why he got himself killed."

"I don't understand."

"John wanted us to move from the Bahamas to some other island far away, maybe in the West Indies. I didn't want to go. I didn't want my family to be like the Haitians here, people with no country, accepted by no one. John begged me. I could see he was afraid of something, but he wouldn't tell me what. He said leaving was the only way, that something bad would happen if I didn't agree."

Even in the dim light Maris could see that Elizabeth's dark eyes sparkled with unshed tears. The sight of the other woman's anguish made her shift uncomfortably on her crate.

"Something bad did happen," Jason said. "He died."

"He was murdered the night before the third Wilkerson ship disappeared—the one he was supposed to sail on!" Elizabeth said, her voice cracking. "He was involved in something dangerous that had to do with that ship. I know it, just as I know my refusing to leave New

144

Providence gave one of the Wilkersons reason to murder John."

"Murder? One of the Wilkersons?" Maris asked, suddenly rising to her feet. She ignored the glare that Jason threw her and stepped next to him. Appalled by Elizabeth Rawlings' accusation, Maris demanded, "What reason would one of the Wilkersons have to do something so horrible?"

Elizabeth eyed her warily. "I don't know, but a few hours before he died John was very nervous. He was talking nonsense, or so I thought then. I didn't pay much attention because I was worrying about his obsession with our leaving the Bahamas. The only thing I remember him saying is that you couldn't trust rich people just because they lived in nice houses and wore fancy clothes. He said they could have hearts as black as their skin was white."

"That's no proof that he was talking about the Wilkersons!" Maris protested. "There are a lot of rich white people on New Providence and Paradise Island."

"But my man wasn't involved with any of the others. He worked for the Wilkersons!" Elizabeth's voice rose as she added, "I wish I'd realized what he was trying to tell me then. Maybe I could have stopped him from leaving our house that night. The next time I saw John was when I found his lifeless body behind a building on the dock where he was to have sailed that morning." She began to cry softly. "Someone had knifed him through the heart."

Maris shuddered at the thought of finding someone she loved like that. Unable to say another word, she turned away and saw that Gallagher was still sitting on a crate, fingering his money. How could the man be so

145

blasé when they were talking about a murder? she wondered.

"Why didn't you report John's death and tell the authorities the things you've told me?" Jason asked. "There's no report of a murder on file. I checked."

"I didn't want to bring more trouble on my family. What else could I expect if I accused the Wilkersons of anything?"

"But the police can't investigate if they don't know about the murder. They'll be as interested as you are in finding the guilty one."

"No! They'll kill me or my babies." Tears streaming from her eyes, Elizabeth paced before them. Maris sensed the woman wasn't far from the breaking point. "I did the best I could in my own way."

"The voodoo curses," Jason said with certainty. "You had the obeah woman Annie send each of them a present. Gallagher took me to her."

A chill ran through Maris as she remembered the chicken head rolling out of Caroline's purse.

"Harold was sent an ox heart carved with a coffin symbol," Jason told Maris. "But the black lamp that Arthur received was even more gruesome. The ingredients appeared to have been soot, castor oil, powdered lizard—and part of a decomposed corpse!"

Maris's breath caught in her throat and her stomach grew queasy as she imagined such a concoction. She waited for Elizabeth to deny Jason's words.

Instead, the islander lifted her chin, saying, "The power of the black lamp was to disrupt the family, to cause the guilty one to lose everything. I wanted to make that person fear something worse than death!"

"The voodoo is what brought us here," Maris told

her. "If Gallagher found this Annie and then you, surely the Wilkersons could do the same."

It was the wrong thing to say. Elizabeth stopped in her tracks and her slight frame trembled. She let out a wail that sounded only half human. "No-o-o!"

"Maris!"

Jason stepped forward as if to calm the woman, but she backed away from him right into a corner where she huddled, her arms wrapped around herself.

"Stay away from me," Elizabeth cried, holding out a staying hand. She was sobbing and her slight shoulders were heaving with her fear.

"Jason." Maris gripped his sleeve so that he turned to her. His angry expression made her swallow hard. "You're not going to get any more information out of her now. I doubt that she knows more than she's already told you. It's my fault she's so upset. Why don't you leave us alone and let me try to calm her down?" He didn't budge. "Please."

He clenched and unclenched his jaw, making her think he might refuse to leave. Then he nodded and signaled Gallagher to follow him from the room. Taking a deep breath, Maris turned to the woman, who still sobbed against the wall.

"I'm sorry," Maris said, approaching her slowly. "I didn't mean to frighten you." She touched Elizabeth's shoulder and the woman turned her tear-stained face to Maris. "I shouldn't have said that. I really am sorry."

The woman clutched at Maris's sleeve. "Don't let them kill me or my babies, please."

"Whoever killed your husband has no reason to come looking for you or your children," Maris said with more certainty than she felt. Who knew the workings of an evil mind? The murderer might suspect Elizabeth knew more than she did. "And I'm sure Jason will do everything he can to find the guilty one and bring him to justice."

"You can't let us die. Help us, please! Promise me!"

How could she make a promise she had no means of carrying out? She could see that the woman was desperate. Taking a deep breath, Maris said, "I'll do anything I can to help you. In the meantime, maybe you should leave Nassau. Do you have any friends or relatives you could stay with on another island?"

"Not another island, but outside the city."

"I think you'd feel safer if you stayed there for a while."

Elizabeth wiped at her wet cheeks with a shaky hand. She took a deep gulp of air that seemed to calm her a little. "I'll go there, then." She closed her eyes and whispered, "So I leave my home now, when it's too late. If I had agreed before when John begged me, he would still be alive."

Not if he'd been on the ship that had disappeared on the following day, thought Maris. Afraid that she'd upset the woman all over again, Maris didn't voice her thought. Elizabeth's strained smile made Maris's heart go out to her. She really wished she could be of some help. The only thing it seemed she could do was to unlock the back door and check the street to make sure no one was watching. She nodded to Elizabeth.

"Take care to watch your back, miss," the island woman whispered. "No one who knows anything about the Wilkersons' business is safe."

Then she slipped out of the opening and quickly disappeared into the shadows, leaving Maris with an uneasy feeling that crawled up her spine. There was no proof that a Wilkerson had anything to do with murder. Somehow that thought didn't exactly ease her mind.

She reentered the tavern in time to hear Monte quietly tell Jason, "So this guy Franklin was seen on Andros Island several times, including the day before yesterday."

Jason muttered down into his stout, his voice so soft that she had to strain to hear his words. "This is getting more and more interesting. John Rawlings was murdered the night before the ship disappeared. Now you're telling me Henry Franklin sailed with that same ship but he's been seen alive and well and walking around Andros."

"That's what I'm telling you, mate, and the information came from one of my best sources." Monte noticed Maris standing there and quickly changed the subject. "I hear you're off of the *Mermaid's Kiss.* Pretty interesting work."

Discussing her occupation was the last thing in the world she wanted to do. "I like it. Jason, do you think we might go now? I've got to get up early, and it's after midnight."

"Sure." He seemed distracted—or was it distant?—as he stood and threw down a couple of bills. "See you, Monte. Keep your ears open."

"Speaking of ears," Maris said, looking around the place, "where's Gallagher?"

"Left, I guess."

Jason headed for the door, his stride long and hurried. Maris kept up with difficulty, realizing he was still angry with her for interfering. She waited in silence as he flagged down a taxi, her mind replaying Elizabeth's last words over and over again: *No one who knows anything about the Wilkersons' business is safe.*

That included not only Elizabeth, Gallagher, and Jason, but herself as well now that she'd forced her way into the intrigue.

She had a hard time imagining any one of the Wilkersons getting involved with sabotage or murder. Brian Nelson was a good judge of character, and he and Arthur had been friends for years. Maybe she ought to talk to her boss about the situation, see what he thought of the moral character of each member of the family. Maris shook her head. No, she couldn't do that. If Elizabeth was correct, it would mean putting Brian in danger as well—if he wasn't already on the list.

"Are you going to get in or are you going to ignore me again?" Jason asked impatiently. He was standing at the open door of a taxi.

"Oh. Yes, of course."

Jason helped her in, but his motions were cool and perfunctory. Waiting only until the taxi took off at his instructions, he said, "I might have gotten some important information if you hadn't interrupted."

"I doubt it, but I apologize for interfering."

He seemed to relax a little. "There's no reason for you to get mixed up in this."

"I feel as though I already am. That poor woman . . ."

"I'll make sure she's all right."

His words made her feel better. Still, Elizabeth Rawlings had been desperate enough to seek help from a stranger, and Maris couldn't forget that.

As though he were able to read her thoughts, Jason said, "Let's forget about everything but getting to know each other better." Inching closer to her, he put his arm around the back of her seat and stroked her shoulder with his fingertips. "How about Saturday night? I know

150

a nice private place where we can be alone—where, for once, business can't interfere with pleasure."

"That would be different," she said, liking the way he was touching her, yet uncomfortable with the way he'd changed the subject.

"If that's a yes, I'll pick you up at six."

"Yes." As the taxi crossed the bridge and Maris looked down into the moonlit waters, she was reminded of the last time they'd been together. She couldn't help herself—she wanted to know more about the case. "Jason, about the other day . . . what exactly did you find when we got separated in the water?"

He sighed deeply. "You don't give up, do you?"

"Not when I really want to know something."

"A boiler from a freighter."

"A Wilkerson freighter?"

"Maybe. I couldn't find any serial numbers when I was down there, so I went back out with a crane to bring it up. The buoy was gone. I went down anyway and found what was left of it—just shards of metal. Someone had used explosives on it."

She heard the frustration and disappointment in his tone and felt a little guilty that she'd added to those feelings. She snuggled closer. "Jason, if there's anything I can do to help, just tell me."

"I'll keep that in mind."

He wrapped his arm around her more fully, yet Maris sensed he was distracted. She was sure of it when the taxi pulled up in front of Brian's villa and he left her at the door with only a quick good-night kiss. Not that she really minded. She wasn't much in the mood for romance at the moment. There were too many things rolling around in her mind. Like the boiler someone hadn't wanted Jason to find.

151

Climbing the steps to her room, Maris remembered Eli saying someone had been following them. More than likely that someone had removed the buoy. She shivered. Danger had been lurking beyond the horizon even as they'd enjoyed themselves playing keep-away with the dolphins.

She was almost to her bedroom when she heard the noise—a curious-sounding thunk—almost as if someone had run into the glass sliding door leading to her balcony. She immediately thought of Jason. He must be at it again. Maris grinned. Maybe she could stand a little romance, after all. It would be days before they'd see each other.

Quickly opening the door, she slipped inside the darkened room. "Jason?" she hissed. When there was no answer she felt her chest tighten in apprehension. Someone had been there—the sliding door was open. Looking more carefully, she saw writing on the glass.

A message was outlined by the glow of the moon in the night sky. Her skin crawled as she read it: "Stay out of other people's business."

She immediately associated "other people's" with "Wilkersons'." Her heart pounding, back pressed against the door, Maris flipped on the light. Whoever had been there was gone. Her eyes wandered back to the message on the glass. It had been written in red. Lipstick? No. The letters seemed to drip. She crossed to the glass and touched one of the letters with a forefinger. It was still wet. She sniffed. Blood!

Her stomach lurched. Before she could think about what she was doing, Maris grabbed the box of tissues from her dresser and wiped away the warning. It was only afterward, when she backed to the bed and sat, still staring at the smeared glass in the door, that she realized she'd destroyed proof that, whether or not she wanted to be, she was now personally involved in the Wilkerson case.

CHAPTER EIGHT

"There seems to be nothing but sand and palm trees." Maris looked out at the small elongated island off the port side of the *Argonaut*. "Is this where we're going? The place looks uninhabited."

"I told you I wanted us to have privacy." Enjoying her surprise, Jason grinned as he brought the boat past the beach side of the island and around one narrow end. "Treasure Cay's not really uninhabited. It just has a small population—four people when everyone's at home."

"Treasure Cay? As in *Treasure Island?*"

"The name has nothing to do with the famous novel. Will Gibbons named this place Treasure Cay because he used the doubloons he found to buy it." Jason watched Maris's face light up as she sighted the building perched on a rocky rise on the island's other side. "That's the house Will built. Like it?"

"It's beautiful," she breathed. "A house the same color as the rocks and sand—it looks so natural, like it rose right out of the sea."

"You'll like the pool in back too," Jason promised. "And we'll have the place to ourselves. Will and his wife are away treasure hunting in the Pacific. The housekeeper fixed us some dinner, but she and the security guard have living quarters at the other end of the island and will stay out of our way."

"Are they expecting us?"

"I called them earlier today."

"They have a telephone out here?"

"Sure, and a CB and a generator for electricity. I keep an eye on Treasure Cay whenever Will is gone and stay here when I get the notion." He glanced at Maris as he cut the boat's throttle, realizing he'd never mentioned the mentor who was like a father to him. "You know who Will Gibbons is, don't you?"

She nodded. "The man who brought up all that treasure off Key Largo." She gazed at the coin he wore. "That was where you got your doubloon, wasn't it?"

"Yes." He let the boat slow even more as he brought it in toward the dock jutting out into the small deep cove below the house. "I never saw so much gold before or since."

"It must have been worth millions. No wonder your friend could afford a private island."

After they'd tied up the boat they headed toward the rock-cut steps that led up to the house. Glancing over his shoulder, Jason paused as he sighted another boat on the horizon. A yacht? It had to be the same vessel he'd glimpsed trailing them earlier.

"Is something wrong?" she asked, halting at the base of the steps. She gazed out to sea, in the direction of his scowling stare.

"No, he's keeping his distance."

"Who?"

"Thorpe Harris. At least I think it's his yacht." Or, rather, hoped it was, Jason silently corrected himself. Knowing Thorpe, he'd be sure to get bored by the time it got dark and take off for the Nassau nightlife. "That boat didn't get close enough on the way over here for me to positively identify it."

"So what makes you believe it's Thorpe?"

"He's followed me a couple of times before, when he thought I was looking for the *Isabella.*"

"Really?" She looked startled.

"I confronted him about it—he said there's no law against his looking for the same sunken ship."

"Caroline told me he fancies himself a treasure hunter."

"Treasure hunter?" Jason had to laugh at that. "If anything, Thorpe's a claim jumper. He's the type who isn't willing to work hard enough to find treasure himself. He'd rather wait and take it from somebody else."

"You think he's capable of thievery? Could he have had anything to do with the missing freighters?"

"Thorpe doesn't have the brains for that big of an operation."

In spite of his remark as they walked up the dozen or so steps, Jason tried to picture Thorpe as a suspect in the Wilkerson case. But it was difficult. The man would have to be a good actor, capable of hiding a very clever mind beneath his doltish exterior. Either Arthur or Harold—if Elizabeth's remarks about the Wilkersons had been correct—were more likely to be at the bottom of the mysterious happenings that had taken place nearby.

For everything was beginning to add up to the fact that the freighters had been sabotaged in local waters, the boiler probably having belonged to one of the ships. The missing buoy, the exploded boiler, and the unusual and consistent presence of another boat following Jason, not to mention the attempt on his life, must mean he was getting too close for someone's comfort.

And now a new twist had been added to the case—a man from a sunken ship had been seen walking on another island. A zombie or someone who was part of a scam? Jason wondered if more dead men could be found alive on other islands. Her husband had tried to convince Elizabeth to move. . . .

He turned to glance back once more when they reached the top of the rise. The boat was still visible. Was it really Thorpe's yacht? If not, Jason hoped his pursuer would be content with keeping an eye on him. Just in case, he decided it would be a good idea to tell the island's security guard to keep watch.

"Is the house unlocked?" Maris asked, drawing his attention back to her.

Not that that was difficult. Standing on the planked deck, the breeze blowing her long hair about her face and billowing her gauzy sea-green sundress out around her long legs, Maris was a sight for admiring eyes.

"I have the key," he said, removing it from his pocket and once more anticipating an evening completely alone with his mermaid.

He'd try to forget about the case while he was with her. The only clues he'd be looking for tonight were the secrets to unlocking Maris's heart and soul.

"This will definitely be more comfortable than sand and palm trees," Maris told Jason, gazing around as they entered the house and thinking how romantic it was to be nearly alone with him on a deserted isle.

The dining room lay to one side and the living room a few steps down on the other. Both were furnished simply and featured displays of shells and dried coral and driftwood. The muted blues, greens, and turquoises of the upholstery set against the sandy whites and beiges of the walls blended with the house's ocean setting and made Maris feel tranquilly at home. The old maps framed and hung on some of the walls spoke of travel and adventure.

"What lovely colors. And look at the view." She stepped down into the living room, drawn to its wall of windows facing the ocean. "You can see for miles."

Jason gestured toward the telescope set up in one corner of the room. "Take a look." He turned to the telephone on one wall, picked up the receiver, and pressed an intercom button. "George?" Jason spoke to the man Maris assumed to be the security guard as she peered through the telescope. "Keep watch on the cove tonight, will you? There seems to be a boat anchored out there." He paused, listening to what the guard said in return. "Right. I'll keep an eye on the pool side of the house and I'll call you if I think there's a problem. Thanks." Placing the receiver back in its cradle, he turned to Maris. "Would you like a guided tour of the rest of the place?"

"I want to see everything," she said pausing. "What's this about the guard watching the cove? Do you think Thorpe . . . or whoever's out there on that boat . . . might visit us?"

"Of course not. The boat is sure to take off any minute. It's probably only a load of tourists anyway. It's just that I feel responsible for Will's place, so I'm taking precautions. On an island like this one, you have to watch out for yourself." He placed an arm around her shoulders as they stepped back up into the dining room. "Come on and see the other rooms."

Maris wished she were so easily reassured by the typically terse answers Jason had given to her leading questions. Who had been following them on the boat? A murderer? She remembered the threatening message she'd found on her glass doors. She hadn't told anyone about the incident, not even Jason. Because of it, however, she felt she had a right to be involved in the case.

Once her initial fright over the bloody words had worn off, she'd been angry. *Very* angry. And more determined than ever to help solve the Wilkerson mystery if she got the chance. She wasn't going to let anyone stop her. Elizabeth's terror was something she'd probably never forget, especially if she didn't try to help. Still, despite her brave resolve, she couldn't help feeling uneasy, knowing how isolated they were on Treasure Cay.

"This house isn't large," said Jason, removing his arm so she could precede him up a narrow set of steps that led to a wing off the dining room. "But it's nice."

"It's more than nice, it's gorgeous," Maris remarked appreciatively.

She pushed her worries aside as they peered into two elegantly understated bedrooms and a bath. All the rooms were decorated in the same sea colors and both bedrooms had double doors that opened onto the spacious deck outside, obviously part of the house's living area in a continuously warm climate.

Heading back to the main section of the house, they crossed the dining room and entered the small but efficient kitchen and office. Although it was now twilight, Maris thought she glimpsed the sheen of water through the kitchen's rear-facing double doors.

"Oh, no, you don't." Placing his hands around her waist, Jason drew her back against him. "No peeking at the pool. I want to save that for later."

"It's that special?" The firm grip of his fingers and his warm breath feathering the back of her neck titillated her, making her anticipate what he might have in mind for the evening.

"So special, mermaids love it."

"Oh?" she said coolly. "How many mermaids have you brought out to this island?"

"One," he said, not blinking an eyelash. "The only mermaid I've ever known is you."

He moved his hands from her waist to her shoulders and guided her toward the stove. "Let's see what Miranda fixed for us. Hmm, barbecued chicken." He lifted the lids on the other pots. "Peas 'n' rice, plantain. There's probably green salad and some fruit in the refrigerator. A nice Bahamian dinner."

"Smells good to me."

Bringing the pots of food, some plates, utensils, and a chilled bottle of wine from the kitchen, they set everything down on the weathered round wooden table in the dining area. Maris pulled out a chair.

"Just a minute," Jason cautioned. "We need more atmosphere."

The beautiful quiet house set on an isolated island amid rolling blue swells was enough atmosphere for Maris. Still, as she watched Jason light several candles around the room—in antique holders and hurricane lamps—she had to admit candlelight would add something more.

When he'd finished he pulled her chair out the rest of the way, his eyes glowing in the flickering light. "Have a seat, lovely lady. There'll be nothing to disturb us now."

Disturb them from what? Having dinner? It would be easy to imagine other activities. . . .

Quirking his eyebrows at her sexily as he sat down, Jason appeared to be thinking along the same lines. But instead of reaching over to take her in his arms, as she almost expected, he picked up the wine.

"Would you like something smooth and intoxicating?" he asked, opening the bottle.

"Definitely," she told him, thinking that the description could apply equally well to Jason.

A salty breeze wafted in a nearby window as they helped themselves to the food and wine. Glancing out at the dark water, Maris nearly jumped when she thought she glimpsed the white yacht again, then told herself she was only imagining things. Once they'd begun eating, Jason pulled a small cloth bag out of his pants pocket.

"And as for dinner conversation," he said with a smile, opening the bag and shaking its contents into his hand, "I know you'll be interested in seeing this, now that I've had it cleaned."

Laying her fork aside, Maris stared at the object lying in his palm. The dull silver of the rather plain piece of jewelry glinted in the candlelight. "The ring?" Excited, she reached for it. "Can I see?"

"Sure. It was your find." He placed the ring in her hand, his fingers lightly grazing her palm. A different sort of excitement fluttered within her at his touch.

But she concentrated on the ring. "Is there an inscription inside?" She knit her brows and tried to read the tiny script, fully aware of his nearness as he leaned closer.

"That's the best part." He grinned. "The letters are partially obscured, of course, the silver having been worn down by its years in salt water. But the words are definitely French, and Carmen thinks they say 'Not gold, milady, but love I give to thee.' " He pointed, his fingers touching her palm again. "It looks like there were some initials here, but they've been worn away."

"Those initials must have been L.D.," Maris said with inner conviction. "I'll bet this ring was given to

161

Doña Maria by Louis Duhamel. Perhaps it was even meant to be a wedding ring." She turned to gaze into his amber eyes.

"It would be great if we could prove that."

"Can't underwater archaeologists date jewelry?"

"Possibly, but there's still nothing to prove this ring was connected with Doña Maria and Louis . . . or the *Isabella.*"

Except her own desire for romance. But what kind of romance did she crave most at the moment? The lure of a romantic tale or the pleasure of being held by Jason? She couldn't help but be disappointed when he removed the arm he'd been resting across the back of her chair and leaned back to sip at his wine.

"The Spanish records wouldn't have listed jewelry that belonged to Louis. But maybe an archaeologist could suggest other kinds of records." He took the ring, which she'd placed on the table, and put it back in its pouch. "I wonder if Frank Parrish, the man who used to work for Will, still lives in St. Augustine."

"Will Gibbons employed an archaeologist?" Maris asked with surprise.

"Yes, he wanted his treasure officially authenticated."

"Why, so he could sell it for a higher price?"

"That, and the fact that it would be accepted as historically important." Helping himself to another piece of barbecued chicken, Jason went back to his food. "Will didn't get the highest price for his gold. Instead of auctioning it off to various bidders, he sold the bulk of the Key Largo find to a private shipping and treasure museum in New England."

"So it would be displayed?" Maris remembered Caroline's assertion that the treasure had been sold piece by piece. What reason could she have had to lie? It was very strange. "I'm glad he cared about history."

"It's not that Will didn't receive plenty of money . . . or pay a good portion of the total amount to his investors," Jason assured her. "The Key Largo treasure was worth millions." He gazed around the room. "It's just that Will's tastes have always been simple. This island is the only piece of property he's ever owned. And, as you may have noticed, there's no expensive art or antiques around here. Will and Darlene value their collection of shells and driftwood more than anything else, except, of course, the thrill of searching for another sunken ship."

"They sound like interesting people."

"I'm sure you'll like each other when you meet them."

She gazed at him curiously. "Are they coming back to the Bahamas soon?"

"Probably not until winter."

Winter? That was months away. Didn't he realize the aquarium crew was in the islands for only a short stay? Not caring to be reminded of the fact that they'd soon part, Maris moved her leg aside when their knees brushed beneath the table.

"I've heard that Will Gibbons is very honest," said Maris as she finished her last few bites of dinner. "And that he always pays off his investors. Is that really true?"

"Absolutely true. That's important when you're in a profession that requires the use of other people's cash. One year, when I was first searching for the *Isabella,* I had to take several months off and do salvaging in order to repay someone who demanded his money."

"It doesn't sound like treasure hunting will make you

rich quick," said Maris, favorably contrasting Jason with her ex-husband. As if he knew what she were thinking, he glanced up at her and smiled.

"It can make you rich, but it's the thrill of the hunt and discovery—rather than the gold—that leads most of us on."

The thrill of the hunt? Maris wondered if Jason really saw her as an elusive mermaid. If he caught her; would he lose interest and simply go on to the next challenge?

Pushing his plate aside, Jason poured them both another glass of wine. "The search is always more intriguing and often as exciting as the find. You'd better love the path you travel, because you're going to spend more time traveling than sitting around at its end once you reach your goal. That's what Will always told me."

"You seem to have learned a lot from him."

"Will is like a father to me," he said warmly. Leaning on one elbow, he turned toward her and sipped at his wine. "I met him when I was young and had been traveling from odd job to odd job, learning about life the hard way."

"What about your real family?" she asked, curious about his earlier background.

"I haven't seen my dad or my two brothers since I was eighteen. After my mother died my father remarried and my stepmother and I didn't get along."

"You left home?" Maris asked with concern. "And you haven't seen your family since? Don't you miss them?"

"I prefer focusing on more positive relationships." Placing his wineglass on the table, he scooted his chair closer to her.

"But you have to take a little bad with the good in most people," she told him, remembering her fear that he was an impractical optimist. Was he unrealistic about relationships? As in treasure hunting, did he prefer the quest for riches to settling down?

"Negative and positive, huh?" He slid his hand down the length of her bare arm, making goose bumps rise on her skin. "Opposites that attract—like male and female."

For the moment she tried to ignore the delightful sensations he was causing. "You can't expect a long-term relationship to have no problems."

"Who said I did?" His fingers traced a playful path up the same arm again, making her want to shiver.

Did he or did he not want a long-term relationship? she wondered. And why did she care so much anyway?

"Your family is a lifetime commitment," she explained, believing it was important for him to understand. "And there's both negative and positive aspects of that relationship. My parents think I'm crazy in some ways—to leave the small town where I was born and work in the city, taking care of a bunch of fish. They're not always supportive of me, but I still love them."

"Your family doesn't support your hopes and dreams?" Instead of talking about his own background, as Maris had intended, Jason seemed to want to discuss her. He placed his arm across the back of her chair again. "Did you always dream of being a curator?"

She could feel the warmth from his flesh through the cotton of her dress. "Nothing that practical. When I was growing up I knew I wanted to live on and in the sea. I chose a profession that's connected to the ocean . . . and more realistic than being a sailor who travels the seven seas or an explorer who discovers uncharted islands, maybe even Atlantis." She laughed, glancing at him from beneath lowered eyelashes. She wasn't about to tell him she'd even imagined herself a mermaid once or twice. "Those were wild dreams."

"Not so wild," he said softly. "Jacques Cousteau has searched for Atlantis."

"Jacques Cousteau is one of a kind."

"So are you."

Did he really believe that? Or was he merely sweet-talking her? She wanted to sigh as he slid his hand across her back to finger one of the thin straps of her dress.

"You have to follow your dreams," he urged. "You don't want to be like Doña Maria, refusing to listen to your heart until it's too late. If she'd listened in the first place, she would have saved herself—and Louis—from a watery grave."

Wondering if her heart was speaking to her now or only her reaction to Jason's warm hand on her skin, Maris turned toward him. The intensity she saw in his eyes made her catch her breath . . . and think about falling in love. But that was ridiculous, wasn't it? She'd known Jason only a few weeks. And the thought was definitely scary. In spite of all they'd shared so far, she still didn't trust the man completely. Furthermore, she'd already made one serious mistake. . . .

"I listened to my heart before and it was totally wrong," she said defensively.

"About your ex-husband?" He shrugged. "That happens. Don't let a bad experience stop you from trying again."

What did Jason want from her? And what was he willing to offer in return? Would he cheat her?

"Bob was irresponsible, emotionally and financially. Since him I've been afraid my dreams will turn into nightmares."

"Well, this dream won't." Jason reached for her, pulling her to her feet and into his arms as he rose.

Could she really be dreaming? she wondered. If so, reality was safer but far less erotic than the feel of Jason's warm lips against her skin. Nuzzling her throat, taking his time, he trailed lingering kisses upward toward her mouth. Lips parted slightly, she waited for him to cover them. She was surprised when, instead of doing so, he turned her in his arms and, with her back pressed tightly against him, walked her across the room.

"Where are we going?" she murmured, thinking he must be in a hurry to get to a bed. And he hadn't even kissed her properly! She started to object until she saw they were heading for the double doors in the kitchen.

"You've told me more than once, you like to spend your time in and on the sea," he said, opening the doors with one hand and holding her against him with the other. "I want to make sure you enjoy the water tonight before I get too distracted."

"Water?" She'd forgotten about the pool. When he let go of her to switch on some floodlights—some of them embedded in the concrete walls of the magnificent free-form pool—she strode quickly to its edge, her eyes widening. "There are fish in there!"

"It's a saltwater pool, open to the sea at the other end." He grinned, obviously enjoying her excitement. "The island's so narrow here, it wasn't difficult to dig a lagoon. Will lined it with concrete before cutting out the final opening and stretched a net across the space so only small fish can get in."

"Fabulous!" Without thinking, gazing down at the blue water rippling gently beneath the lights, she slipped off her sandals.

"Want to swim, huh?"

"You said I should enjoy the water."

"That I did." Slipping off his knit shirt first, he removed his rubber-soled shoes and unfastened his belt.

She watched him for a moment, then quickly stepped back across the deck, skirting a chaise lounge and a table as she headed for the door.

"Wait! Where are you going?"

She stopped and turned around. "I left my swimsuit inside."

"Since when does a mermaid need a suit?"

He grinned wickedly, the doubloon swinging gently against his muscular chest as he unzipped his pants and drew them down over his long legs. The skimpy briefs he was wearing followed. He threw the clothing onto a nearby canvas chair and gazed at her, standing only a couple of feet from the water.

"Come here, Maris," he said low and invitingly.

She'd already raised her eyes to his face, suddenly a little shy. He was fully aroused. But hadn't she been imagining they'd make love all evening? Hadn't she even allowed herself to think about falling in love with him? How could she not love a man who believed in her dreams?

Mesmerized by his gaze, she walked slowly back across the deck, boldly stopping mere inches away. Warmth rose within her, but also fear. . . . Jason placed his hands on either side of her face, then slid them back to entangle them in her long hair.

"My beautiful mermaid," he said huskily, moving one hand down her back to undo the buttons of her dress.

Once open, the light, gauzy garment slipped easily off her shoulders and whispered down the length of her body into a puddle of soft fabric at her feet. The air felt cool to her exposed skin, now covered by only a wisp of lacy bra and briefs.

Heat seemed to emanate from Jason's flesh as he drew her even closer to unhook her bra and slip her briefs down over her hips. Throwing the undergarments aside, he ran his hands lightly over her body, pausing to cup her full breasts and kiss their aching tips. Shuddering, she grasped the strong arms that held her. She was oblivious to everything but the heady, spiraling sensations engulfing her and the man who was causing them. She wanted him and his love passionately, fiercely. She hardly realized they'd somehow gotten nearer the pool.

"Like to join me in the water, Maris of the Sea?" he raised his head to murmur softly. How could she refuse to answer the merman's siren call? To give her heart to him?

They both stepped off the side of the pool at the same time, their plunge taking them down the full ten-foot depth. Hair flowing around her, toes barely grazing the bottom, Maris opened her eyes. Blinking against the salt water's sting, she saw Jason hovering before her. She flowed into his waiting arms, their lips meeting and legs entwining, their bodies slipping and sliding over one another like natural creatures of the sea. For it was the sea that had brought them together and the ancient sea that could bind them forever. In Jason, Maris had found a man who loved the ocean and its deep and briny secrets as much as she.

Kissing her sweetly, he held her against him and let a hand glide over the sleek curves of her breasts, the indentation of her waist, the flare of her hip and thigh. When his exploring fingers delved between her legs, caressing the sensitive skin of her inner thigh and moving higher to touch her intimately, she gasped, breaking the kiss with a stream of bubbles that rose upward.

The bubbles reminded Maris that she needed oxygen. Motioning to Jason, she clung to him as they propelled themselves to the surface. She came up laughing with the joy of their newfound intimacy. His hair water-slicked, his wet body gleaming in the moonlight, he was an irresistible sea creature. Openly admiring him, she'd hardly gotten her breath when his salty-tasting lips settled possessively over hers again.

But not for long. Loosening his hold as they treaded water, he took a deep breath and swam toward the pool's shallower side, drawing her along with him. Soon her feet touched the slope of the concrete as it rose to shoulder-high depth.

"Come here, my mermaid," Jason whispered, taking hold of her waist and lifting her easily in the buoyant water.

He let her slide down again, skin gliding sensuously over skin, before he caught her, hands cupping her hips, anchoring her firmly against him. He lowered his head to sip at a nipple exposed at the surface of the water. Reacting to the heat of his mouth and the velvety hardness nestled against her, she instinctively opened for him, wrapping her legs around him. He groaned and lifted her again, this time bringing her down to join them completely. He nibbled at her mouth, softly biting her lower lip.

She took a shuddering breath as he undulated his hips, rocking them in the age-old rhythm of the sea. It was wondrous, this first glimpse into loving him, as wondrous as the water's magic. Ripples surrounded them, reminding Maris of inexorable ocean currents and the endless play of frothy waves.

From deep within she called forth the magical creature she'd once allowed herself to imagine she could be.
Maris the mermaid embraced her lover as they swam
closely together in a brilliant turquoise sea. Golden hair
intertwining with silver, jewel-like scales flashing, they
kissed, melding souls as well as bodies. . . .

"Maris?" he questioned softly, prompting her to look
at him. Her breath was ragged. "You love me, don't
you?"

"Yes," she answered without hesitation, letting her
heart speak. "I do love you."

"I love you too."

She closed her eyes again, clinging to him when he
began moving his hips faster. She caressed the flexing
muscles of his back, Jason the only solidity in a world of
foaming, surging waves. The ancient rhythm carried her
blindly toward resolution, just as tides move into shore.
She cried out when the wave she rode finally reached
the sand, crashing forward, spray rising high into the
air, the insistent rhythm of the water slowing and turning into itself as it receded, flowing out to sea. . . .

She collapsed against Jason, who shuddered with his
own release. Half floating with him in the water for a
few seconds, she placed soft kisses along the curve of his
throat before returning to reality. She opened her eyes,
gazing at the dark water sparkling with light from the
floodlights. Suddenly she became aware of nibbling sensations along the calf of her leg.

"Jason!" she exclaimed, stirring in his arms. Peering
beneath the water, she saw small flitting shapes and
laughed. "Something's chewing on me. Look, I think
they're little angel fish."

"Little devil fish is more like it." When he laughed,
too, she felt the vibration through his chest. "They ex-

pect to be fed. Will and Darlene treat their fishy visitors like pets. I'll see if I can't find some bread or rolls in the kitchen after we get out."

"Do we have to get out?" Loosening her embrace as she smiled sexily at him, Maris stretched her long legs, letting her toes touch the pool's bottom.

"You'd prefer to stay in the water all night?" He grinned, running an appreciative gaze over what he could see of her body. "Okay, I'm game, fair mermaid. We might get a little wrinkled, though."

"I guess I would be willing to settle for a nice swim back to the deck."

"You're on," he told her, drawing her out into the deeper water for a quick kiss before they swam for the ladder leading up to the deck. "You know, fish aren't the only authentic addition to this pool." He paused, treading water. "Take a look down there."

"What is it?" In the darkness she could make out only an elongated shape sitting motionless on the bottom.

"That's one of the cannons from the Key Largo galleon," he explained. "Will kept it for sentimental reasons. There's a small chest full of coins down there too. You'll be able to see them better in daylight."

"Doubloons?"

"A few."

"No wonder this island needs a security guard."

Later, having dried off with towels, they used another to lightly cover themselves as they stretched out together on the chaise lounge.

After a few minutes Maris wriggled against Jason, trying to get comfortable. "This lounger is hardly big enough for the two of us."

"I know. Cozy, isn't it?" He turned over farther on

his side, cradling her against him. Smoothing tendrils of hair back from her face, he gazed at her intently. "I knew our lovemaking would be good from the first time we met—and you kissed me."

Thinking of the day she found him struggling alone beneath the sea, she disagreed. "Me? It was *you* who kissed *me,* remember?"

"I distinctly recall regaining consciousness with you kissing the hell out of me." He raised himself on one elbow and stared down at her.

"Then you remember wrong. But I suppose that stands to reason . . . since you were hallucinating."

He laughed, his teeth flashing white in the dim light, though the expression in his eyes looked serious. "Next you'll be telling me I only imagined you told me you loved me tonight."

She was speechless for a second, then shook her head. "No, you didn't imagine that."

But she'd almost forgotten about it. Drugged by passion, inspired by his belief in her, had she really meant what she'd said? Was she ready for a deep involvement with the man?

Obviously ready to take her at her word, he placed soft kisses on her forehead, then lowered his mouth toward hers. "You're a dream come true," he whispered.

Still musing on the fact that she'd actually said she loved him, Maris passively watched his lips come closer. He froze at the sound of gunshots.

"What the hell?" Jason rose up on his elbow, then slid from the lounger, quickly rising to his feet. "That came from the dock."

"Good lord! Is someone attacking the island?" Maris exclaimed, grabbing the towel as she got up to follow him into the house.

His long stride outdistanced her easily, and somehow he was able to pull on his briefs much faster than she could wrap the towel around her naked body. By the time she reached the front door, her heart pounding, it stood wide open and Jason had already descended the rock-cut steps. The moonlit cove was empty except for the *Argonaut* tethered at the dock. The only sound to be heard was the murmuring of masculine voices coming from below.

"Climbing on the rocks?" exclaimed Jason before muttering something unintelligible to the security guard. George, in turn, murmured back in a singsong island lilt.

Had someone been climbing on the rocks that lined the small harbor? Had a stranger invaded their private island? Looking around nervously, wanting to hear exactly what the men were saying, Maris was tempted to walk out onto the front deck. But her hold on the towel was precarious. She waited a few more seconds, letting her breathing slow, trying to decide whether to go back to the pool and get her clothes. Before she could turn around, she spotted Jason striding rapidly up the steps.

He hurried faster when he caught sight of her. "Don't worry," he assured her when he reached the door. "It was nothing."

"What's this about someone climbing on the rocks?"

"George heard some noises out by the cove—pebbles bouncing around and so forth. Because I'd warned him to keep watch, he took a couple of shots, then investigated. But there's no one around but us. It was probably only some of the small lizards that infest this island."

"He was shooting at lizards?"

He nodded as he closed the door behind them. "It

174

was a waste of ammunition, but he was trying to do his job."

"And scare us to death in the process!"

"Were you afraid?" he asked with concern.

"It's easy to feel a little nervous after hearing about that murder the other night." And, she silently added, remembering the warning on the glass door.

"That seaman was killed in some kind of cover-up," Jason told her as they headed back toward the kitchen. "He was poor and a nobody. The person who sank the Wilkerson freighters surely wouldn't try to murder someone like you . . . or me." He paused thoughtfully. "Unless they're stupid or crazy."

Stupid? Wasn't that how Jason had described Thorpe Harris? Frowning as she remembered Thorpe's lewd suggestions at the casino, an exaggerated example of his usual sleazy behavior, Maris could easily imagine the man as some kind of criminal. But was he really bad enough to be a murderer?

"Hungry?" Jason's question interrupted her musings. "There's still fresh fruit in the refrigerator. Want me to take some out to the pool?"

"That sounds refreshing. Is there anything to drink?"

He opened the refrigerator door and looked inside. "What would you like? Cola, bottled water, more wine?"

"I'll take a cola, thanks."

As he got out the can of soda and piled some mangoes and grapes in a bowl, she wondered if his frown of concentration meant he was thinking about the investigation. Perhaps if he told her a few more details, she could figure out what was going on, guess who'd had enough gall to sneak into a private house to warn her. She decided to try to probe, maybe work some information out of him. "Are you going to look into what Monte Adams told you? About the man on Andros Island?" she asked Jason.

"Probably."

"And what else? What's the next move you plan?"

He glanced at her curiously, then grinned. "Why? Are you planning to come along to guard me?"

"Well, if nothing else, I can certainly serve as a distraction for the criminal." She adjusted her towel, accidentally letting it drop lower, revealing the tops of her breasts.

He gazed hungrily at the lush flesh she displayed. "That's distracting, all right."

"So what are you going to do?" she insisted.

"About the towel . . ." He moved toward her.

She held one hand up to slow him down. "No, about the investigation."

He stepped even nearer. "I don't know. It's about time I checked the records, I think."

"The records?" She seized upon the subject and stared him in the eye. "You're going to check out the shipping records? What good will that do?"

"I don't know. Though I've already seen a copy of the manifests that were presented to Intercontinental Mutual, I have a hunch I should check the originals."

"Are you going to have the insurance company request another set of manifests?"

"Maybe."

"And maybe not. I love your nebulous answers."

"And I love you," he murmured before encircling her with one arm and leading her toward the double doors. "Forget about the Wilkerson investigation. A night with a full moon and a mermaid isn't one to waste on work. Let's have our dessert by the pool."

Acting as if he wanted *her* for dessert, Jason nibbled her ear playfully as they strolled out to the chaise lounge. He let go of her for a moment to pull over a small table for their drinks and fruit as Maris stepped toward the pool to slip on the sandals she'd left lying beside it. Gazing at the water glistening in the play of the subdued recessed lights, she opened her eyes wider when she noted a strange shadowy substance rising ribbonlike from the spot where the cannon lay.

"Jason?"

"Maris," he answered huskily, quickly coming up to slide his hands around her waist.

"What is that?" she asked tensely.

"What is what, lovely lady?" He kissed her throat, but she was too distracted to fully appreciate the touch of his warm lips. She clutched her towel more tightly.

"It looks like blood."

"Blood?" His head suddenly jerked up and he stared out at the pool. He removed his hands from her waist and walked closer to the water. The dark ribbon flowed gently up from the bottom of the pool, drifting and dissipating at the surface. He frowned. "There's something down there . . . by the cannon."

Chills climbed up her spine as a feeling of foreboding swept through her. They'd been talking about murder. She only hoped . . .

"What is it?" she asked tensely. "A dead fish? That's what it's got to be, although I swear I didn't see anything in the water before."

"Looks a little large for the kind of fish that inhabit this pool." But surely it was too small to be human. Besides, everyone on the island was accounted for, weren't they? Jason peered down into the water. "I'll have to take a closer look."

"You're not going in there, are you?"

"Not at the moment."

Striding back toward the house, he picked up the long pole that had been resting against one corner of the outer wall and examined the curving hook at its end. "Will uses this to clean debris out of the pool."

Both anxious and curious, her eyes glued to the dark stream that continued to rise in the water, Maris moved closer as Jason knelt at the pool's edge. Using the pole, he poked around the area near the cannon. The hook scraped against the cement bottom, then finally snagged on something.

He frowned in concentration as he lost his hold on the mysterious object, then caught it up again. "Heavy." He jerked on the pole. "And there seems to be fishing line attached to the thing—that's what got caught on the cannon."

"Fishing line." She let her breath out in relief and stared at the shadowy lump as he drew it up. "A fisherman's catch that got away?" Leaning over for a closer look, however, she wasn't prepared for the sight of the bloody mass he suddenly pulled from the water. "Oh!" she cried, jerking away.

They stared in silence at the gutted three-foot-long shark. At least it wasn't a human body, Maris thought, shaken. Its sandpaperlike skin ripped open across its belly, its triangular teeth set in a permanent dead smile, the creature had been snagged on a large hook that stuck out of its jaw. Taking hold of its tail, Jason pulled the dead fish away from the water's edge.

"How did . . . that thing get in the pool?" Maris asked, shivering. Suddenly the balmy wind that stirred the palms surrounding the house seemed cold.

Jason didn't answer her question. He was busy examining another piece of fishing line that had been tied around the shark's throat. Tied?

Instantly reaching the same conclusion as Maris, Jason muttered, "Well, one thing's for certain. No other fish did this." A small disklike object dangled from the line. Snapping the disk off with a quick jerk, Jason gazed up at Maris. "Damn shark's been executed."

"Executed?"

He gestured toward the shark's ripped belly. "Sliced open with a knife." He rose and turned the disk over in his hand. Of some kind of cheap metal, the circular piece was inscribed with wavy lines. "And this appears to be someone's crude version of a doubloon—like the one I always wear. Whoever made it must have cut the net and swum into the pool in order to leave this amulet and corpse for me. Looks like the Wilkersons aren't the only ones being cursed by voodoo."

Someone swam into the pool? When?

Stunned, Maris gazed out to where an opening cut in the island's sandy soil to let in the sea. Although it gave her the creeps, she couldn't help imagining the diver who'd swum into the island—invading their sanctuary. She clutched the towel even tighter to her body, thoroughly chilled. Had the trespasser glimpsed Maris making love with Jason? Waited for them to leave the pool so he could enter with his grisly gift?

"Those noises George heard could have been a diversion," said Jason before throwing the disk aside. He continued to gaze at the shark thoughtfully. "They wanted to get us out to the front of the house."

"They? You think there was more than one?"

Aware of Maris's thinly veiled terror, Jason rubbed her shoulder soothingly. But his touch nearly made her jump out of her skin. "You can relax. I don't think anyone's here now. As soon as they'd left their present for me, they'd have no reason to stay."

Relax? How could he take this so calmly? Trying to maintain some semblance of composure, Maris insisted, "But we can't stay here now."

"Do you want to go?"

Why couldn't he understand? "Of course I want to leave! We're all alone out here!"

"All right. Just give me a few minutes to get rid of this thing. I'll also need to dive down and tie up the net. Otherwise the pool will fill up with all kinds of unpleasant creatures."

Maris's mind was already filled with thoughts more unpleasant than any creatures the sea could produce. As she watched Jason dive cleanly into the pool, she couldn't help remembering what Elizabeth Rawlings had said. Only the people who were suspected of being guilty of theft and murder were supposed to receive voodoo gifts. Did someone believe that Jason was involved in the case along with the Wilkersons?

CHAPTER NINE

Nassau seemed deserted as Jason and Maris walked from the dock down Bay Street on Sunday night. The straw market and the rest of the shops were closed, the street empty of cars, and the only other pedestrians in sight—a couple of native women—quickly disappeared down a dark alley.

"There was more life on Treasure Cay," Maris commented, unable to keep an ironic tone from her voice.

"Would you like to go back there?" he asked softly, sliding an arm around her shoulders and drawing her against his side. "I know the night on the boat wasn't that restful." After the wonderfully intimate time they'd spent together, he hated having to part.

"Go back there?" Maris asked, incredulous. "I couldn't wait to leave! I don't care to have any more sharks delivered at midnight."

He frowned, still puzzled and angry about the voodoo gift. He supposed he should have immediately approached the boat that had been watching the island that evening. The invaders probably would have been driven away before they had a chance to leave their grisly gift.

"I'm sorry our time together was interrupted in such a disturbing way. I tried to get us some privacy . . . to no avail. This case is becoming more and more complicated."

"And I suppose you should get back to work. I need to leave—Brian's expecting me tonight."

"Don't you want to have dinner first?" As they stepped off a curb he gazed up one of the dimly lit side streets that climb the gentle hill on which Nassau is built. "If we can't find a restaurant that's open around here, we can always head for the Sheraton."

"I'm not really hungry. But if you want to eat . . ."

"I'm not hungry either." He let go of her so she could precede him as they skirted several large crates piled up in front of a store. "I suppose all that's left for us to do then is find you a taxi."

"Do you think there're any around on Sundays?" she asked as they crossed yet another deserted side street.

He didn't respond, his attention wandering elsewhere. A few blocks up the quiet street, fronted by a row of tall palms, stood the multistoried office building that served as the Wilkerson Industries headquarters. Jason frowned in concentration as he got an idea. There'd probably be only one guard watching that building tonight.

"Where are they hiding?"

Maris's question startled him. He stopped in his tracks and turned back to her. "Who's hiding?"

"All the taxis."

"Taxis?" He had to grin. "Right, we're looking for a taxi. There're probably only a few on duty, but we'll be able to find one near a hotel." He glanced back up the side street, resolving to come back there as soon as he got the chance. "I'll walk you to the Sheraton."

"All right, but you won't have to escort me over to Paradise Island this time."

"Okay," he agreed, quickly accepting the offer.

That meant he could return in a few minutes. And then, later, still have time to talk to Alonzo. His mate had surely returned from Andros by now with a report on the "dead" seaman. Slipping Maris's arm through his, Jason set off.

"Wait a minute." She pulled on his arm to slow him down. "Why aren't you arguing with me?"

"You want to argue?" he asked, puzzled.

"No." She stared at him suspiciously. "It's just that you've always insisted on seeing me home before. Why the sudden change in character?" He started to tell her he'd accompany her in a taxi if she really wanted when she craned her neck to gaze back at the side street they'd passed. "And what was so interesting . . ." Realization dawned on her face. "Oh, I get it. No wonder you're so agreeable about my leaving alone. That's the Wilkerson building back there, isn't it? Brian once pointed it out to me. You're planning to check out those records."

He raised his brows in admiring surprise. "Are you psychic?"

"No, I'm simply skilled at using my logic." She stared at him. "I assume you know that breaking and entering is against the law."

"Who said anything about breaking and entering?"

"How else are you going to get into that building?"

He shrugged, hoping to avoid sharing the dirty details. "I have my ways."

"Are they any more legal?"

"I have to look at those records, compare their information with the manifests I've already seen," he said simply, attempting to set off again. "Let's go find a taxi."

"No." She literally dragged her heels, effectively stopping him. "I don't want to go until I know what you're planning."

He frowned. From the way she was acting it seemed as if she had a personal stake in the investigation. She'd probably never be satisfied unless he explained.

"I'll bribe the watchman to get into the building."

"And what if he reports you anyway?"

"I'll have to take that chance."

Her eyes glimmered in the dim glow of the streetlights. "Is it really that important?"

He realized she expected him to justify his actions. Normally he wouldn't think of doing so, but the closeness they'd recently shared must have loosened his tongue, because he found himself saying, "The answer to this mystery could be tied up in those records." But should he divulge something that might scare her? He decided it was necessary. "I've got to get a handle on this situation. Things are getting too hot. There's been one murder and who's to say there won't be another. I avoided telling you last night, but I'm sure someone tried to kill me."

"There's been an attempt on your life? I thought you said they'd never do that," she exclaimed softly, her eyes widening. "But how? When?" She stood ramrod straight, an odd look on her face. He could almost swear she was relieved, as if some doubt was suddenly lifted from her mind.

"You should remember that attempt," he told her. "You were there."

"The carbon monoxide—someone tampered with your tanks?"

"Right. And murder makes a case a bit more complex than simple piracy or in-house sabotage, don't you

184

agree?" He gestured toward the Sheraton, its towering wings visible at the end of Bay Street. "Now, how about that taxi?"

She shook her head and frowned as if she were considering something. Finally she said, "I can't go off and leave you when you may be in danger."

"Going into the Wilkerson building won't be that dangerous," he insisted.

"How do you know it won't? At least I can stay outside and keep watch."

"Watch for whom?"

"Why, the police," she stated. "Or anyone else who looks suspicious. At the least you don't want to be recognized entering or leaving, do you?"

He shook his head perplexedly. "I can't believe it. First you're concerned that my actions will be illegal. Then you're willing to serve as a lookout."

"I only hope the records will shed some light on the case," she said, sounding worried as she started walking back in the direction from which they'd come.

He followed. Not mentioning the fact that her safety would also concern him now, he swallowed his annoyance and accepted the circumstances. She was capable of being almost as persistent as he was.

"Having a partner is a good idea, you know," she told him.

He didn't respond as they made their way up the side street toward the office building. Other than their footsteps the only sounds were the buzz of insects hovering around the streetlights and the distant horn blasts of a boat far out in the harbor. The street remained empty until they turned off the sidewalk and started down the walkway that led to the Wilkerson building. When a car suddenly rounded the street corner some yards away, Jason drew Maris against him.

"Police," he whispered near her ear, recognizing the car's markings.

"What shall we do?" she whispered back.

He pulled her along quickly. "Let's go inside."

The watchman was sitting at a desk at the building's entrance, observing the intruders curiously.

"Now what?" muttered Maris.

Motioning for her to stay near the door, Jason approached the uniformed man with a grin. The man grinned back when he saw the bills Jason pulled from his wallet. Soon they were on their way to the central offices via elevator. In spite of her cool demeanor, Maris was tense. Jason could feel it.

"Why don't you go back outside and keep watch, as you first suggested?" he asked her, not wanting to involve her any more than he had to.

"I'm already inside now—the guard saw me."

"I'm certain he won't report our visit to anyone. He'd be indicating his own guilt."

But she didn't offer to leave, nor did she visibly relax. Darting a gaze at him as they exited at the fourth floor, she asked tautly, "So what are we going to do? I might as well help."

"You don't have to do anything."

"Two people can get a task done more quickly than one."

Though that was true, Jason still hesitated. He glanced around at the rows of desks in the floor's open central area and at the doors of the private offices that faced the street. Reluctantly he finally said, "I suppose you could look at the shipping books while I check out the private offices."

"Okay. Show me where the books are."

It wasn't hard to locate the accounting department. When Jason had visited Arthur at the beginning of the investigation, the older man had mentioned the fact that it was across from his own office on the same floor. Dragging out a couple of huge ledgers from the record shelves, Jason gave Maris the missing freighters' titles and serial numbers, suggesting she check all the ships' cargoes. He'd look at what she'd found later, after he'd returned from his own explorations.

He picked the lock on Arthur Wilkerson's office first, but found nothing out of the ordinary in the huge walnut desk's drawers or on the wall of shelves behind it. The desk itself hadn't even been locked. Just in case, Jason also examined the oil painting hanging above the desk, thinking it might hide a safe. But he was wrong. After further searching, careful to leave nothing out of place, he moved on.

Several doors down, after breaking into Harold's office the same way, he found the younger Wilkerson's rolltop desk securely locked. Using a letter opener to pick the mechanism, he managed to get inside. Poking around the many small drawers and spaces, he was surprised when what had looked like a strip of molding suddenly sprang aside. A hidden drawer? He must have released the spring lock accidentally.

Eagerly reaching inside the narrow opening, he withdrew a thin spiraled notebook. Did this contain Harold's secrets? Jason raised his brows as he read the figures listed in small precise printing on the graphed pages inside—Five thousand dollars, thirty-five hundred, seven thousand. . . .

Such large amounts of money! What had Harold been doing with it? Quickly leafing through the rest of the notebook pages, Jason paused when he found the name and address of a company in Florida. He frowned and picked up a ballpoint pen to copy it down. Was Harold channeling his illicit funds into investments in the United States? Planning to have Intercontinental Mutual Insurance check out the company the very next day, Jason was sure he'd found the information he'd been seeking.

Sitting in one of the accounting department's steno chairs, Maris placed another slip of paper in the second ledger's pages and hoisted the large book from her lap back to the desk. Using the titles and numbers Jason had given her, she'd found the records of all three freighters, but she didn't see how the details of their cargoes would help solve the case.

She gazed around the spooky, empty office. Where was Jason? When would they be leaving? In spite of her willing participation in the search, she couldn't help feeling uncomfortable about snooping around in someone else's private records. Nor could she stop herself from wondering about Jason's rather questionable regard for legality.

But at least he wasn't guilty of anything worse than some illegal prying. Despite the fact that she'd spent the night in her lover's arms, Maris hadn't been able to elude the small nagging doubts she'd felt since Jason had received the voodoo gift of the dead shark. A lot of money was involved in the Wilkerson case, money a treasure hunter could definitely use. But Maris couldn't force herself to believe that Jason was involved in any plot concerning the Wilkerson ships or murder. She'd concluded with relief that the person who'd left the shark had probably been conveying a message similar to the bloody words that had been left for her. Now that she knew Jason's tanks had been tampered with, she was even more certain of his complete innocence.

She'd even insisted on coming along tonight in hopes that Jason would find more proof implicating the real murderer. . . .

Maris sighed with relief when she saw her lover come out of an office and stride toward her. She stood up before he reached the desk. He gazed at her questioningly.

She pointed to the books. "All three freighters are listed in these. I marked the right sections for you with slips of paper." She watched as he flipped through the ledgers' pages. "One of the ships was carrying industrial tools and other high-tech products." She moved closer to gaze over his shoulder. "The third ship was carrying nuclear-energy rods. Does this information mean anything?"

"It coincides with the records I've already seen." He leafed through the pages on the third ship a second time. "They all had easily disposable cargoes."

"Disposable?"

"It would have been simple to unload the ships before getting rid of them." He checked his watch. "We'd better get out of here—it's been almost an hour."

"So what good have we done? Did you find anything that will shed new light on the case?" Maris asked as he quickly replaced the ledgers on the shelves.

"I found something," he said cryptically, motioning for her to accompany him to the elevator.

"What?"

"A notebook."

Maris could tell she was going to have to drag the

information out of him as usual. "Exactly what was in that notebook?" she asked pointedly.

Jason hesitated before saying, "One of the Wilkersons seems to have an overabundance of personal funds."

"From embezzling?"

"Maybe. Or from selling off those disposable cargoes."

"Which Wilkerson?" she inquired insistently as they entered the elevator and it started down. "Who's the guilty one?"

She could tell he didn't really want to share the information, but he answered her anyway. "I don't know if it proves his guilt—but it looks as if Harold has been investing quite a bit of money in a company in Florida."

"Harold?" she repeated the name breathlessly as the elevator doors started to open. Somehow she'd been hoping Jason would find something that would indicate Thorpe Harris. He was nearly a Wilkerson by marriage, wasn't he?

But she had no more time to speculate. She and Jason had to get out of the building. Although the guard carefully looked away as the couple exited the elevator, there were still several yards between them and the front entrance. Maris began to breathe a little easier when they'd finally gotten out of the door and were descending the building's front steps.

Then Jason stopped dead. And Maris looked up, her throat tightening convulsively at what she saw—a white Rolls-Royce pulling up to the curb! It was easy to recognize Arthur Wilkerson's car. They surely couldn't escape his attention. What now?

Before she could even say a word, Jason dragged her down the rest of the steps and pushed her to one side. "Go on, hide!" he whispered urgently as she slipped away from his grasp. "I'll think of something to tell Arthur."

Heart pounding, trying to stay hidden in the shrubbery that grew around the place, she sneaked around the side of the building and stopped there, resting her back against the structure's solid stone wall. She could hear the men's voices coming from the vicinity of the front steps.

"Well, if it isn't the intrepid Jason Price," boomed Arthur.

"I thought I might find you here tonight," said Jason, doubtlessly trying for an excuse.

But the older man went for it. "You did, eh? Is there anything in particular I can do for you?"

Maris couldn't hear Jason's low reply. Not daring to peek around the corner at the men, she only hoped Jason would find some way to get rid of Arthur so she could safely get away. Her chance came sooner than she expected.

"Come along inside then, Price," urged Arthur in his usual loud tone of voice. "We can talk about those cargoes over a stiff drink. I've got some good Scotch in my office. You've seen the ships' manifests—would you like to compare them with the original records? Be happy to get them out for you. . . ."

Arthur's voice faded with the thud of the front door as the two men entered the building. What must the guard think? The Englishman was going to show Jason the ledgers again? How ironic. It was daring of Jason to have even mentioned the cargoes. Maris was sure she'd never have been able to remain cool enough to do so. At the least, Arthur would have read the guilt written clearly on her face.

In a few more seconds, assuming the coast was clear,

she pushed herself away from the wall with sweaty palms. Crouching as she made her way through the shrubbery, heading toward the sidewalk, she peered over her shoulder to see that the entrance to the building was indeed empty. Taking a deep breath, she straightened up and hurried on, passing the Rolls-Royce to creep into the long shadows of some palms that grew near the sidewalk. From there she paced swiftly to the end of the block and crossed the street, wanting to put as much distance between herself and the Wilkerson building as possible.

But physical distance couldn't stop her from thinking. Mind whirling, she sped along for several blocks. Had Harold really sunk his family's ships? And stolen their cargoes? What kind of proof had Jason found? Did Arthur have suspicions about his son? What were the men discussing right now over their Scotch?

Arthur had seemed extraordinarily accommodating. Recalling the unpleasant side of the Englishman's personality that he'd exhibited while gambling, Maris suddenly wondered if Arthur had been a trifle too helpful toward Jason. If she'd still been wondering about Jason's involvement in the case, she would have suspected the two of being in collusion.

An uneasy feeling made her pause for a second. She glanced back over her shoulder at the deserted street. Why did she have the feeling she wasn't alone? Maybe it was because she was spooked by the murder involved with the Wilkerson case. She frowned as she realized it was easier to imagine Arthur, rather than Harold, as a killer. Had she gone off and left her lover alone and in even greater danger? Surely not. Arthur Wilkerson was Brian's longtime trusted friend. But hadn't she once heard that even a normally peaceful man could become violent when desperate?

Telling herself that she was letting her imagination run wild, Maris glanced around once more before staring up at a street sign. Not recognizing either street name, she stopped short and gazed around at the unfamiliar buildings. Where was she? Distracted by her thoughts, she must have been wandering aimlessly. Where was Bay Street? She'd better return there and go to the Sheraton if she was ever to find a taxi tonight.

Only one of the intersecting streets at the corner led downhill. Assuming that it would descend to Bay Street and the harbor below, Maris turned, crossed the intersection, and almost tripped over a broken slab of concrete curbing on the other side. Several small rocks rolled away from beneath her passing feet. Their skittering sound seemed to echo behind her on the sidewalk.

Or was she hearing another set of footsteps?

Startled enough to stop and whirl around, Maris stared back up the deserted-looking street. But the only movement she observed was in the long, shifting shadows of palm leaves as they were stirred by a slight breeze. She was definitely becoming far too paranoid.

Cautioning herself against imaginary dangers, Maris turned to go on. Just ahead she spotted the Little Yellow House, a national landmark of sorts, and beyond that, she knew, was the Nassau library and other public buildings. Bay Street was only a few more blocks away.

She was tired by the time she passed the limestone walls of the small garden fronting the empty and shuttered Yellow House, her adrenaline high slowly seeping away. She couldn't wait to get back to Brian's villa and crawl into her own comfortable bed. But she wasn't sure she could sleep, not knowing if Jason was all right.

Once at the villa, perhaps she'd have a snack and a talk with Jo, who was undoubtedly waiting up for her return. That would relax her.

Thinking about her friend and the censored details she'd be willing to tell Jo about her night with Jason, Maris almost missed the muffled sounds behind her. But she *did* hear them, and quite suddenly, within the space of a heartbeat. She became instantly alert, adrenaline shooting through her once more. For this time she was certain the furtive sounds were footsteps, not echoes.

Pulse racing, Maris whipped around fast enough to spot a dark figure slipping behind a tree. She swallowed hard and had difficulty taking an even breath. There was no doubt about it. She was being followed.

Deciding the brighter lights of Bay Street might dissuade a possible mugger, she walked faster, her long legs taut with tension. She cast a cautious glance back over her shoulder. Just as she'd suspected, the person who'd been hiding slid out from the shadow of the tree to creep along the wall she'd passed.

Maris speeded up her pace even more. Was she being tracked by a mugger? Or by someone even more sinister? Whoever was following her had been doing so for quite a while, perhaps directly from the Wilkerson offices. Unbidden, the words from the message she'd found in her room flashed through her mind: *Stay out of other people's business.* Was her would-be assailant connected with the case? If so, was he intent on silencing her? As it was, she felt she couldn't make a sound, even if she had to.

The lights of Bay Street seemed miles away as Maris nearly sprinted toward them down another deserted street. What if she found no safety there? She had no time to contemplate the possibilities when she realized her tracker had somehow gotten much closer, approaching her swiftly through the shadows of the great palm trees that grew in the garden surrounding the library.

Leaping forward into a full run, Maris flew toward Bay Street, ignoring the fact that her legs felt like rubber. Concentrating on that one and only goal, breath labored, pulse pounding in her ears, her small shoulder bag slapping against her side, she let the downhill momentum carry her out to the middle of the street—and into the direct path of a car!

Brakes squealed and lights seemed to flash as the vehicle came to rest mere inches away from her body. Maris draped herself gratefully over the taxi's hood and tried to catch her breath.

A taxi. The island gods must be smiling on her.

The shaken driver cursed at the top of his lungs. "Hey, lady, what's the matter with you?" he stuck his head out to yell. "You trying to get yourself killed?"

"No, I'm trying to stay alive." Still panting, she pushed herself up off the hood and frantically ran to the rear door, opening it while promising, "I'll give you a big tip if you take me to Paradise Island as quickly as possible."

"A big tip?" The man's outraged tone softened slightly.

"A really big tip."

As they drove away she jerked around in her seat to gaze back at the dimly lit streets. She saw the furtive figure gliding out from the shadows only a few yards away. She did a double take. It couldn't be.

But it was. Eyes glittering behind his wire-rimmed glasses, Davey Watson—Jason's diving partner—stared after the taxi, then slunk back into the darkness from which he'd come.

CHAPTER TEN

"Davey Watson was only looking for you on Sunday night?" Maris repeated Jason's explanation, unable to keep the edge from her voice. "He says that's why he chased me through the streets?"

"He was worried because I'd been gone so long and knew I'd been with you on Treasure Cay. When he saw you walking down the street he followed, thinking you'd lead him to me. At least that's what he claims." Jason frowned as he pulled the car out of Brian's driveway and turned it into the road. "I questioned him thoroughly after I'd spoken with you on the phone this morning. He says he didn't mean to scare you. Davey's a little strange, but that's probably because he's shy."

"He's shy all right," agreed Maris sarcastically, recalling the skulking figure she'd sighted two nights ago. "He hid behind trees rather than let me catch clear sight of him."

Jason turned his eyes from the road to glance at her inquiringly. "That *is* odd behavior. Do you want to talk to him yourself, then? Demand an apology?"

"No."

She thought hard for a couple of seconds, trying to force herself to be less angry and more understanding. But she could only wonder if Davey were some kind of voyeur who had a weird crush on her. The kid always stared when she was around. She decided she should keep her distance from him.

"You were probably in a particularly jumpy mood on Sunday—after the voodoo visit on Treasure Cay, then our snooping around in the Wilkerson building."

"I might have been a little tense," she admitted grudgingly, remembering her nervousness as she'd inspected the shipping ledgers, then creeping away from the Wilkerson building before Arthur saw her. She could never have pulled off the innocent act Jason had gotten away with. "What did you and Arthur talk about anyway?"

"I already told you—he brought out the records and showed them to me all over again."

"Then invited you and your 'girlfriend' to his birthday party tonight. That's all?"

"The records are the best thing Arthur can offer. I don't think he knows anything else about the case."

"So the elder Wilkerson isn't guilty? And he doesn't suspect Harold either?"

"That's what it looks like," said Jason, slowing the car before taking it up the curving rise of the Paradise Island bridge. Upon descending the other side, he turned the car onto the drive that would take them to Cable Beach.

"And what's our next move?"

"Our move?"

She nodded. "Surely I can do something else to help."

"Well, since you volunteered," he said with a slow smile. "I do have a task for you tonight."

"You do?"

She was pleased but a little disbelieving. She'd been

half joking when she'd tried to make him include her in the investigation again. When he stretched an arm across the back of the seat, his hand lightly touching her shoulder, she leaned into his fingers' warmth. She couldn't help thinking about the havoc those fingers had caused when he'd stroked her all over as they'd made love on Treasure Cay. The short kiss they'd shared when he'd picked her up at Brian's this evening had hardly been enough.

"I'd like you to keep an eye on Caroline Wilkerson at the party," Jason said, interrupting her erotic thoughts. "Perhaps you can ask her a few discreet questions about her brother."

"As to what?"

"Harold's position in the company, his wages, his relationship with his father, whether or not he has any trust funds or private investments that Caroline knows of—"

"Hold it," she demanded. "You call those discreet questions? What makes you think Caroline will tell me any of that?"

"She might not." Did the glance he gave her hold a hint of challenge? "Just glean whatever information you can, try to get some insight into Harold's character and the Wilkersons' familial relationships. I have a hunch Caroline's more likely to talk to you than to me. In the meantime, I'll question Arthur before cornering Harold himself."

"Are you sure Harold's guilty?" asked Maris, once again thinking of Thorpe. "Exactly what evidence did you find against him last night?"

"Only a notebook, some figures and an address—but today Ray Turner at Intercontinental checked out that address, proving Harold has some substantial investments in a company in Florida."

"Money from the disposable cargoes?"

"That's what I'm thinking."

She knit her brows, considering the next step in logic. "And that would also mean Harold is the one responsible for a murder. Do you really think he's capable of it?"

He shrugged. "Who knows? From what I can tell, Harold isn't working very hard on the in-house investigation. Why should he if he's guilty of the crime himself? And he's an odd duck, a loner who's obsessed by money and who doesn't seem to have any friends." Jason scratched his jaw thoughtfully. "No one knows much about Harold except for the fact that he's always had problems getting along with his father—something about the old man being reluctant to give his son any power within the company. Of course there's always the chance that the family's problems may have been exaggerated by rumor. That's why we need to question them ourselves."

"All right, I'll try my best to cozy up to Caroline."

"Don't overdo it. Just use your intuition about the right way to approach her."

"I'll use my logic," she replied firmly as he turned the car into the curving driveway of the huge mansion on Cable Beach.

A liveried footman helped them out of the car, and Maris wondered if her cocktail-length silk dress and Jason's sporty jacket were dressy enough. But she didn't have time to worry any more about it as she followed the servant into the house. A butler led them through the mirrored, marble-floored hallway to a huge room that was just as elegant and even more expensively furnished.

A fine oriental carpet covered the polished wooden floor, real crystal chandeliers hung overhead, plush velvet couches and antique chairs were arranged before a massive traditional English fireplace built into one wall. Caroline Wilkerson and her mother, the party's hostesses, were greeting guests as they entered the room and directing them to the linen-covered refreshment table.

After they'd paid their respects to the ladies Jason clasped Maris's hand and drew her aside. "We'll have to split up now," he whispered near her ear. "See you around."

Feeling deserted, she watched her escort stride off across the room to join Arthur Wilkerson and a group of men gathered around the party's open bar. That feeling of longing was only intensified by the knowledge that she'd have less than a week with Jason—a man she was now certain she loved—before returning to Florida. Was there some possibility he'd ask her to stay in the islands with him? If so, would she be willing to consider such a hopelessly impractical idea?

Forcing herself to get her mind back on the investigation, Maris glanced around at the other numerous guests, almost all of whom were absolute strangers. Brian wouldn't be dropping by until later. Caroline was busy playing hostess. What was she to do with herself until the young woman had time to talk?

Deciding she might as well help herself to some refreshments, Maris joined the people circling the table and picked up a cup of champagne-laced punch. There were also nuts and little candies to eat. From the substantial space that had been left clear in the middle of the table, she assumed there would eventually be a large birthday cake.

Making her way over to a tall potted palm, she stepped out of the murmuring crowd to survey the room. Jason had already gotten into a discussion with Arthur, while Thorpe Harris looked on. Caroline's fiancé was wearing a bright lavender jacket tonight and seemed to be swigging down generous servings of rum. As Maris watched he drank one full glass of the dark-colored liquor and had the servant acting as bartender fill it up again.

As soon as he got the refill Thorpe moved away to approach two pretty young women sitting on one of the couches. They smiled flirtatiously up at him and made room for him to sit between them, surprising Maris. Did other women actually find Thorpe attractive? Perhaps she was just immune.

She glanced toward the other corner of the room. Standing apart from the rest of the men—and everyone else at the party—Harold Wilkerson leaned against the carved mantel of the fireplace and sipped a cup of punch.

Staring at the bespectacled young man—he had to be in his early thirties—Maris tried to picture him as the perpetrator of the crimes that had been committed. Was he so consumed with resentment for his father that he'd been trying to steal the old man blind? Did power mean that much to him? Born to a wealthy family, he surely hadn't needed the money from the freighters' stolen cargoes.

"Attention! Attention, everyone!" Caroline suddenly cried, stepping to the center of the room and clapping her hands several times. "Almost everybody's here—so we're going to serve the cake."

The crowd parted as Caroline spoke, allowing the entrance of the butler and another servant carrying a long tray on which sat a three-tiered cake in the shape of a ship. Candles blazed atop the edible freighter. While the guests sang "Happy Birthday" loudly and off-key, Arthur made his way to the forefront to blow out the candles. The servants set the cake on the table and began to cut it as Arthur shook the hands of well-wishers.

"Yes, hope to have another good healthy year," he boomed to everyone in general as they gathered to get a piece of cake. "Lovely piece of pastry, isn't it? The ship was Caroline's idea."

The Englishman beamed down at his petite daughter as he gave her a one-armed hug. Dressed in a frilly, puffy-sleeved white dress that made her resemble a twelve-year-old, Caroline gazed back at her father adoringly. Maris frowned. Had Caroline always been Arthur's favorite? Had that fact added to Harold's resentment of the old man?

Moving among the other guests, Maris got herself a piece of cake, all the time keeping her eye open for a chance to approach Caroline. That opportunity soon occurred when the young woman separated herself from the crowd and hurried over to one of the large room's sets of double doors to peer out. Maris immediately followed.

"Caroline?"

"Yes?" Caroline whirled around to face Maris in a flurry of stiff, ruffled white skirts. "Oh, Maris. Hello."

"I didn't mean to startle you."

Caroline blinked. "You didn't. I'm only a little anxious from the demands of hostessing a large party like this."

"I can imagine how you feel." Maris smiled back

agreeably, wondering exactly how to get into a more extensive conversation. Perhaps she should try to put Caroline at ease. "And you've done a wonderful job with this party—such a beautiful cake." Maris took a bite of it from the plate she held. "Delicious too. Of course, how could a party miss when it's being held in a mansion like this? Have the Wilkersons always lived here?"

"For the last three generations."

"There's a lot of history tied up in this house then."

"And more to be made in the future," said Caroline. She raised her brows at Maris. "I see you came with Jason Price tonight. Have you two been treasure diving again?"

"No treasure diving, I'm afraid." Remembering Caroline's strong opinions on that subject, Maris said quickly, "I've been diving off the *Mermaid's Kiss,* though. I've spent several days a week looking for various kinds of fish."

"Fish? Oh, right, you work for an aquarium, don't you?" Caroline looked her up and down. "Is that why you often have a fish or sea theme to your clothing? That dress is beautiful, by the way—the same color of dusty lavender as the coral in your necklace."

"Thank you," said Maris, fingering the multiple strands of shell and purple coral.

"It must be nice to have a job that's so all-consuming, it even affects your wardrobe," remarked Caroline.

Job? Suddenly wondering what the young woman did with her time and hoping it might give her an opportunity to talk about Harold, Maris asked, "Do you work for the family company?"

"Well, of course—I'm a Wilkerson, am I not?"

Caroline sounded surprised that she would even ask.

Before Maris could figure out a way to question Caroline further without raising her suspicions, an elderly dowager approached.

"Caroline—what a lovely little party!" the lady raved. "The cake was an especially clever idea."

"I'm so happy you think so, Mrs. Stewart," Caroline said, responding graciously.

"I always know we'll be well entertained whenever you're in charge of a social occasion. You're such a competent young woman."

As the women discussed the Nassau social scene Maris finished her cake and gazed across the room. Harold had moved to the other side of the fireplace. Leaning against the mantel there, he sipped at his drink and stared at an attractive woman as she passed by. Was that a flicker of sexual interest Maris saw in Harold's eyes? Why hadn't he brought a date for the party instead of standing around alone?

When the dowager moved away Maris asked, "Does Harold have a girlfriend?"

Caroline turned and raised her eyebrows quizzically. "Why, no. Not at the moment. Are you interested in meeting him?"

Maris grinned self-consciously. "I was only curious— I'm already involved."

"You're probably better off. Much as I love my brother, he has an odd attitude toward dating." Caroline shook her head ruefully. "Unless he can bring a woman to a family dinner, he doesn't take her anywhere. Harold is very . . . thrifty when it comes to money."

Maris jumped on the topic. "Isn't such frugality a little strange, considering that Harold's going to inherit

204

the family business someday? He *is* going to be the next president of Wilkerson Industries, isn't he?"

"He's always been groomed for the presidency, yes," said Caroline sweetly, an unreadable expression in her eyes. Then the young woman looked away, scanning the room as if in search of someone. "But Daddy isn't going to give up the presidency until he absolutely has to. He doesn't believe anyone else can do as good a job."

"Really? That must be disappointing for Harold."

"Needless to say."

"I don't mean to be nosy, but I can't help wondering . . . why does your father think Harold could never replace him? Your brother seems like a responsible, businesslike person."

Caroline sighed. "Responsibility is not one of the traits my father feels that Harold lacks," the young woman stated. "But there are others. Are you sure you don't want to meet my brother? You seem frightfully interested in him." When Maris started to say no Caroline continued, "Poor Harold. He could stand to have something nice happen to him. He can't do anything right according to Daddy, not even the in-house investigation that he seems to have given up on. I've tried to give Harold some pointers myself, but he never listens. I suppose he thinks I don't have anything worthwhile to contribute. . . ."

Before Maris could say something reassuring to put the smile back on Caroline's lips, they were interrupted again.

"Caro, darling . . . and if it isn't the lovely Maris Collier as well."

Thorpe's fawning words abruptly halted any further conversation between the two women. Having suddenly appeared before them with a crooked smile plastered across his shallow handsome face, Caroline's fiancé was holding two cups of punch.

"Liquid refreshment for the beautiful ladies," he said, offering the cups. The slight slur in his voice told Maris that Thorpe had already had more than enough to drink. She wasn't surprised, considering the rum she'd seen him consuming earlier.

"Thank you, Thorpe, sweetheart," said Caroline, reaching for one of the cups. "So thoughtful of you."

"Thanks." Maris took the other cup reluctantly, moving her hand away as Thorpe tried to caress her fingers. The punch sloshed and almost spilled.

"Be careful," cautioned Thorpe, moving nearer, his eyes caressing her from head to toe. "You won't want to get anything on that gorgeous . . . dress."

No, she'd prefer to spill it all over him and his intensely lavender jacket. Honestly, didn't the man realize his fiancée was watching his tasteless flirting? Didn't he care? Maris carefully stepped away from him with a polite smile.

"Thorpe?" said Caroline, the edge to her voice finally capturing his attention. "Did you do that errand I asked you to do? It was of the utmost importance. . . ."

As the couple drew away for some personal words, Maris glanced around the room again and spotted Jason talking to Harold. The younger Wilkerson seemed genuinely interested in what Jason was saying, nodding and interjecting comments from time to time. Once Harold even smiled, his boyish expression making him look even less like the criminal he was suspected of being.

Maris's glance swung back to Thorpe. Obviously a fortune hunter, why couldn't it be he who was responsible for theft and murder? How had such a sleazy guy gotten in with the proper, powerful Wilkersons anyway? Had Caroline become so besotted with him, she'd forced her father to accept him? Brian had told her Thorpe had a job at Wilkerson Industries too. Why couldn't Jason have found damning evidence about Caroline's fiancé?

Maris was relieved when Thorpe finally took his leave, obsequiously kissing Caroline and smirking at Maris before he left the room. The young Englishwoman, on the other hand, now seemed irritable and tense.

"Boys will be boys, I guess," Caroline remarked with a wry smile, obviously referring to her intended. "Thorpe can be a little absentminded at times. Luckily, he has other merits."

"He's colorful," agreed Maris, hoping Caroline would miss her dry humor.

She had no reason to be concerned. The other woman's attention had suddenly switched to the nearest double doorway. A hulking figure of a man stood there for a second, gazing around, then quickly disappeared. Who was he? Maris wondered, staring after the man curiously. She hadn't recognized his rough features, but then she knew very few of the guests.

She was about to ask when Caroline hastened to excuse herself. "I'm afraid I'll need to interrupt our little chitchat again. I have to give the servants their final instructions for the evening." She smiled, nodding toward Harold and Jason as they conversed. "Why don't you go talk to Harold? He needs some diversion, some inspiration to get him going again on the investigation . . . though the case is probably hopelessly unsolvable anyway."

The young Englishwoman departed, hurrying out into the hallway. Gazing across the room at Jason—

who was still talking to Harold—Maris wondered disconsolately if she'd found out anything worthwhile to tell her lover. Jason already knew Harold had problems with his father, was crazy about money, and hadn't been doing much about the company investigation. Had she failed to ask Caroline the right questions? What *were* the right questions? Perhaps if Maris had had more experience in detective work, she'd know.

With a big sigh she left the crowded room, intending to go outside for a few minutes to get a little air. Maybe she'd feel refreshed enough to think of another way to approach Caroline when the young woman came back to the party. Once in the hallway, however, instead of heading for the front door Maris turned in the other direction, following a scented breeze that seemed to waft through the house.

The fresh air was coming from a set of French doors that stood open at the end of the long hallway. Breathing in the perfume of blooming hibiscus and other island flowers, Maris stepped out onto the terrace of the mansion's carefully landscaped rear garden. White statuary—dimly visible in the light from the windows of the house—nestled amid shrubbery and flower beds. Some yards beyond the garden lay a stretch of sand that served as the Wilkersons' private beach. Strolling forward and breathing deeply, Maris listened to the hypnotic murmur of incoming waves.

"Looking for me, beautiful?"

She almost jumped out of her skin at the sound of the low ingratiating voice coming from behind her. And she knew exactly who that voice belonged to before its owner placed his greedy hands around her waist.

"Let go of me!" exclaimed Maris, leaning back to

shove Thorpe away. She whirled around to escape, only to find him blocking the pathway that led to the house.

"Relax," said Thorpe, grinning lecherously. "Your boyfriend's inside. You don't have to play hard to get out here."

Maris clenched her jaw angrily. Why wouldn't the man leave her alone? "I'm impossible to get as far as you're concerned. It doesn't matter where Jason is."

Stepping sideways, she attempted to skirt by him. But Thorpe moved with her, once again blocking her way. She backed away from the hand that reached for her. "Come on, give it a chance, baby. We're made for each other. Look." He gestured toward her dress and his jacket. "We even like the same colors. We're a perfect couple."

"No, you're a perfect idiot. What do I have to say or do to prove that I'm not in the slightest bit interested in you?"

"Idiot?" Thorpe's leer changed to a belligerent scowl. "Jason's the idiot—letting you run around by yourself." He moved toward her purposefully, and she became aware of the strong odor of rum clinging to him. He was obviously drunk. Balling up her fists in case she had to hit him, she backed away farther. "What'sa matter, baby? Old Jase giving you money or something? Hell, I'm gonna have money, too, when I marry Caroline and it'll be a damn sight more than he's being paid by the insurance company to find those ships. . . ." Thorpe paused, looking sly. "Or the payoff he's getting to *not* find them."

"Payoff?"

Maris was so startled by Thorpe's words, she stopped short. He had her in his arms before she got the chance to say anything else. His wet lips moved over her face while his hands lifted the skirts of her silk dress to slide underneath and caress her nearly naked brief-clad hips.

"Stop it!" she yelled, furiously hitting at him.

"Come on, I know you're a hot number."

He nuzzled her neck, holding her against him in a suffocating squeeze. Maris tried to lever herself against him so she could aim her knee, but Thorpe kept a tight grip on her.

Just as she was able to shift herself so she could try to get free, she heard an anger-filled voice shout, "Let go of her, you bastard!" Jason sprinted across the terrace. "Get your filthy hands off her!"

Grabbing the back of Thorpe's collar, Jason yanked. Thorpe let go, a look of surprise on his drunken face. Then Jason whirled him around and punched the man soundly in the jaw. As if in slow motion, Thorpe opened his mouth in surprise—or pain—and toppled backward into a flower bed.

Breathing unsteadily, golden eyes glowing, Jason reached for Maris. "Are you all right?"

"Don't worry, I'm fine," she insisted, smoothing her skirts and nestling into his embrace. She was relieved to be offered his protection. Over his shoulder she glimpsed a splotch of white moving in the half-darkness as Caroline came flying out onto the terrace. A hulking figure lurked in the doorway behind her.

"Thorpe!" the Englishwoman yelled. "Thorpe, darling, are you hurt?" Caroline knelt by the prone man and glared up at Jason. "What have you done to him? He's probably got a concussion."

"I doubt that," remarked Jason as Thorpe let out a loud groan. "He's not seriously injured—he sounds as obnoxious as ever." Maris drew away and tugged at her lover, indicating that they should leave the sordid scene.

But before they could turn toward the house Thorpe managed to struggle to his feet.

"Let go, Caro," Thorpe complained, shaking off his fiancée's restraining hand. He took a couple of steps toward Jason, rubbing his jaw. "Think you're a big important treasure hunter, don't you, Price? And think you're smart, too . . . gonna make double money, aren't you, big man?"

Jason frowned. "I don't know what you're talking about."

"Sure you don't." Thorpe addressed Maris and looked from her to Jason and back again. "You better ask your big man where his money comes from. And why it's taking him so long to solve this investigation." He sneered. "Has old Jase been busy looking for the *Isabella* . . . or has he been protecting someone who doesn't want those freighters found?"

"What kind of accusations are you trying to make, Thorpe?" From the stiff way he was holding himself, Maris could tell that Jason was furious.

"You're taking a payoff, aren't you, Price?" Thorpe accused. "That kind of money should keep you in treasure hunting for quite some time. I know how expensive it is."

Jason glared coldly at the disheveled man, then gazed down at Maris. "Come on, let's go. I'm tried of listening to a drunk's ravings." He turned to go, guiding her along with him. "A claim jumper would have no idea of how expensive treasure hunting is anyway."

"Claim jumper, am I?" snarled Thorpe, addressing Jason's retreating back. Then he lurched forward, trampling through another flower bed to cut them off. "I'm not the shady character around here. You're in thick

211

with the criminal who sunk those ships, Price, and I'm going to prove it if it's the last thing I ever do."

Jason shoved the man aside, muttering darkly, "Your proving it *would* be the last thing you'd ever do all right."

"You threatening me, Price?" yelled Thorpe, striking out.

Jason blocked the punch, knocking the man against the side of the house. Surprisingly agile for someone in his inebriated state, face mottled with rage, Thorpe pushed himself off the wall and came at Jason again.

"Thorpe!" cried Caroline from somewhere behind Maris. Both women jumped aside as Thorpe slammed into Jason, knocking him breathless.

"Think you can push me around, huh?" shouted Thorpe, trying to strike Jason in the chest and face.

The two men struggled, exchanging punches until Jason's fist connected with Thorpe's already swollen jaw in a loud smack. Toppling backward onto the stones of the terrace, Thorpe lay still.

Caroline ran to her unconscious fiancé, throwing herself across his body. A crowd had been slowly gathering, attracted by the noise, and now began to collect around her. She turned an anxious face up toward them. "Someone help!" she cried. "I think Jason's killed him!"

"The world should be so lucky—to be rid of a jerk like Thorpe Harris," muttered Jason as Maris gently cleaned his cut lip with some antibiotic. Sitting on his bunk in the captain's cabin of the *Argonaut* while she leaned over him, he inhaled the pleasant scent of her perfume. Usually fiercely self-sufficient, he suddenly realized how much he enjoyed being taken care of. It was

212

almost worth being in a fight. "Thorpe may wish he were dead, though, when he wakes up tomorrow with a hangover and a sore jaw."

"Whatever he gets, he deserves," she assured him. "And he was awake before we left—I saw the butler and Caroline helping him inside the mansion." Jason winced slightly as Maris applied more antibiotic to the wound, though the pain didn't stop him from appreciating the concern he read in her eyes. "Did I hurt you?" When he shook his head she went on, "I couldn't believe it when Thorpe sneaked up on me in the garden." She made a face and put the bottle of medicine down, then sat on the low cupboard to gaze at him. "Thorpe also made some terrible accusations . . . about you."

"Consider the source."

"Are your sure he's not guilty of the crimes himself?" she asked, sounding hopeful.

"I haven't found any kind of evidence against him."

"Too bad. I don't know how Caroline can stand Thorpe. It's obvious he doesn't really care about her."

"Perhaps he has his uses."

"Caroline said something to the same effect tonight." She fingered her necklace, looking thoughtful. "But I have no idea what she sees in him. I don't find Thorpe the least bit charming or smart and he's always running after other women. Surely Caroline wouldn't want to make love with someone who cheats on her, even if Thorpe is a good lover, which I doubt. It's strange. . . ."

"All the Wilkersons are strange," Jason told her. Noticing with regret that his mermaid's ministrations were over, he rose from the bed to hang up his jacket. "Harold actually seemed friendly when I asked him for some pointers on investments tonight. He said he'd be pleased to give me some advice."

"So that's why Harold was smiling."

"You're observant." Jason turned back to her, appreciating the fact that she was as sharp as she was beautiful. "Money is Harold's favorite topic. I could tell he loved talking about it. But when I mentioned the in-house investigation he just changed the subject. He even ignored me when I mentioned the fact that a 'dead' man was reported to be living on another island and that I had sent someone to look for him."

"It's unfortunate that Alonzo couldn't find that man."

"Yes—he'd conveniently disappeared."

Maris got up from the bedside cupboard and smoothed her skirts. He noted that the lavender of her dress brought out the unusual color of her eyes. "I don't really know if I got much useful information out of Caroline, but she indicated that Harold has been having problems with his investigation, that he's almost given up on the case because it's unsolvable."

"She said it's unsolvable?" Jason frowned.

"You have to admit there have been a lot of stray clues."

Jason rubbed his swollen lip gingerly. "But that doesn't mean the case isn't solvable. In fact, I have a hunch we're getting close now."

Maris gazed at him, concern once again on her face. "Oh, look. Now you've gone and split your lip open again."

He hadn't meant to do so, but now that he had . . . "I guess you'll just have to treat it some more," he murmured happily.

Sitting back down on the bunk, he turned his face up

toward her when she picked up the medicine and another cotton swab. A tendril of her long hair brushed against his face, bringing with it the warm scent of her body mingled with perfume. As she leaned over him the soft mounds of her breasts pressed against the dress's low-cut front. Desire surged through him and he slid his hands up her smooth arms with a groan.

She looked alarmed. "Now I know I'm hurting you."

"Just a little—actually, I think I may have a few injuries that you've missed."

"You do? Where?"

"My chest is sore—it's probably bruised. Why don't you take off my shirt?"

She did so immediately, then ran slender exploratory fingers over his breastbone and nipples, down toward his flat belly. His skin felt scorched where she touched him. It was all he could do to keep himself from dragging her down onto the bed. But he wanted to postpone the pleasure.

"I don't see any bruises," she told him. She pressed gently against his rib cage. "Does it hurt here?"

"Lower," he gasped, catching another whiff of her intoxicating scent. She gazed at him curiously. "Take off my pants—I think something's swollen."

Now she looked really worried. "You could have internal injuries. Maybe we should take you to a doctor."

"I don't think a doctor will be necessary."

She'd unfastened his belt and undone his zipper before she realized his ploy. "Swollen! O-oh, you aren't hurt. . . ."

"No, but I'm in desperate need of a lusty mermaid."

Lying back, he pulled her down on top of him, melding their lips more softly than he really wanted because of his injury. When he cupped her breasts, caressing her

215

nipples through the thin dress fabric with his thumbs, she shivered and squirmed deliciously against him.

Flipping her skirt up above her waist, he rolled her over beneath him on the narrow bunk. She murmured deep in her throat as he explored the satiny skin of her thighs, his hands moving up over her hips and gently rounded belly. Hooking his fingers beneath the elastic of her lacy briefs, he slipped them off and threw them aside.

She tugged at his open pants, sliding them the rest of the way down over his hips, along with his briefs. Kicking aside his canvas shoes and his socks, he crouched over her, almost seeing exploding stars when she touched him intimately and started to guide him to her. Wanting to prolong their lovemaking, he removed her insistent hands, lowering himself so that her limbs twined about him like fronds of magical seaweed.

He gazed down into her hazy violet-blue eyes. Lying in a bed of her long silvery hair, her pale flesh luminous, she seemed to beckon, a mermaid who'd captured him with an enchanted spell. Wanting to bind her just as thoroughly to himself, Jason lowered the top of her dress to kiss and suckle at her breasts, hoping to draw forth her soul along with her impassioned cries.

Finally, when he felt he could continue no longer, he plunged into her, joining them completely. Moaning into his mouth as he kissed her deeply, she arched her back and tangled her fingers in his hair.

He couldn't seem to get enough of her as they rode the swift and powerful current they were both swept up in. Bodies moving rhythmically, they sought the ultimate release. They found it almost simultaneously, with dizzying intensity.

Slowly they drifted down from the heights they'd

climbed. Kissing Maris over and over as he gazed into her pleasure-satiated eyes, Jason finally rolled onto his side and cradled her against him. He smiled and sighed contentedly. Even in the narrow bunk, she seemed to fit perfectly.

What would it be like to share a bed—as well as life and dreams and love—with Maris every day? In spite of his reluctance to rely on anyone, Jason knew he'd found the woman he'd always been looking for.

CHAPTER ELEVEN

Jason walked into the offices of Wilkerson Industries early Thursday morning after being summoned there by Arthur Wilkerson himself. The message delivered by an islander had been nebulous, but Jason hadn't doubted that the shipping magnate had commanded his immediate presence since the messenger had been instructed to drive him to the meeting. The obvious urgency of the summons made Jason think that Arthur had gotten hold of some important information having to do with the disappearance of his freighters.

He stopped in front of the secretary's desk. "I'm here to see your boss."

"Go right in, Mr. Price. He's expecting you."

Jason opened the door and strode across the threshold—directly into what he could only describe as a hornet's nest. Waiting for him were an impatient Arthur, two red-faced uniformed members of the local police, and an hysterical Caroline.

"There he is!" she cried, pointing an accusing finger at Jason. She swayed slightly as she rose from her chair. "That's the man who threatened my fiancé. Arrest him for the murder of Thorpe Harris!"

"What?" The accusation against him barely registering, Jason looked from Caroline to her father, who sat behind his massive mahogany desk. "Thorpe's been murdered?"

His face more florid than usual, Arthur Wilkerson cleared his throat. "Hrumph. Well, Price, we don't know that for sure, yet."

"What do you mean you don't know, Daddy? Have you seen Thorpe since the party broke up?"

"No, I haven't, but you don't have any witnesses to foul play, dear girl. Nor a body."

As if crushed by her father's disloyalty, Caroline sank back down into her chair with a small whimper. She stared up at Jason with a teary, accusatory gaze.

"Your father has a point, Miss Wilkerson," the older officer, who seemed to be in charge, told her. "You're making a very serious accusation against this gentleman."

The fact that Jason was being accused of murder finally struck home. "Would someone mind explaining exactly what's going on here?" he demanded, incredulous.

Caroline sobbed as she spoke. "D-don't pretend you don't know. You th-threatened him. . . ." She paused to blow her nose, and Jason almost felt sorry for her until she glared at him and informed the officer, "At Daddy's party this man struck my fiancé several times, and all b-because Thorpe threatened to expose him."

"That's not exactly how the fight started," Jason objected. He'd seen no reason to inform her otherwise the other night, but now she obviously needed to have her eyes opened about her wonderful *fiancé.* "Thorpe was—"

"A moment, Mr. Price," the officer in charge said. The other man stayed in the background, obviously there merely for support. "Miss Wilkerson, you made a claim to that effect before. Would you care to explain more fully?"

Seeming to get herself under better control, Caroline nodded. "He accused Jason Price of being in collusion with the horrid person who's been sinking Daddy's ships. Thorpe said that's why Jason has so much time to go treasure hunting, because he's not really investigating. I'm sure you've heard about his search for the *Isabella*. Well, Thorpe thought Jason was being paid off to *not* find evidence . . . and said so. There were witnesses to all this," she added earnestly.

"Go on," the officer told her.

Jason gritted his teeth as she took a calming breath and continued. "Thorpe assured Jason that he would prove he was guilty of collusion if it was the last thing he ever did." Then she began sobbing again. "J-Jason said if he could p-prove it, it *would* be the last thing he ever did. Then he p-punched Thorpe and kn-knocked him out!"

When all eyes in the room turned to him, Jason admitted, "I finally lost my temper at those ridiculous accusations."

The questioning officer's stare was shrewd. "Exactly how far might you go when your temper is lost, Mr. Price?"

"Not far enough to kill a man, unless it was in self-defense."

"Now he's trying to say he killed Thorpe in self-defense!" Caroline cried.

"That's not what I said."

"And there's nothing to indicate a murder has been committed," the officer stated, his island lilt even, his tone kind. "Maybe your fiancé went off and had himself a good time. You know, prospective bridegrooms often

220

get edgy before the wedding and need a way to let off steam."

"No!" Caroline said, seeming truly shocked at the man's insinuation. Her fingers worried the tissue in her hand. "When he came to Thorpe told me that he was going to start investigating on his own in the morning. *Yesterday* morning. He said he'd find out the truth and throw it in Jason's face! I didn't really believe him, or I would have stopped him from doing something foolish. But I thought it was his pride talking." Caroline bent her head. Tears rolled down her cheeks to her chin. Her voice was a hoarse croak when she added, "He never showed up to work yesterday." She turned to her father. "Did he, Daddy? Tell them."

"No, he didn't. But, Caroline—"

"He'd never let a day go by without calling me, no matter what the circumstances. He *loved* me! He must have found out something that Jason didn't want him to know," she cried, glaring at Jason once more. "You've got to arrest this . . . this . . . murderer before he harms anyone else."

"I'm sorry, Miss Wilkerson, but I'm afraid we can't arrest a man merely because he made a threat in the heat of the moment, and especially when we have no proof that anything happened to your fiancé."

"P-poor Thorpe," Caroline whispered to herself. "His body could be anywhere and nobody cares. He could be weighted down with chains at the bottom of the sea. I don't understand why no one cares but me."

Before anyone could answer, the office door burst open and Harold came flying through it. "Father, you won't believe what happened!" Noticing the other people in the room, he adjusted his glasses and took a step back.

221

"What is it, Harold?" Arthur asked wearily.

"It's the *Caroline*. She's disappeared!"

"W-what!" Arthur thundered, almost knocking his chair over as he jumped clumsily to his feet.

"My ship." Caroline's voice was faint as she stared wide-eyed at Jason. "First my fiancé, and now my ship."

"When did this happen?" Jason asked.

"A little after six this morning." Regaining his poise, Harold stepped more fully into the room. "The captain was in radio contact with the harbor authorities. Right in the middle of an exchange about docking procedure, the transmission cut out. Dead air."

"How did you find out about it?" the older police officer asked.

"The harbor master got worried when he couldn't raise the *Caroline* again. He called me at home." Harold turned to his apoplectic father. "You and Caroline were already on your way here."

"And you could have called us here almost two hours ago!" Arthur raged. "Why the bloody hell did you wait so long to give me this news, Harold, you dimwit! Did you think that if you ignored the situation the *Caroline* would come waltzing into the harbor on schedule?"

Cringing, Harold cleared his throat nervously. "I didn't want to upset you if it wasn't absolutely necessary, Father. Within minutes of receiving the information I had the helicopter scouring a ten-mile radius around the coordinates the captain gave the harbor master. There was nothing to find. She's gone—disappeared—like all the others!"

Arthur mopped the sweat now pouring from his face and sat back down in his chair with a loud thunk. "My

God, we can't afford another mishap like this. What will people say? We won't be able to get cargoes. . . ."

"Or crews," Harold added. "Rumors are already circulating that none of the local seamen will sign on with us. They're saying we send out death ships into the Bermuda Triangle."

Jason had never believed in the Bermuda Triangle nonsense, and he wasn't about to give it credence now. But a fourth ship had disappeared—and with him on the job! At least it had happened only a few hours before. Surely there'd be some sign of the wreckage. Before he could organize his thoughts, Caroline attacked.

"Are you proud of yourself, Jason Price? Not only are you responsible for Thorpe's death, but the death of all those men on the ship as well. That's why you killed him, isn't it? Because he found out about the plans of the one you're protecting. Who is it? Who's trying to ruin my family?"

Jason stared at Harold briefly, tempted to mention her brother's Florida-based company. He decided it would only waste time, and he intended to find that ship —or what was left of it—before all traces were gone.

He headed for the door immediately. "I'll gladly tell you, Caroline, as soon as I find the answer for myself!"

Maris entered the Rum Keg, wondering if she had, indeed, seen Jason come in here. It had taken her taxi driver several minutes to negotiate traffic, circle around, and deliver her in front of the tavern. Squinting as her eyes adjusted to the dingy interior, she glanced around. In spite of the early hour, there were several customers in booths. Jason was standing at the bar talking to Monte in a low tone. She could sense his agitation by the set of his jaw and his body's stiff stance.

223

"Jason?"

He whirled around to her, startled. "Maris, what are you doing here?"

She stopped abruptly, perplexed by his unwelcoming tone. "I was on my way to Bay Street and I spotted you as my taxi sped by."

"Bay Street? Why aren't you out on the *Mermaid's Kiss?*"

The question sounded like a reprimand, and Maris frowned. "Matthew Kearns won't take her out without a crew member," Maris said, remembering the captain's irritation that morning. "Last night Gallagher told the captain that someone was out to kill him and he was going to lay low for a while. Kearns thought it was just talk until this morning—when he couldn't find Gallagher anywhere."

"So Gallagher's disappeared too," Monte mused.

"Too?" she asked as a strange look passed between the men. She approached them, demanding, "Who else has disappeared? What's going on?"

Jason explained. "Thorpe Harris hasn't been seen since the night of the party. Wilkerson had me summoned to his office this morning. The police were already there. Caroline wanted them to arrest me. She said Thorpe must have found out something about the disappearing ships that I wanted to keep secret. She accused me of murdering him to keep his mouth shut."

"Murder?"

He nodded. "And while we were in the midst of this confrontation, in comes Harold announcing the fact that a fourth ship disappeared early this morning. The *Caroline.*"

The ship that had been christened on the day she met Jason.. "Do you think there's a connection?"

"Could be. Caroline Wilkerson certainly thinks so," he muttered.

"What a bloody mess," Monte said. "Another ship gone—vanished without a trace."

"That's not exactly true."

Maris and the two men turned at the softly slurred words. The voice came from one of the booths.

"What do you know about it?" Jason demanded.

A rumpled-looking old man slid from the booth and shuffled over to the bar, holding out an empty pint. "I could probably remember better with a little encouragement, if you gets my drift. The name's Pinder."

Monte took the glass from him and refilled it. "Here you go, mate."

The seaman took a long swig, then said, "I was out fishing early this morning as usual when I hears this thunderous crack—like an explosion, you know? Well, I decides to investigate. Wasn't getting hardly nothing in me nets anyhow." The man finished his pint and held it out for a refill. "I saw this freighter sink—at least what was left of her."

"Did you report this to the authorities?" Jason asked.

"Don't like to involve myself, if you knows what I mean." The old man grabbed his ale and downed half, then wiped the foam from his whiskers. "Besides, I figured the captain of that yacht had already called a report in."

"What yacht?"

"The one heading from the area. Her captain must've heard the explosion and gone to investigate too."

"Or sank her himself," Jason mused thoughtfully. "Where did she go down? Can you show me?"

"Ain't about to go out there, not if someone sank her. Don't like the idea of trouble. But I could use a little pocket change. How much would it be worth if I showed you on your charts?" Jason pulled money out of his pocket and held it before the old man's eyes. A grimy hand swiped the bill and tucked it into a pants pocket. "What're we waiting for?"

"Not a thing." Jason hooked a hand under Pinder's elbow. He called back to Monte, "Should Carmen or Alonzo show up, tell them what's going on."

"You've got it, mate."

Maris followed Jason out of the tavern and toward the slip where his boat was anchored and tied, hurt that he seemed oblivious of her. She told herself not to be so sensitive, that he was merely distracted by the events of the morning and the new turn to the case. Still, she couldn't help but feel strange about the situation. They were as close as a man and a woman could be, and yet Jason didn't seem willing to share this part of his life with her. Why?

"Aren't the Ferraras on board the *Argonaut?*" she finally asked.

"When I got the message from Wilkerson I told them to take the morning off. I didn't figure we were going anywhere before this afternoon." Jason barely glanced at her as he headed swiftly to his boat. The deck stood empty. "They weren't here when I got back from Wilkerson's office, so I told Davey to call around while I checked the Rum Keg and filled Monte in."

"Maybe Davey has tracked them down already," Maris said hopefully. "I assume you're going out to try to find the *Caroline* whether or not they've returned."

"If I want to find her before all traces have disappeared, I have no choice."

Frowning, Maris kept her opinion to herself. Objec-

226

tions wouldn't do any good where Jason Price was concerned, so she might as well save her breath.

"Lucky you spoke up when you did," Jason told Pinder while helping the old man board his craft. "I've already gotten the *Caroline*'s last radioed coordinates from the harbor master, who's an old friend of mine. I wonder how far she actually got before they blew her up."

Obviously having heard them board, Davey came out of the cabin. "Hey, boss, I can't find the Ferraras," the young man said, studiously avoiding looking at Maris. "I guess we'll have to wait, huh? And I've got to tell you, we won't be able to go out this afternoon, either. I radioed the harbor authority to inform them of our plans. The guy warned me a storm's coming up fast."

"We're heading out in a few minutes, without the Ferraras." Though Davey seemed surprised by Jason's words, he didn't object. "Tell Eli to get ready to cast off."

"Eli?" Davey shook his head. "He's not here, either. I sent him over to Bay Street. Carmen mentioned she wanted to do some shopping."

"So, there's only the two of us." Jason swore softly. "Well, it can't be helped. I'll be ready to leave as soon as Pinder here looks at our navigational maps. Get that anchor up."

The old man followed Jason into the cabin while Maris stayed behind. Expecting Davey to do his captain's bidding immediately, she was surprised when he hesitated.

"Something wrong?" An odd feeling made Maris suddenly feel uncomfortable. She stared at his youthful features, now drawn into a scowl. "Or is it my presence

227

that's stopping you from your work? I've been told how incredibly shy you are."

Though he avoided direct eye contact with her, Davey looked in her general direction and said, "Uh-uh, it's just that I can't believe he's planning to go out there alone again." Then he shook his head and spun on his heel as Jason came out of the cabin followed by the old man.

"Well?" Maris asked.

"I think it's possible to find her. Pinder confirmed the coordinates almost to a tee." Jason handed another bill to the old man, who grinned toothlessly as he stepped back onto the dock. Then Jason held his hand out to Maris, as though he were going to help her off the *Argonaut.* "I'll let you know what I find as soon as we come back in."

Hearing the sound of the winch motor—Davey raising anchor—Maris crossed her arms and stood firm. "That won't be necessary. I'll be out there swimming alongside you every stroke of the way."

Jason frowned. "Oh, no! I'm not letting you get mixed up in this mess."

"I'm already mixed up in it," she said, thinking of the bloody message and the other incidents she'd witnessed. She remembered Elizabeth's terror and heartrending plea for help. Maris's chest tightened as she pictured the moment she'd first seen Jason. Disoriented. Helpless. Another intended victim! "I'm coming with you."

"Just because I let you help me search through a few company records doesn't mean I'll let you put yourself in real danger, Maris," Jason said heatedly.

"Just because you're stubborn enough to go down alone doesn't mean I'm going to let you!" Maris retorted, locking gazes with the man she loved, wondering how he thought she could worry about her safety when he was diving headfirst into danger. Why wouldn't he admit that he needed help? Well, she could be as stubborn as he! She wouldn't let Jason lock her out of this part of his life any longer. "I'll dive with you while Davey guards the boat."

Jason suddenly changed his tactics, gently cupping her shoulders with his hands. "Arguing about this is ridiculous. Please, just do as I say and go back to Brian's. I promise I'll be careful."

"I know you will. I'll make sure of it."

Cursing softly, Jason tightened his grip on her shoulders and gave them a sharp shake. He ignored her wince of pain. "You're getting off this boat—now—if I have to carry you over my shoulder!"

"Go ahead. I'll go straight to the harbor authorities and have them call the RBDF," she threatened, referring to the Royal Bahamas Defense Force, responsible for national security. Jason let go of her and stepped back, standing frozen as she continued. "Their patrol crafts will be buzzing you in minutes if they think you're trying to usurp their authority. And then I'll call the Wilkersons. I'm sure they'll get their helicopter out there searching for you in no time!"

"Maris, solving this case is important to me!"

"Not as important as you are to me, Jason," she assured him. "I'm not afraid to go down with you. But waiting, doing nothing to help you—knowing you're diving alone in a situation like this—that would truly terrify me."

Hands on his hips, Jason stared at her for a moment, clenching and unclenching his jaw. Maris stared boldly back, daring him to force her hand. He gave in more quickly than she would have thought possible.

"We're wasting time."

She helped Davey with the lines as Jason took over the wheel and guided the *Argonaut* out of the slip and into the channel between New Providence and Paradise islands. It was only later, when they were out in open water heading for the Bahama Banks, that she wondered at Jason's sudden acquiescence.

Had it been her threat to involve the authorities or the Wilkersons that had changed his mind? Staring at the back of Jason's familiar broad shoulders, Maris rubbed her stomach absently. No, he'd just been in a hurry to get to the site before what was left of the *Caroline* was impossible to find. He hadn't wanted to put her in danger. She tried to convince herself that the answer was that simple.

However, she didn't feel any better when he turned the wheel over to Davey and she helped him prepare the diving equipment.

Their conversation was cursory, and Jason made it clear that her interference was not only unwanted but resented. When he looked at her with angry golden eyes, the tightening knot in her stomach made Maris wonder if she'd pushed Jason too far.

That was an odd thought. Too far for what?

Ignoring her growing trepidation, she climbed into Davey's bright blue wet suit. It fit her a little too snugly in the hips, but it would do. She busied herself with preparations for as long as she could. Then, unable to stand the rift between them any longer, Maris attempted to heal it.

"Am I mistaken or is this familiar territory?" she asked, breaking the silence.

"Our destination isn't too far from the area where I took you diving to find the *Isabella*," he admitted.

Nor was it so far from the area of water where she'd saved his life. Maris looked around them at the darkening sky in the southeast and the choppy water surrounding the boat. Her flesh crawled at the thought of diving under such adverse conditions, something she'd never before done.

"That storm may hit sooner than we thought," she said, hoping her voice didn't betray her growing uneasiness.

"It'll be rough going. You can stay up here."

"No."

Tight-lipped once more, Jason turned away from her and headed for the wheel. A minute later the boat slowed and stopped. Jason headed for the back of the boat, where he threw the magnetometer into the water behind the *Argonaut*.

"So, you're going to mag the area to find the metal hull of the freighter," Maris said.

"This is going to be a crude method." Jason set a buoy in the water and dropped a line tied to a stone, thereby marking their present position. "But it's the best we can do."

"I don't understand, I've never seen magging done before."

"You can't just wave this thing over the sea," he explained impatiently. "To register a hit on the *Caroline* we have to get within sixty feet of her. We need to mag the area in a rigid grid pattern, making each line parallel to and about fifty feet from the last."

Quickly catching on, Maris nodded. "But how can you draw straight lines in open sea with no land to parallel? We don't even have a tower where we could station Davey to give us readings."

"All we can do is drop buoys at the start and end of

each run and hope we're accurate. But we're not far from the Tongue of the Ocean," he told her.

He didn't have to finish. Maris knew the steep drop-off would make the work more difficult if not impossible.

"Davey," Jason yelled, "move her out!"

Jason watched the unreeling graph paper coming from a meter attached to the magnetometer. In theory, Maris knew the line it drew should be straight if there was no large amount of metal present. The seas were rough, however, and the line wiggled around on the paper. She wondered how Jason would be able to tell the difference between the waves that were assaulting them and an actual hit.

For the next hour Maris was sure she'd never find out. Davey moved the *Argonaut* back and forth, stopping only so Maris could drop a buoy. The blue-black of the Tongue of the Ocean drew ever closer, its fathomless depths theatening as the skies above turned dark and the wind picked up in intensity. She knew diving would be dangerous if they ever did find the *Caroline*. Maris was beginning to hope that Jason would give up, even while knowing he wouldn't.

Suddenly the needle went wild, zigzagging from one side of the graph to the other, sending her already shaky stomach spiraling like crazy. They were suspended over waters mere yards from the Tongue of the Ocean.

"Davey, cut the engines!" Jason yelled. "We got a peg reading!"

The boat stopped and the engines died. The rising wind was mournful in its intensity. A warning shivered through Maris, making her feel cold as ice. She told herself she'd be fine once she got below the surface of the waves, but she wasn't sure she believed it.

"Maris." Jason made her turn to him. He stood less than a yard away, filled with a viable strength that irritated rather than reassured her. "Don't be foolish. Stay up here."

It sounded like a command rather than a plea.

"Is there some special reason you want me to remain on board the *Argonaut?*" Maris asked suspiciously.

"I'm thinking of your safety."

"Because of the weather? We'll have limited time below the surface. Our tanks will run out of air long before the storm hits," she reminded him. "We'll find what we're looking for and then we can return to Nassau, where we'll *both* be safe."

It was obvious that Jason was growing as angry with her interference now as he had the night they'd met Elizabeth Rawlings.

And she knew he was worried about the dive when he shook his head ominously and muttered, "I've got a gut feeling that there might be trouble down there—"

"All the more reason for me to be with you. I thought you didn't want to waste time arguing."

That wasn't what she'd wanted to say. She wished she could simply tell Jason how much he meant to her. She wanted to feel his comforting arms around her for just one moment before diving into the unknown. The distance he'd put between them stopped her. For an instant it seemed as if he was reaching out to her. Her pulse surged in jagged strokes because she wanted his touch even while the indefinable expression in his eyes made her breath catch in her throat.

What was it she saw in their golden depths?

Regret?

Jason dropped his hand and turned away, leaving her strangely shaken.

They both donned their gear, including headlamps. It would be murky below the surface. Then, with Jason carrying a guide line from the *Argonaut*, they stood on the diving platform. He touched her, a fleeting caress on her cheek. His eyes glittered strangely through the tempered glass of his mask, which was already in place.

"I'm sorry you got involved in all this," he said, his tone confirming his words. "It's my business, not yours."

A moment later they entered the same waters Maris had explored so many times before. Familiar but different. For her the watery fantasyland had been transformed into something more ominous.

Something uninviting.

Alien.

Dangerous?

Fighting the unusually strong current and waves that buffeted them, they hung suspended for a moment a few yards below the surface while they got their bearings. Then Jason took the lead, slowly heading downward, following the beam of light from his headlamp that cut through the sunless waters. Maris stayed close, forgetting to look around and take stock of their fishy companions as she normally would.

She found no pleasure in this dive—only fear and the dark magic of island superstition.

Though she'd insisted she wouldn't be afraid diving with Jason, she'd been mistaken. Instinct triumphed over logic. As they descended fear closed in on her, trying to suffocate her like an airless coffin.

Breathe! she thought, her hand automatically shooting to her regulator. She'd forgotten to breathe. . . .

She noticed she was lagging behind. With a series of powerful kicks of her flippers, she caught up to Jason.

No need to panic. There was always the guideline to follow. Still, she made a point of keeping up lest the current take her too far away to find the nylon rope.

Suddenly Jason stopped, signaling to her. She swam next to him. Her headlamp illuminated his face. His expression seemed . . . triumphant. Following his pointing finger, she saw why. Off to their left where the bottom dropped off sharply into the Tongue of the Ocean, a man-made shape seemed to cling to the reef, precariously suspended at its edge, rocking gently with the current. As she focused on it the dark shape gradually emerged as the outline of a ship. The *Caroline*?

Jason swam toward it, descending more quickly. Maris followed within touching distance. Her eyes were everywhere now, darting around them, looking for danger.

They found it in a deadly form at least a dozen feet in length. This was no dolphin! A tiger shark circled near the ship. It must have been drawn to the area by the explosion that sank the *Caroline*. How many other sharks lurked nearby? She didn't want to guess.

Instead, Maris concentrated on breathing evenly so she wouldn't use up her oxygen supply too quickly. She kept up with Jason even though she dreaded reaching the ship, which loomed ever closer. As they approached the sabotaged freighter, which lay before and below them like a broken child's toy, she saw no signs of human remains, nothing to indicate there had ever been life on deck. Only a few oil drums littered the tilted surface. Otherwise, the submerged structure seemed deserted.

Quickly looking at Jason, she expected to see the same amazement she was feeling. Instead, his eyes seemed to glow with knowledge behind the tempered glass of his mask.

While Jason tied the guideline to a railing Maris swam toward the pilot house, which seemed intact. She carefully shone her headlamp in its interior, on the alert for another shark. Empty. Had the captain and navigator been able to escape? she wondered. Pinder hadn't said anything about survivors in the water. What he had mentioned was a yacht leaving the scene. Maybe the men had escaped on that.

And yet she knew there were other decks, other spaces to trap unwary souls. She didn't want to think about what she and Jason might find below.

But it seemed that her lover was in no hurry to descend through the open companionway. Instead, he stopped in front of one of the steel drums wedged against a broken part of the railing. He righted it and worked on loosening the lid.

Maris caught up to him just as he succeeded. As the lid lifted and the water shifted the drum's contents were forced out. A human form shot upward, twisting crazily in the water. Maris's sharp outtake of breath forced an explosion of bubbles to surround her. Her light shone on the corpse's back, covered with vivid lavender. It turned, facing her. Even lifeless and water-bloated, he was easily recognizable.

Thorpe Harris.

And Jason had gone directly to the dead man's final resting place.

She looked beyond the corpse to the man she loved. The man who Caroline Wilkerson had accused of killing her fiancé, who'd done his best to stop Maris from helping him with this case, who'd tried to prevent her from diving with him to find the *Caroline*. And who—

from the beginning—could have easily made a lucrative deal with Harold, or Arthur, or someone else. . . .

I'm sorry you got involved in all this. It's my business, not yours were the last words he'd spoken to her. She remembered the bloody message on her glass door: *Stay out of other people's business.*

Eyes wide, she watched Jason Price draw his knife from the scabbard on his thigh. When he raised his head she couldn't read the expression behind his mask. His movements toward her appeared menacing, making the blood pound in her ears. Hooking a flipper through the rail to steady herself, she snatched at Thorpe's slowly rising body and pulled it down between them.

A few minutes ago she'd been afraid of the tiger shark circling overhead.

Now she was so terrified, she was frozen to the spot, her fingers clutching a dead man's coat, knowing that if she were truly trapped underwater with a murderer, there'd be nothing she could do to save herself.

CHAPTER TWELVE

Jason briefly noted the fear in Maris's eyes before using his diving knife to cut a length of the guide rope. He planned to secure the body before going on. From the way she was clutching at the dead man, he figured she'd second-guessed him. He didn't want evidence of a murder floating off somewhere while they searched the rest of the ship.

He suspected they wouldn't find anything when they did. No cargo. No bodies other than Thorpe's. The man must have become a nuisance to whoever was behind the crimes against Wilkerson Industries.

Jason tied the rope around the dead man's waist, remembering how he'd thought he'd had it all figured out: Harold transferring and selling off the cargoes, investing his illicit profits in his Florida-based company; sinking the ships to get rid of the evidence and transporting their crews to some other part of the Caribbean after paying them off. There was only one thing wrong with the theory. An irritating hunch had niggled at Jason until he'd admitted that he didn't believe Harold was cunning enough to pull it all off.

It wasn't until he'd secured the other end of the rope to the railing that Jason realized that Maris was staring at him strangely, giving him the most peculiar feeling. . . .

The powerful woosh of a projectile cut through the water between them. A spear now stuck out of Thorpe's body. Jason's heart thudded as he realized that death had missed him by mere inches. A dark shadow moved toward them and Jason grabbed Maris instinctively. Though she started struggling, she finally seemed to see the spear and the human menace that followed it.

Before the black-garbed diver could reload, Jason kicked him in the chest, loosening the man's hold on the spear gun. Then Jason plunged ahead through the water, leading Maris toward the pilot house. He planned to hide until he figured out a way to overcome their attacker or until he was sure it was safe to ascend without being a slow-moving, open target.

Instead of going inside where they would be trapped, he swam around the structure, planning to use it as a shield. He pushed Maris in front of him, farther away from danger. Before they switched off their headlamps, Jason saw the fear darkening Maris's eyes. Covered by the dusky darkness, they flattened their bodies against the metal housing. At that moment he spotted their attacker in pursuit.

Instinct told Jason to hold his breath, but quick thinking saved him from doing so—he didn't need a possible embolism added to the dangers he was facing. He just had to hope their air bubbles would go unnoticed. The sound of his own unnatural breathing reverberated through his head.

The black-garbed diver stopped and gazed around, trying to spot his prey's hiding place. He raised his arm, signaling for someone to join him. Jason saw that there were two more of them, and all three carried pneumatic spear guns and, strapped to their thighs, shafts full of extra spears.

Damn! Why hadn't he thought to arm himself with something more intimidating than a diver's knife? Jason wondered. But then he'd had no reason to suspect the enemy would track him down far below the surface of the sea. Someone was obviously desperate to get rid of him.

Maris touched his arm and pointed in the direction away from the men. Stealthily they slid along the tilted deck of the *Caroline,* playing hide-and-seek with their pursuers behind parts of the broken structure. If she was afraid, the woman he loved didn't show it. She seemed level-headed and as cunning as the men who stalked them. When the three divers finally split up, each going in a different direction away from them, Jason snapped on his headlamp. He then searched the area for something he could use as a more effective weapon than his knife.

His light fell on a stretch of metal railing that had been twisted and bent, the angle so severe, the thing appeared ready to snap. Maybe, if he and Maris could get at it, they could pry part of it loose. Having a length of metal pipe might come in handy, especially since the range of a spear gun was so limited. It was worth a try. Using sign language, he conveyed his plan to Maris as best he could. Her eyes alight with understanding, she nodded.

He switched off his headlamp once more. Hopefully they'd blend into the bulk of the ship until they'd succeeded at their task. Once at the railing, they floated through to the outside so as to have the camouflage of the ocean rather than the white deck behind their bright blue wet suits.

He'd barely turned to their task before a long shadow crossed in front of them—the tiger shark coming nearer to investigate the unusual activity. The shark swam over them so closely that Jason felt as though he were looking into its deadly jaws. Maris stiffened next to him. So his mermaid could be frightened of a sea creature, after all.

The shark seemed merely curious. Ignoring it, Jason signaled that they had to work fast. He levered himself against a solid part of the deck while they tugged at a broken section of the railing. The first end pulled loose just as one of the divers came into view.

Jason touched Maris in warning, but she was already aware of the man's presence. Jason froze, completely alert, waiting until their pursuer's back was turned. Then they attacked the railing again, this time more vigorously. As he worked at loosening the stubborn metal Jason felt a sense of desperation growing within him.

What if he couldn't get them out of this one? He'd never known what it was like to depend on anyone else —and there was certainly no way that he could start now!

There was a muted crack and a burst of bubbles as the second end of the metal shaft finally gave. Whipping around toward them, the villain shot without aiming his spear gun. Maris and Jason were already in motion, and he missed them widely.

Figuring it was now or never, Jason signaled to ascend, letting Maris lead the way. She was holding on to the upper end of the railing. They'd gone only a few fathoms when the other two divers rounded a corner, looked up, and spotted them. The larger, hulking man shot quickly, missing them both by a wide margin.

Then the third diver aimed his spear gun, the careful movement seeming as if it were practiced in slow motion. Jason knew the damned weapon wasn't aimed at him, but he couldn't get to Maris fast enough—and she was looking up, unaware of the immediate danger to herself!

He shoved at her with the pipe, but his warning came too late. The underwater missile found its target. Maris's body jerked and she let go of the metal rail. Panicking for a second, she dropped her regulator, which let out a steady stream of air bubbles. A small black cloud seeped from her thigh where the spear tip had grazed her. She pressed a hand against the wound, trying to stop the flow, and grabbed for her regulator.

Jason could feel her terror and pain as clearly as if his own life's blood were spilling into the sea. The very water surrounding them vibrated with menace as the tiger shark swooped in close, drawn by her blood. Placing himself between it and Maris, Jason poked at its head with the ragged edge of the metal piping. The shark turned away, daunted.

But it would return, bringing others with it—of that Jason had no doubt.

Maris was still trying to stop the bleeding from her wound. Jason rose to her, planning to release the carbon dioxide cartridge that would inflate her buoyancy compensator vest and take her to the surface. It would be dangerous—they were in more than fifty feet of water and the fast emergency ascent could mean the bends or worse—but she'd die a horrible death if he didn't get her out of the area and quickly.

For now a double threat pursued them.

The other divers were suddenly cut off when the tiger shark circled between them and its intended victim.

While Jason struggled with Maris's vest with one hand, still holding on to the pipe with the other, one of the black-garbed divers panicked, aiming his spear gun at the shark. Struck broadside, the great fish jerked as Maris had done a moment before. More spears were hurtled into its flesh, but not before the shark plowed into the first of its attackers.

The broken human body went sprawling. As his companions left him and slipped away into the dark waters beyond, the tiger shark went into convulsions from its own wounds, its jaws snapping reflexively.

Jason released the valve of the carbon dioxide cartridge on Maris's vest, expecting her to shoot to the surface. Instead, she wrapped an arm across his neck and under his armpit and slipped her good leg through and around one of his, bringing him upward with her, whether or not he intended to go.

Why was she doing this? It was slowing her down. He was sure he could save her if only she'd let him. As it was, their tanks would be almost empty. They'd be out of oxygen at any moment, probably before they could get to the surface. If the sharks didn't get them, they'd undoubtedly drown, lovers to the bitter end, like Doña Maria and her Frenchman.

Suddenly the sea below them became a churning mass of confusion and death as another shark sped out of nowhere and hit and gutted the wounded one, the violent action drawing even more deadly attention from the dark depths of the sea. The gathering sharks were attacking not only it but each other, mindless in their blood-frenzy.

As he and Maris rose toward the surface Jason kept a careful watch around them. He felt the tension in

Maris's body as she did the same, facing in the opposite direction.

The churning waters spread upward toward them. Jason reached for his own emergency cartridge, hesitating only because any extra thrashing might bring the attack upon them immediately. Then a ten-foot lemon shark broke from the pack and came straight for them at top speed—and it was too late to do anything but use both hands to wield the metal railing.

Jason swung at it and missed. The shark slipped under his arms, its powerful tail knocking into them hard enough to make him drop the pipe and to force Maris to let go of him. Without his weight to anchor her, she was propelled upward—a perfect, helpless target. The slim lemon shark circled wide and came straight at her, its long nose lifting, its mouth opening. Drawing his knife from the sheath strapped to his thigh, Jason struggled to reach Maris, fearing that the gesture was useless. He was too exhausted to save her or himself.

They were both about to die!

The knowledge screamed through his mind, creating a worse case of squeeze than any deep dive or too-quick ascent ever could. Ripped apart by a shark—he couldn't think of a more horrid way to go. He could almost hear the click of the shark's jaw as it dislocated for the attack, could almost see the whites of the creature's eyes as they rolled back into its deadly head.

Then a shot of silver streaked from the side—another shark to finish them off!

It was all over and they were mere yards from the surface!

Jason's eyes widened when the silvery body plowed into the muddy yellow one. Not a shark, after all! A dolphin—the shark's only natural enemy—rammed into the creature's ribs to break them! The shark spun crazily, its equilibrium destroyed. Heart pounding with hope, Jason looked up. Maris had reached the surface and was moving away toward a dark shape close by. He imagined he heard her yelling to him. Adrenaline pumped through him as another streak of silver joined the first—and another. Three dolphins surrounded them, keeping the enemy at bay.

Jason recognized them: Freckles, Spot, and Puff. Had a few games of keep-away sealed a bond so strong that the sea mammals would risk their lives for those of mere humans? Or were they merely protecting their territory from their enemy?

Jason gasped as he broke the surface and sucked in fresh air. He swam the few yards to the *Argonaut* through the wind-tossed seas. Maris had already reached the boat but seemed too weak to pull herself up onto the diving platform. She was struggling to rid herself of her tanks while trying to fight the waves that slapped at her mercilessly.

No one was trying to help her. Where the hell was Davey? Had he been murdered at his post?

Jason reached Maris seconds later, barely aware that the *Argonaut*'s engines were running and that her anchor was being drawn up. He threw his knife on the diving platform before giving Maris a boost. She crawled up onto the slippery surface, then reached down to give him a hand in return. Chest heaving with the effort to breathe, he collapsed next to her. "You all right?" he gasped.

She nodded, coughing up salt water as she finished removing her equipment. Jason ignored his exhaustion and stripped off his own gear. Hearing a boat's engine, he looked out in the direction he guessed New Providence to be. A white yacht was speeding away in the distance, quickly becoming a speck on the horizon.

Maris grasped his arm, distracting him. "The dolphins!" she gasped, pointing in the other direction. The magnificent sea creatures leapt in graceful arcs through the water, moving away from the ship. "Jason, they saved our lives!"

Attempting to rid her voice of its remaining quiver of fear, Jason joked, "Whoever said a dog was man's best friend?" He was rewarded with a sight that, a few minutes ago, he wouldn't have thought he'd live to see: The woman he loved smiled at him through saltwater tears. "My God, Maris," he whispered, gathering her shaking body in his arms, "we are alive, aren't we?"

Jason kissed her desperately, an affirmation of life. If his own tears mingled with the salt water on his lips, Maris would never know. . . .

Maris clung to Jason for all she was worth. If she couldn't stop shaking, at least she could take comfort in his embrace. She could hardly believe that she'd escaped the cold hands of death that had reached for her underwater. Right now she couldn't think of a place she'd rather be than pressed against his warm solid chest with the feel of his strong arms wrapped around her. Only moments ago her life had flashed through her mind. The inner vision had been quite vivid, and in a matter of seconds she had faced both the joys and disappointments of her past.

The *Argonaut* heaved and twisted in the water, the abrupt motion ending their kiss. A strong gust of wind sent a deeper chill through her, making Maris admit she'd learned one thing that day: Life was too tenuous for regrets. Jason touched her face with a gentle hand,

and tears of love and relief streamed down with the sea water on her cheeks.

"Shh, it's all right," he assured her. "We made it, and that's all that counts."

"I know. If it weren't for you . . ." Thoroughly ashamed of herself for ever doubting him, she forced a smile to her lips. "We make pretty tough shark bait, huh?"

"Shark bait . . . good lord, Maris, your leg! How could I have forgotten?"

Jason pulled away and gently turned her thigh toward him, carefully parting the torn material of the wet suit to inspect the wound. Though she knew the bleeding had stopped, Maris was afraid to look at the damage too closely. Now that her adrenaline was wearing off, she was becoming aware of a dull, hot throb in that vicinity. The boat continued to thrash in the water, the jarring movement sending occasional sharp pains shooting up and down her leg.

"It's only a flesh wound," Jason told her as she tried not to wince. "Not as bad as it looked underwater. We'd better clean it out and get an antibiotic cream on it right away, though. I don't want to take any chances with a possible infection." He stood and held out his hands. "It's bound to be sore. Do you think your leg will hold your weight?"

She nodded and placed her hands trustingly into his just as she felt the first drops of rain on her upturned face. He pulled her up into his arms, but before they reached his cabin they nearly collided with Davey. Thoroughly shaken, Davey stared at them as though he couldn't believe what he was seeing.

"Jason." The word came out in a strangled sound and his eyes darted from Jason to Maris to a fixed point beyond them. Then he closed them, his expression and deep breath indicating his relief. "You're all right. Both of you. Thank God."

"But no thanks to you." Jason gritted the words out, making Davey's lids fly open in alarm. "What the hell have you been doing while we were almost killed? You weren't even around to help us back onto the boat."

His Adam's apple bobbing as he gulped, Davey hastily explained. "Hiding—I was afraid those men would kill me. I figured if they didn't see anyone on deck, they'd assume everyone was diving."

The explanation didn't soften Jason's rigidly held body. Maris could feel tension oozing from the arm he'd wrapped around her back to steady her against the thrusts of the boat in the rising waves. Clenching her teeth against the pain that shot through her leg, she moved closer to Jason, only his nearness keeping her warm. The rain was already beginning to pelt them steadily. They should be heading for Nassau immediately, before the storm broke for real.

Jason ignored the weather, challenging Davey. "I suppose you have an equally satisfying explanation as to why you were hauling anchor. And you started the engines before we were even aboard!"

Davey blinked. Maris could see the fear in his hazel eyes as he said, "I—I saw them climb back onto their yacht. There was a big commotion, and I could tell they were preparing to leave. I did the same so I'd be ready to take off as soon as you surfaced."

"You knew the boat would drift the moment that anchor was up," Jason said accusingly.

"I didn't want to leave you down there, Jason," Maris thought Davey's expression seemed stricken as he added, "Believe me, if anything had happened to either of you, I would never have forgiven myself."

Davey's sincere words were almost drowned out by a rumbling from the east. Then a moment later the heavens opened and poured down on them. It was too late to beat the storm back to Nassau.

With an arm securely guiding her, Jason led Maris toward the cabin, shouting at Davey, "Take the wheel and get us back to port. And radio the authorities. Tell them what happened and give them our location. We'll finish this discussion later, after I take care of Maris's leg."

It was a relief to enter the small cabin. Although chilly, it was dry. Jason helped Maris out of her wet suit, moving slowly so as not to hurt her leg. She was getting used to the steady pain. Or so Maris tried to tell herself. After climbing out of her tank suit, she gratefully accepted the towel Jason threw to her.

"I'll get my first-aid kit. Crawl under those covers and keep warm," he ordered. "It's bad enough you're wounded. I don't want you to be sick as well."

"I'm fine," she insisted even as she pulled a blanket free from the bedding.

She was arranging it around her shoulders when he reemerged, a kit in his hand. Interest shone from his golden eyes, but he focused on the task of cleaning and medicating her wound. He did it all so gently, in spite of the rising swells of the storm-tossed seas, as though she were some precious treasure he'd found on a dive.

Remembering how she'd suspected Jason, guilt nagged at her. As he bandaged her thigh Maris rested her head against the pillows, then closed her eyes only to picture Thorpe's body whirling in the water, Jason unsheathing his knife, and her own hands reaching out to pull the corpse to her as a shield against the man she loved.

The man who would have given his own life to save hers.

Who, then, was Thorpe's murderer? And why had Thorpe been killed? Because he'd discovered the person who'd been behind the ships' disappearances?

"There, you're all set," Jason said, bringing her back to the present before she could logically think it all out. "How badly does it hurt? Do you need a painkiller? Or will aspirin do?"

Maris opened her eyes and stared up at the ceiling. Knowing she had to say something about her suspicions —not telling Jason was on the same level as lying to him—she had trouble meeting his eyes. "What I could really use is a nice dry set of clothes."

He raised a brow and let his golden gaze travel along her legs and over the parts of her body that were exposed. He stared meaningfully at the rise of flesh where she clenched the blanket together at her breasts. "You look better without any clothes." But she couldn't return his inviting grin.

"Don't start looking at me like that," Maris warned him, trying to figure out how to word her apology. He was merely teasing her anyway—he'd never leave the *Argonaut* in Davey's hands in this weather. She tried to scoot up and away from him without losing her cover. The seductive, loving side of Jason was the last thing she was capable of dealing with at the moment. Even so, she added, "I doubt if we could accomplish anything satisfying in this storm, anyway."

As if the elements were cooperating with him, the boat rose with a swell and then dropped, making Jason pitch forward. He landed neatly, half over her, resting on his flattened palms. "I've always liked challenges," he admitted.

A tiny smile slipped past Maris's lips in spite of her purpose. "So that's why you like me, huh?"

"I *love* you because you're a very special mermaid. Beautiful. Courageous. Loyal."

"Well, usually I am," she said, quickly taking the last attribute as her cue.

"So your hair's a little straggly," he teased, reaching out and tangling a finger in the braid dangling across her breast. "That doesn't mean you're not beautiful."

"No, it was the loyal part . . ." Maris let her words trail off. His expression was so warm, so loving, she almost lost the courage to tell him. But she had to. She had hated his keeping secrets from her. How could she do the same to him? She touched his cheek, needing the reassurance of his warmth. "I, uh, feel awful for giving things Thorpe and Caroline said any credence."

"What things?"

"About your being paid off."

His grin faded a little. "You're kidding, right?"

She shook her head and swallowed hard, feeling suddenly suffocated by his nearness. "It was just that you were so secretive. I had to drag any information out of you. Then someone left that shark, just like the voodoo warnings the Wilkersons received. Then, when you tried to keep me from diving with you, I—"

"You what?" Jason drew back, away from her hand, disbelief hardening his features. "You thought I might be a murderer?"

"Well, no, not really." But she had, if only for a fleeting moment. "I—I don't know how to explain what I felt. You were treating me oddly. And I was so frightened. I know I said I wouldn't be, but I've never dived

251

in rough seas before. And then, when you went straight to Thorpe's body . . ."

His golden eyes smoldered with anger as Jason finished for her. "You were afraid that you would be my next victim."

The silence between them stretched tautly. Jason stared at her, his expression unreadable. Then he rose, went straight to the built-in dresser, and found a sweatshirt and shorts. As he passed the bunk he dropped them on it and kept going without looking at her.

"Jason, wait a minute." Her words stopped him, but Maris had never felt so unsure of herself. She was staring at his rigid back, could see the corded muscles in his neck. "I want to apologize for distrusting you. I'm sorry. I'm so sorry."

She hoped for forgiveness or at least his understanding. All she got was a cool glance over his shoulder. Jason stared at her steadily before shrugging and saying, "You won't ever have to worry about that again."

"Jason!"

But he was already out the door.

Dropping the blanket, Maris quickly picked up the clothes he'd left for her, anxious to go after him. Things couldn't end like this. They'd defied death together! She scrambled into the shorts and sweatshirt, surprised the task was so easy. The boat seemed steadier. Had the storm abated already? She listened intently and heard the howling winds. But where were the engines?

A thrill of anticipation shot through her as Maris headed for the door, knowing that only the current and winds were moving the boat at the moment. She was barefoot and barelegged and heedless of the dull, throbbing pain in her thigh. Unable to find a slicker, she left the cabin, resigned to being wet until they got back to Nassau.

Maris barely got outside the door before plowing directly into Jason's tense back.

"What's going on?" she asked, steadying herself as best she could when the boat rose on another swell.

"Why don't you tell her, Jason?" came a familiar voice.

But he didn't say a word, didn't acknowledge her presence in any way. Maris pushed around Jason to see for herself. And when she did her eyes were wide with disbelief.

There stood Caroline Wilkerson.

The woman Maris had pitied wore a smug smile on her lips—and held a deadly-looking gun in her hand!

CHAPTER THIRTEEN

"You!" Maris said breathlessly. "You were sabotaging your father's ships all along!"

"Guilty."

Caroline Wilkerson looked even more fragile than ever with her lank brown hair plastered around her small pale face and loose men's clothing clinging to her slight frame. But her smile negated the impression of innocence. Its malice chilled Maris more than the rain that whipped around her bare legs. The other woman appeared to be very self-satisfied. It was as if she took real pleasure in her criminal activities. Maris couldn't forget that they included murder. She glanced at Jason to see his reaction, but his face wore a closed expression.

What was he going to do? Did he have a plan? She knew he'd try to save her, even though she'd hurt him so badly. She wished she could reach out and touch him, tell him how much she loved him, but that moment was past. Maris swallowed hard when she realized she might never have another chance.

"Both of you move," Caroline snapped, waving her gun to indicate the direction. "And quickly. I have little patience left."

For the first time Maris saw the large yacht tied to the *Argonaut*. On the deck, still in wetsuits, two armed men guarded Caroline. The other boat must have approached while Jason was taking care of her leg. They'd been so intent on other things that neither of them had realized what was going on until it was too late.

Maris looked over her shoulder as she crossed from one boat to the other. A white-faced Davey stood near the wheel of the *Argonaut* watching the proceedings. Bare feet gripping the slippery wet deck, Maris passed the hulking man she'd glimpsed at Arthur's birthday party taking shelter under a canopy.

"Get over here, Davey, and untie the *Argonaut.* On the double," Caroline ordered shrilly as she followed Jason, who swiftly crossed to her yacht. "It was bad enough having to wait aboard the boat, not knowing what was going on down there. Then you couldn't even follow simple directions like hauling anchor and clearing out before these two resurfaced—not that I actually expected them to do so! It's just a good thing I intercepted the message you radioed asking the harbor authorities for help."

"Jason would have been suspicious if I hadn't followed orders," Davey protested.

Another chill shot through Maris. Caroline had hoped the sharks would get them! It was no wonder Jason's diver had been acting so peculiarly. She stared at the innocent-looking young man, who even now appeared uncomfortable. Though he seemed reluctant, Davey followed Caroline's orders, as he must have done all along. Waiting for the swell to crest, he jumped from one boat to the other, then swiftly untied the lines that held the craft together.

Maris turned to Jason as the *Argonaut* drifted off into the storm, which was beginning to let up. How could he remain so calm at his loss? His expression remained blank, only a muscle twitching in his clenched jaw revealing his true feelings.

"She'll eventually wreck herself on the reefs," Caroline said, seeming as if she were enjoying herself.

"I'm surprised you didn't tie us up on her," Jason said. "Then you could rid yourself of all your problems at once."

"Oh, I plan to rid myself of you all right, but nowhere in the vicinity of your boat. When her wreckage is found without any trace of bodies, the superstitious islanders will claim the Bermuda Triangle has struck again."

Her laugh raised the flesh on Maris's arms. Could Caroline really be so evil? Or was she merely insane? It didn't matter—their fate would be the same.

"For the moment you can wait in the salon," Caroline told them. "You'll be dry and warm—and tied up, of course. Davey, bring the rope."

Maris saw that Jason's body was taut with tension and wondered if he'd try to overpower the two thugs, who herded them inside. She hoped not. He had no defense against their weapons and would only get himself killed. Although she was relieved when he followed orders, walking to the back of the long room and sitting where they told him to, Maris also tried desperately to think of some plan to get away.

"What are you waiting for?" Caroline demanded, shoving Maris down into a seat with her left hand. She backed off toward the windows, still clutching the gun in her right. "Davey, Felix is waiting," she said impatiently, shifting her body with the movement of the yacht as it rode out another crest. "Tie up Maris."

Davey threw a length of rope to one of the hulking men, who quickly restrained Jason with it while the other man held a gun in Jason's face, daring him to try something. Then Davey approached Maris. When he couldn't look her in the face she knew he was the weak link in Caroline's plan. It was plain to her that he didn't like what he was doing.

Even so, he tied her hands behind her in back of the chair. Maris wondered if she could get to him somehow. Caroline was looking out of the window. Was it possible other boats would be out searching for them?

"Why, Davey?" Maris asked in a low voice, hoping to appeal to the young man's conscience. "Why did you get yourself mixed up in this?"

Davey's eyes looked luminous behind his glasses. He swallowed and glanced at Caroline. Then he said softly, "Thorpe talked me into taking the job with Jason and spying on him. He said we'd both be rich if I cooperated . . . if I helped to make sure no ships were found. He didn't say anything about anyone getting hurt." As he talked Davey wound the rope around Maris's body and secured her to the chair. The bindings were loose enough to be comfortable, if not enough to allow her to escape. "I didn't know what I was getting into, and then it was too late. I trusted Thorpe. I never thought my own cousin would—"

"Enough!" Caroline shouted as she turned back from the window. "I want you on deck, Davey, on watch while Felix and Luther take us farther out. Where no one will ever find their bodies."

The Englishwoman was suddenly on edge, Maris realized. Why? Swallowing hard, Davey backed to the door more slowly than the other two men. Now he couldn't seem to take his eyes off of Maris. Her eloquent gaze held a silent plea. She was sure that he was their only hope.

Jason seemed to realize it too. "So you were really going to leave us in the water with those sharks, Davey." He shook his head. "I didn't want to believe it."

"Just like you didn't want to believe I was clever enough to fool the great Jason Price," Caroline said with a contemptuous laugh. She stared at Davey until he finally slipped out of the salon. Then she turned back to Jason. "Actually, if it hadn't suited my purposes, I would have been really angry that you didn't even add me to your list of suspects—"

"Ah, but I had," Jason told her.

"What?" Caroline sounded disbelieving, yet, thought Maris uneasily, strangely pleased. "Of course you say that now! You're probably just like everyone else. They're all so stupid, they can't see past their noses. They have no idea of how intelligent or clever I really am."

"I must admit the revelation came to me late in the game," Jason went on. "And quite suddenly, as a matter of fact, when we found your latest victim in the oil drum. But I still can't figure out the angles. You seemed to have everything a woman could want—"

"Except power," Caroline finished just as the yacht lurched, making her stumble. She sank down onto a settee opposite them and placed her gun on the cushion next to her. "People have always underestimated me, especially my own parents. While Daddy was determined to keep control of Wilkerson Industries in the family, he never gave me credit for being the strong one, the smart one, the logical one to succeed him."

"And how were you going to get Harold out of the way? Kill him too?"

"No, Jason, I had something far more clever in mind. By sinking ship after ship I reduced the trust of our stockholders. They didn't care if Wilkerson Industries was plagued by curses or by my father's incompetence. The important thing is that they were more and more willing to sell their shares. I, of course, was willing to buy. The irony is that I've had to spend very little of my own personal fortune to do so."

"The disposable cargoes," Jason said.

"Disposable, *valuable* cargoes, especially the nuclear-energy rods. I very carefully chose which ships I sank—after removing the cargoes and transporting the crews, of course."

"What about John Rawlings?" Maris asked, appalled by the other woman's smugness. *"He* didn't come out of this alive."

"Rawlings agreed to my terms, then wanted to back out on them. At the last minute he decided he wasn't willing to be relocated."

Elizabeth had been right, Maris thought sadly. "You had a man killed because he wouldn't move to another island."

"I had him killed because I couldn't trust him to keep his mouth shut."

Maris glared at Caroline. "Why didn't you just leave him a warning on his door like you did to me?"

"What warning?" Jason thundered, making Maris cringe inwardly. She was sure he saw her secret as another violation of his trust.

"The night you left me at the villa—after we spoke to Elizabeth—I found a message on my sliding doors telling me to stay out of other people's business."

Caroline chuckled. "Having someone use chicken blood was appropriate since you'd just been grilling the Rawlings woman about voodoo—though the trappings of superstition disgust me," she said, shuddering slightly. "Elizabeth Rawlings was a fool to think that voodoo could stop me. Where did you hide her, anyway?"

"Someplace where she's safe," Maris told her, praying that Elizabeth stayed hidden with her relatives until Caroline was stopped. Jason's questioning gaze made her flush uncomfortably.

"Never mind," Caroline finally said. "I'll get the Rawlings woman as well as Gallagher. I don't leave loose ends. Too bad you didn't heed my warning, Maris, because I rather like a woman with brains and strength. If only I'd been able to convince you to stay away from Jason, you wouldn't have to die with him. And if he'd taken Thorpe's dead shark as a serious warning, he wouldn't have to die either."

"So it was Thorpe who left it," Maris said distractedly, thinking back to Caroline's speech about irresponsible treasure divers. "How did you and Thorpe know I'd be at the Bayside Restaurant?"

"After returning to port himself, Thorpe was waiting for the *Argonaut* to come in that afternoon—Davey had radioed the fact that you'd found something but wouldn't talk about it. It was the boiler that we later found and blew up, much to Jason's dismay. When you left the *Argonaut*, Thorpe thought you might know something. He followed you, then called me when he realized you were settling in for dinner."

It seemed that talking about Thorpe finally got to her —as if she might have really cared about the man. Caroline rose to look out the window, turning her back to the room. Maris eyed the abandoned gun on the settee, then looked toward Jason and saw that he, too, was aware of it. If only one of them could get to the weapon!

260

Twisting her hands behind her, Maris tried in vain to free them from the ropes.

"Ah, well," Caroline sighed. "All this will be over soon. I already have enough money. And after word of the *Caroline*'s disappearance is spread around, I'll be able to buy all the stock I need to take control of the company."

She turned from the window and approached Jason. As Maris followed with her eyes she noticed the door was cracked open. Someone stood outside listening. The eavesdropper had to be Davey. What did he expect to hear? Suddenly it hit her—she knew the reason Caroline had gotten so edgy. Davey must be wondering where his cousin was. He must not know that Thorpe was dead! Maybe that would be all Davey would need to hear to decide to help them.

"My weakling brother, Harold, was groomed for the presidency ever since I can remember," the other woman was saying. "He was always a poor businessman —slow, timid, needing direction. Daddy gave me a pathetic excuse for a job with the company—public relations—and only at my tearful insistence that I wanted to be of some use to him. He's under the impression that women are meant for nothing more than breeding, a ridiculous notion fostered by my spineless mother. Daddy even planned to retire me when I married Thorpe!"

Maris said, loud enough so that Davey would hear, "Is that why you killed Thorpe?"

"You're the reason Thorpe is dead," Caroline stated evenly.

"Me? I didn't have anything to do with it."

"No, perhaps not. But you were the catalyst. When I met him Thorpe was a pauper with no prospects, working at a clerk's job in Miami. I picked him to be my partner, groomed him for the task, gave him everything. And how did he repay me, except by cheating on me at every opportunity? You were probably the only woman the ingrate couldn't get. If you'd have given in, he wouldn't have become obsessed with you, constantly throwing you in my face."

The door burst open and a wild-looking Davey stood at the threshold. "Caroline!" he shouted. "Felix picked up a transmission. The Defense Force is after us!"

Caroline swore and raced out of the room. "Come with me!"

Maris's eyes darted to the gun, which had been abandoned, and then to Davey, who stood staring at her strangely while the boat tilted with a wave.

"Is it true?" he asked, his voice choked with emotion. "Did she really kill Thorpe?"

"His body was in an oil drum on the *Caroline*," Jason said.

"He didn't deserve to die and neither do you!" Davey cried, leaping forward as the boat steadied. "We've got to hurry. She won't be fooled for long." Behind Maris now, he was already working on the knots at her wrists with cold, wet fingers. "I didn't know about that Rawlings guy, either. You've got to believe me."

"Save it for later, Davey," Maris told him.

"The gun!" Jason growled softly. "On the settee."

"One second." Davey gave the ropes a good yank and Maris pulled her hands free. "Now I'll get it."

"You're going to get it, all right!" shrilled Caroline as she burst back into the salon. "I should have known I couldn't trust you."

Freed of her bonds, Maris rushed forward, ignoring the pain streaking up her thigh as she made for the settee. Lunging for it, the other woman reached over the seat back and grabbed the gun.

"Caroline, don't!" Jason shouted as a sharp crack reverberated through the salon.

Maris turned and her stomach churned with nausea. Jason was splattered with blood.

"Oh, God!" Davey groaned, holding his shoulder as bright red blood oozed through his fingers. "She'll kill me!"

Jason was safe for the moment.

With one instinctive movement, Maris lunged with the uneven motion of the yacht and pushed the settee into Caroline. Thrown off balance, the Englishwoman stumbled backward. The gun flew out of her hand and through the doorway, skittering to a stop on the outside deck.

Caroline darted after it, Maris close behind, following in a limping run. As the smaller woman bent to get the weapon, Maris grabbed her stringy hair and yanked back with all her strength. The Englishwoman turned and kicked out, missing her bandaged wound by mere inches. Even so, the contact with Maris's thigh brought a pain-filled moan from her lips.

She let go of her handhold, aware of commotion behind her and the thundering of footsteps from the other direction. Felix and Luther!

Caroline held the gun.

"No, you don't!" Ignoring her pain, Maris sprang forward, ramming Caroline with her shoulder.

Both women hit the deck hard and slid through the rainwater, their tangled bodies shooting out from under the canopy. As the storm pelted them with renewed energy Maris tried to grab the weapon, but Caroline was quicker and strong for her size. Aware of angry male grunts mere yards away, Maris caught a glimpse of two struggling men. She rolled on top of the smaller woman, momentarily subduing Caroline with her greater weight.

"Don't move, Luther!" Davey yelled from somewhere behind them. "I swear I'll shoot!"

Davey had gotten a spear gun!

Maris recoiled as Caroline attacked her face with her free hand. Fending off the clawlike fingers took all Maris's concentration and she barely heard fists making bone-cracking connections. She couldn't miss Felix, however, as he came sprawling out next to them on the deck with a loud splash.

The ship rolled and the hulking body came tumbling heavily toward them! Fearing she'd be crushed, Maris immediately scrambled out of the way. Suddenly the Englishwoman froze. Her mouth gaping open, she stared in horror across the yacht. Before Maris could turn to look, the boat lurched again. Arms outstretched, Caroline flew backward, landing hard against the railing.

Then, as they all watched, Caroline fell overboard in slow motion. Still clutching the gun, her mouth opened in a silent scream.

"A life preserver!" Maris yelled, looking around wildly. "Where's a life preserver?"

Jason was busily tying up Felix, who was already coming around.

"Right next to you," Davey called from where he guarded Luther.

Maris threw the preserver out to Caroline, whose small body bobbed in the turbulent sea like a drowning rat. She rose above the yacht on a great swell of water.

"Get it!" Maris yelled. "I'll pull you in!"

Caroline thrashed around, submerging and coming up again. Finally she got hold of the doughnut-shaped preserver.

"Hang on!" Maris called out, pulling on the line. She heaved with all her might, when suddenly the line cut through the water easily as the preserver slipped from Caroline's hands. "Caroline, I'll toss it to you again. Try to hang on this time."

Before Maris could throw the preserver, a huge swell carried the Englishwoman up and away from the boat. Caroline's eyes were wide and fixed, as though she were staring at something on the yacht. Maris turned, searching.

A chill shot through her.

There, dangling from the yacht's canopy, was a primitive doll stuck with pins. The thing bore an amazing resemblance to none other than Caroline Wilkerson. Maris turned back to the water, already knowing what she would see.

An open, empty sea tossed by waves . . . devoid of human life.

The voodoo had done its work, after all.

As Jason guided the yacht toward an empty slip near the harbor authority office, Maris couldn't help but feel sorry for Caroline. Would there be anyone to mourn her death? She could see Harold waiting for them on the wet dock, surrounded by officials, but she doubted that there'd been much love lost between the odd successor to Wilkerson Industries and the sister who'd betrayed him. Arthur and his wife were nowhere to be seen.

Love. Such a complex emotion, Maris thought, her mind spinning. She and Jason loved each other, yet they hadn't touched, hadn't spoken more than a few cursory words since Caroline had disappeared from sight. . . .

She stared at him now, at the clear-cut profile against a sky as gray as her thoughts. Shaken by uncertainty, she glanced away. She watched Davey, who was still tensely gripping the gun although both Felix and Luther were securely tied.

Davey had loved his older cousin Thorpe, his idol since their poverty-stricken childhood. He had walked the fine edge of the law because of it, spying first on Jason, then on her. Had he been truthful when he'd vowed he hadn't known about Jason's fouled tanks the fateful day Maris had saved the man she loved? They'd learned that Thorpe had been on the boat to see him earlier that day. Davey said he hadn't wanted to believe that his cousin was guilty of switching the tanks, but how else could it have happened?

Davey had also confessed that he'd faked an allergy to shrimp so he wouldn't have to dive, assuming his employer wouldn't be foolish enough to go without his partner. Other than that, he'd insisted he merely kept tabs on both Jason and Maris—like the night he'd followed her down the dark streets of Nassau. He'd done so on Caroline's direct orders, while she'd stayed behind to spy on Jason and her father.

Whether or not he was as innocent as he claimed, Davey had promised to make a complete confession, naming names and anything else he could. Maris figured that would be enough to get him leniency and to satisfy Intercontinental Mutual. The mystery had come to an end at the same time as her work in the Bahamas.

Had her relationship with Jason come to an end as well?

Before she could gather the courage to find out, Jason growled, "Maris, pay attention."

He'd already killed the engine and the yacht was slowing to a halt. "Yes, sir!" Maris picked up a line and stiffly jumped onto the dock. Before she could finish securing the line to a post, Harold ran up to them, leaving the other men strolling behind him.

"I heard what happened. We've already sent search ships out for Caroline."

"Don't be too hopeful," Jason told him.

"I'm not, but father . . ." Harold shook his head. "I suspected her for quite some time, you know. That's why I slowed my in-house investigation. I didn't want to know for sure."

"It sounds like you cared about her," Maris said gently.

"Of course I did—she was my sister." He was staring at Davey, Felix, and Luther when he added, "Caroline always was a strange girl. During the past few years she could hardly hide her resentment of me and my position as heir apparent of the company. She worked on our father constantly, trying to turn him against me. I figured she'd succeed eventually. Father would realize his favorite child wanted Wilkerson Industries—and would be willing to give it to her."

"So you were building your own company in Florida," Jason added.

"You know about that?" Harold sighed. "I was planning to leave the Bahamas within the next six months. She could have had it all, but patience was never one of Caroline's virtues."

"Save the details, Mr. Wilkerson," a uniformed official said. "We'll take your statement as soon as we take care of those two thugs."

Several of his men attended to Felix and Luther as Harold followed the official back toward the harbor authority's office. "Are you coming, Price?" he called over his shoulder.

"I'll be right there," Jason assured him while staring at Maris. "Get a doctor on the way. I have a woman here who needs looking after."

Anticipation crawled through Maris's stomach, but the feeling turned to dread when she realized he was frowning at her. "I'm all right. Really. I could get to a doctor's office in a taxi."

He didn't seem to hear her protest. Looking right through her, to the depths of her soul, he said, "Oh, Maris, if only you'd listened to your heart."

"I'm listening now."

But he looked as angry as the clouds that were still rolling behind him, and she began to doubt that anything could save their relationship. The rain had started coming down again, this time in a fine mist.

"I could tell you all kinds of things," he finally said, "but I don't know if you'd believe me. Trust is a fragile thing."

"And it goes both ways," Maris told him. "If you hadn't been so evasive, kept so many secrets, I would never have doubted you."

"Keeping those secrets was part of my job."

"You mean keeping those secrets from someone you didn't trust," Maris said, turning the tables on him.

"I trusted you."

She remembered all the times she'd had to drag information out of him. She'd even had to blackmail him into allowing her to come along to look for the *Caroline.* "Then why wouldn't you let me be of more help?"

Jason's golden eyes seared into her. "I don't need anyone's help."

His ridiculous statement made her angry. Did he think he was above normal human frailty? "That's a pompous assertion if I ever heard one! Everyone needs help sometimes. Even you." She had a fleeting image of Jason, helpless and confused, the way she'd first seen him. He might have drowned if she hadn't spotted him. "I'm speaking from experience, remember?"

"When my tanks were fouled? That was different. It was an unusual situation—"

"You dived alone," she said accusingly.

Jason's eyes flashed. "And I'll do it again too. I like being self-sufficient!" With that he turned his back and strode off.

Feeling sad and angry, Maris watched him leave, wondering if one day's worth of doubt would truly separate them forever.

CHAPTER FOURTEEN

The Goombay festival was in full swing in downtown Nassau the day after the storm. Maris could smell the aroma of barbecued food and hear the beat of amplified calypso music as she and several of the other members of the *Mermaid's* crew walked from the dock toward Bay Street.

The late afternoon sun was bright, the harbor water sparkling. It seemed as if the storm and all the tragic events that had taken place during it had never happened. But Maris couldn't forget, though her injured leg felt almost as good as new. She only wished her spirits could mend as easily. It was to be the aquarium crew's last night in the islands. Gallagher had shown up once the danger was over, and the *Mermaid's Kiss* was set to take them back to Florida the next morning.

"Are you sure you don't want to just turn around and head back to the villa?" Jo asked, obviously sympathetic.

"I'm here because I needed to get out," Maris told her, wondering if her sadness showed on her face. She didn't want everyone feeling sorry for her. "And don't let me slow you down. There're plenty of other people to have fun with."

"Nonsense—good friends always mope around together."

"I have no intention of moping," Maris stated.

"Really? Okay, but if you change your mind, I want you to know moping's fine with me."

Maris shook her head wryly at the woman's persistence, giving Jo a warm smile. She knew her friend was only trying to be supportive. And Jo's warmth had been a lifesaver while Maris had waited in vain to hear from Jason.

But he hadn't called or dropped by the villa. And racked with shame and guilt, she hadn't had the courage to try to contact Jason herself. Not that there was an *Argonaut* tied up in Nassau's harbor anymore. The boat had been lost the night before, doubtlessly broken up and sunk by the wind and sharp reef.

Maris wondered if Jason was through clearing up the details of the Wilkerson case. When they'd returned with Caroline's yacht they'd both been thoroughly questioned by the police. Today, only twenty-four hours later, the entire affair had already erupted into a scandal, with photos of the prominent family displayed in all the local newspapers and television reports. Although the authorities had searched a wide area, Caroline's body hadn't been found. And purportedly Arthur was so distraught over his daughter, he was refusing to leave the mansion or talk to anyone. Harold would run Wilkerson Industries in the meantime.

And who knew where Jason was.

"Don't expect me back until morning, folks! I'll meet you on the dock at dawn."

Paul Martinez's jovial announcement interrupted Maris's thoughts. Looking up as the small group reached the entrance gate of the festival, she saw that

Paul had been joined by the pretty dark-haired woman he'd been dating since the night he'd "consoled" her at the casino.

"Raquel and I are going to boogie all night," Paul boasted as his girlfriend clung to his arm. "I need some warm human companionship to offset that shipload of cold-blooded fish I get to escort back to Coral Gardens." He glanced around, his eyes meeting Maris's. His wide smile narrowed into a more serious expression as he addressed her personally. "I can change my plans though—if you need me to look up that jerk of an Adonis for you, Maris. Where is he?"

"You don't have to do anything. Go have fun." Maris spoke adamantly, though she appreciated the young man's concern. She knew everyone in the crew was aware of the relationship that had become so important to her, but she hoped they also realized she was far from being devastated by Jason's obvious absence. To establish that point she lied, "If I want Jason Price, I'll find him myself."

As if there were any question about her wanting the man.

After the harrowing experience of a life-and-death situation, Maris had come to terms with what was most important to her in life. She'd already spent too many years without the kind of love she needed and the outdoor adventure she craved.

She wanted to stay in the islands as a professional diver.

And she wanted to stay there with Jason Price.

She'd take him any way she could get him. She knew by now that he lived in the present, preferring to take each day as it came. He probably wasn't the marrying kind. The only question was . . . did Jason want her at all? He'd had good reason to stalk off and leave her on the docks.

Maris tried to forget about her concerns—she'd already brooded on them enough—as the crew strolled through the wooden horses and down the street that had been blocked off for the celebration.

Food booths featuring island specialties—conch fritters, pralines, key lime pie, the inevitable peas 'n' rice—lined the street near the sidewalks on both sides. A stage had been set up farther on where a band was still playing calypso. Dancers, many wearing masks and brilliantly colored costumes, cavorted to the music, adding an even more festive, carnival touch to the setting.

"Want to try some barbecued chicken?" Jo asked Maris, stopping by a booth where the meat was roasting on an open grill. "It looks great." The native islander in charge of the booth moved toward the women expectantly.

"Sure, I'll take a piece," Maris told her friend.

The food seller collected their money and placed their selections on paper plates. Munching on a succulent wing as Jo wandered off to inspect the food in other booths, Maris was reminded of the wonderful Bahamian dinner she'd eaten with Jason on Treasure Cay.

That was the night she'd told him she loved him, completely surprising herself. But then she'd always hidden from her feelings, chosen logic over intuition . . . distrusted the more colorful and adventurous part of herself.

That same distrust had driven Jason away. Would he ever forgive her for doubting him?

"Maris?"

"What?" Her faraway gaze suddenly focused on Jo, who had returned from her foraging.

Her friend observed her questioningly. "I guess you didn't hear me. I asked you if you thought daiquiri pie was better than key lime. I've never tasted either."

"They're both delicious," Maris assured her, then hastened to add, "Why don't we get a serving of each and split them?"

"Sounds good. Come on." Jo motioned for Maris to follow her through the crowd of celebrants. "I found the pies in a couple of booths farther down."

Their journey took them even closer to the music platform. Maris glanced at the band and at the graceful dancer moving across the stage in front of the musicians. He was wearing an elaborate King Neptune costume, complete with shimmering cape, long white beard, gold crown, and trident.

"They really go all out for these festivals, don't they?" Jo remarked, stopping to watch the dancer more closely. "We're even getting entertainment. Interesting that the special occasion coincided with this particular night. It seems like an exotic going-away party."

Going away!

Once more Maris was reminded that they'd be leaving in the morning. And even if she quit her job in Florida and returned to the Bahamas on her own, she might never see Jason again. . . .

She gulped, fighting the sadness that suddenly threatened to overwhelm her. Through a veil of unshed tears she watched King Neptune wave his trident aloft and jump from the stage into the applauding crowd. As if the flamboyant action were inspiration, she blinked fiercely and considered a different tactic.

She simply couldn't give up so easily. If Jason weren't going to seek her out, she'd just have to go searching for him. What did she have to lose? He already owned her heart. And she'd prove she'd picked up a thing or two about detective work by hanging around him. As soon as she got the chance she'd visit the Rum Keg and question Monte about Jason's whereabouts. . . .

"Wow, this is some party!" exclaimed Jo, moving closer to Maris as a group of costumed people surged by.

"It certainly is," agreed Maris, observing a woman wearing nothing but a couple of silvery sequined bands wrapped around her mahogany body and a four-foot-tall headdress of brilliant turquoise plumes.

The masqueraders circled around Neptune, who waved his trident again, seeming to urge them on. Then, quickly assembling themselves behind the mythical god, the entire group danced forward in a fantastic sea-serpentine line. Various spectators, costumed or not, joined in. The musicians picked up their driving calypso tempo.

The sea serpent wove its way down the street through the crowd, undulating from side to side. Maris stared openly when she caught sight of Alonzo and Carmen Ferrara somewhere near the middle of the line. They were smiling at her. Surely the Ferraras would know where to find Jason.

Attempting to keep the couple in sight while at the same time avoiding the final wave of the serpent's tail, Maris stepped back. But she was too late. The long arm of the end dancer reached out to sweep her along. The last she saw of Jo was her friend laughing and waving good-bye.

"Wait a minute!" Maris struggled against her masked captor's strong grasp as he danced her along for several yards. When she managed to glance up her heart leaped into her throat. There was no mistaking the lambent golden eyes glowing behind the iridescent blue half-mask. "You!"

"A mermaid always knows her prey. I see my disguise is useless." Jason grinned and removed the mask. Steering Maris away from the dancers to a quieter place in back of the refreshment booths, he told her, "Siren that you are, I'm surprised you didn't magically call me to you before now."

Ignoring his poetic reference to sirens and magic, Maris fumed, "How could I call you?" Though elated by Jason's presence, she also couldn't help feeling defensive. The responsibility for their separation wasn't totally her fault. "I don't have Alonzo's phone number. And it isn't listed in the book—I looked." But if it had been there, she probably wouldn't have called anyway. She went on, "Why didn't *you* call *me?*"

"I let your phone ring at least a hundred times today —no one answered."

He still clasped her firmly by the arm, his fingers feeling hot against her flesh. Her eyes hungrily digested his familiar features. Still, she stopped herself from melting into his arms. Instead, she said, "You should have called earlier. You must have waited until after we'd left."

"So I was told. I went over to the villa to wait for you and met Brian coming home from the Wilkerson's."

"Brian told you where I was?"

"And that Arthur has recovered enough to talk to him." He paused significantly. She thought about the case that had first joined then separated them. He drew her closer, his golden gaze penetrating. "We've been through a lot together, haven't we, Maris of the Sea?"

"Are you still angry at me?" she breathed.

"Are you still distrustful of me?"

"No . . ." They both answered in unison.

As he wrapped her in his arms she tried to explain. "I didn't trust myself, you know. And I was always focusing on my doubts. I even compared you to my ex-husband." She wondered how to go about the next part. She finally blurted it out. "But that was nothing compared to the suspicions I harbored against you, for however short a time. Can you forgive me?"

Jason knew he'd never forgive himself if he let her go. "Can you forgive my bullheaded insistence on relying on no one but myself?" After a bitter night of self-examination, he'd come to a few conclusions. He gazed at her searchingly as he admitted, "I didn't exactly trust you either—at least not with the details of my work."

She nodded knowingly, looking as vulnerable as he felt. "But I also forced you to involve me in the investigation, whether you liked it or not. It's not as if I was one of your hired employees."

"No, you're only the woman I love, the most important person in my life. And I guess that should have made me trust you enough to confide in you. It's just that I've been on my own too long and had never really depended—"

"Stop." She placed a hand over his mouth, her blue-violet eyes glowing like a banked fire. "I understand. We both love each other. And I've had enough of words for the moment." Her expression told him what she wanted and he was happy to oblige.

Swiftly enclosing her in his arms, he molded her curves tightly against his body. Last night, alone, he'd felt empty without her. Maris responded passionately to his fervent kiss, winding her arms up about his neck and entangling her tongue with her own. His pulse pounded raggedly. Caught up in heart-stopping sensation, he still

277

managed to force himself to loosen his hold when she moaned.

He gazed down at her with concern. "I didn't hurt you, did I? I forgot about that cut on your leg."

"It's fine." Attempting to repeat the humorous trick he'd played on her the night of Arthur's birthday party, she told him, "But you'd better inspect my leg later—along with the rest of my body—just to make sure."

He smiled sexily. "I'll be happy to oblige, though I'd prefer more privacy. My boat's down at the dock."

"The *Argonaut?* I thought the storm—"

"I was insured. I already had my eye on a newer boat anyway. I bought her this afternoon—the *Argonaut II.*" He released Maris reluctantly, placing an arm around her as he led her away. "She's a real beauty—perfect for treasure hunting." He looked at her questioningly. "Treasure hunting's what I'd like to do for the next few months, using the fee I'll collect from Intercontinental. Want to search for the *Isabella* with me?"

"Yes," she answered without hesitation.

"Is that your heart speaking?"

"Absolutely."

"And what does your heart say to getting married before we head out to sea?"

She stopped short. "You're asking me to get married?"

He nodded. "I'd like to settle down . . . now that I'm feeling more comfortable about depending on someone. How do you feel?" He knew she could tell he was vulnerable now. The expression on his face gave him away.

"I'll marry you," she said, a huge smile spreading joyfully across her face.

He embraced her again. "And you won't mind living on a boat? I also have a small place in Key Largo."

"A house? You'd dare to separate a mermaid from the sea?" She undulated her hips against him, making him catch his breath. "I want to live on and in the water—"

"And sail the seven seas, look for uncharted islands, maybe search for Atlantis," he finished for her, cupping her hip with one hand while stroking her beautiful face with the other. She shivered. "I'll make you a deal, mermaid. If we locate the *Isabella,* our next project will be finding the lost continent. I want to make your dreams come true."

"You *are* a dream come true," she told him softly. Then she pushed away to take hold of his hand and pull him along the sidewalk. "Come on, let's find the *Argonaut II.* And quickly. I'm beginning to long for that privacy."

They hurried forward, exchanging mischievous loving glances that almost made him believe they were alone in the midst of the festival. But of course they weren't. The sidewalk was only a little less crowded than the street. In the lead, Maris almost ran smack into the small native woman who darted out from an alley as they passed.

"Annie," muttered Jason under his breath, recognizing the wizened elderly lady.

Maris stepped back a pace and stared at the small lady wearing a scarf on her head and, it seemed, yards and yards of colorful beads over her shapeless dress.

Annie's black eyes darted from Jason to Maris and back again. She stood proudly, smiling enigmatically as she spoke. "Only true love will uncover the gold." Leaving the couple with that mysterious pronouncement, the native woman then glided away, disappearing into the crowd.

"Annie? Is she a friend of yours?" asked Maris, staring after her. "And what was she talking about?"

"Annie's an obeah woman," Jason said, leading Maris forward again. "The islanders believe she can foretell the future, cast spells, do other kinds of magic."

"Voodoo . . . Elizabeth Rawlings," Maris murmured, making the connection.

"Forget about that." Turning the next corner, they headed toward the dock. Jason pressed Maris close against his side. "I have a hunch Annie was only giving us her blessing."

"I've learned that your hunches are often right. But do you think it was a magical blessing?"

"Our love is the only magic we'll ever need," he told her, speaking from his own heart.

EPILOGUE

The watery landscape near the Tongue of the Ocean was a misty aqua, nearly opaque with the sand that had been hurled into its currents. Listening to the even bubbles of her escaping oxygen, Maris treaded water and watched her husband swim upward toward the *Argonaut II.*

She knew he'd order Eli to move the boat, then direct the prop wash downward in a slightly different place. Having found a gold chain, two cannons, and a pile of ballast in the same vicinity during the last two months, Jason was certain he was about to uncover the *Isabella*'s mother lode, her main treasure stronghold.

Not that he hadn't been equally certain several other times. But Maris had learned to appreciate the man's constant positivism. Perhaps today his hunch would actually pan out.

If not, she'd just as thoroughly enjoy the diving.

And she always loved being with Jason.

Maris waved to Alonzo and Carmen, swimming on the other side of the crater that the prop wash had already dug. Then she signaled for them to wait and that Jason would soon be returning.

After both divers had replied to her gestures Maris turned around in the water, gliding off a short distance with a kick of her flippers. She squinted her eyes behind her mask, trying to see through the murky water, to catch sight of the submerged reef.

On her very first treasure dive she'd discovered a silver ring near the reef, an artifact she still firmly believed had belonged to Doña Maria and Louis Duhamel. Wondering if today's search would reveal their ship's final resting place, she felt her usual nostalgia for the romantic story. In four months of marriage she and Jason had already spent far more time together than had the doomed lovers. Unless there really were ghosts. Imagining the seventeenth-century couple locked in each other's arms, Maris once again hoped they were together somewhere. . . .

She returned to the present when she glanced up to spot Jason descending from above. He motioned to her as he swam closer, his eyes alight behind his dive mask. The mag reading today had been very strong. If nothing else, they would probably uncover some more cannons.

Before another crater was dug, Maris and Jason took up their positions on one side of the boat, Carmen and Alonzo on the other. When the blast of air began— moving water directed downward by chutes fixed to the *Argonaut II*'s propellers—it formed a column of nearly clear water all the way to the bottom. Once there, the powerful rush blew away the sand, sending shells careening through the water.

Maris moved a little closer, hovering, attracted by a glimmer she expected to be shiny exposed rock. Except that it looked distinctly yellowish. Or golden.

Then it all seemed to happen at once.

Maris froze as her eyes beheld the precious secrets the prop wash was revealing. The bottom of the sea was a carpet of gold! Time stood still as the mythic power of the metal hypnotized her. And the sand kept blowing away, exposing more and more: piles of doubloons, gold bars, chains and other jewelry lay amid the rotting remains of ship timbers. Was that really a huge emerald over there?

Heedless of the blowing sand, Alonzo plunged into the crater to fill up his gloves with coins. Then he rose to grab Carmen and execute a crazy, happy dance. They were rich! Some of the doubloons fell out of the mate's gloves, drifting back to the bottom. But they'd soon find them again.

And where was Jason? Maris whirled around in the water only to find him swimming toward her, tiny brilliantly colored fish seeming to dart through his hair. His golden eyes caressed her, glowing as brightly as the doubloons that lay below them on the ocean bed. She flowed into his arms, knowing their love had already made them wealthy.

They'd use the earthly treasure only to propel them further down their chosen path. To help them search for other dreams.

Floating upward in Jason's arms, heading toward their boat, Maris gazed into her true love's eyes and knew she'd have to begin doing serious research on Atlantis. And he'd willingly follow her to her dream. For once kissed by a mermaid, he belonged to her forever.

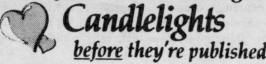